THE TENSION HAD BEEN
BUILDING FOR THREE DAYS

By the time they reached the outdoor dance
floor, Erin was almost afraid to touch the
flawlessly muscled man who drew her into
his arms.

PATag

It was starlight dark on the wooden deck, and
they were almost alone. Sea-shanty lanterns shed
a faint light at the edge of the wharf where Erin
and Kyle drifted, the sultry music overpowered
by the thunder of their own heartbeats' duet.

Ever so slowly Kyle's hand began a caressing
search, coming to rest on the swelling curve of
her breast. Gently he stroked, circling toward
the center.

Suddenly Erin could bear no more! In
desperation, she all but pushed him away. But
Kyle held her fast, his fingers burning, and her
hunger grew to dizzying proportions....

ABOUT THE AUTHOR

Suzanne Ellison teaches school in rural California, where she lives with her husband and daughter. After researching and writing *Wings of Gold,* her second romance, she became an avid fan of NASA's space program. She also gained deep respect and admiration for the Navy and for the wives of naval officers.

Suzanne Ellison

WINGS OF GOLD

Harlequin Books

TORONTO • NEW YORK • LONDON
AMSTERDAM • PARIS • SYDNEY • HAMBURG
STOCKHOLM • ATHENS • TOKYO • MILAN

Published May 1985

First printing March 1985

ISBN 0-373-70165-9

For every brave man
who has ever worn
wings of gold.

CHAPTER ONE

"ERIN! ERIN NESS! Are you in there?"

In that misty world between sleep and consciousness, Erin battled for full awareness. She recognized
the urgent voice that accompanied the heavy fist thudding on her front door; a wafting surge of sensual
dream told her that she'd heard it somewhere before.

"Dammit, Erin! Open up!" thundered the now-
familiar baritone outside.

Even in her sleepy haze, Erin realized that there was
something wrong with the voice. It belonged to a man
who always wore courtly manners and self-control like
a pair of ancestral side arms...a man who always said
her name like a caress instead of a command. In her
mind's eye she saw his dark, muscular form dressed in
white and navy with gold wings above his pocket, a
uniform she saw every day on the pilots who strutted
through her life at NASA. But this one was different.
He was the only one that Erin, as a woman, had had
difficulty ignoring.

"Dammit, Doctor, this is an emergency!"

Now fully alert, Erin sat upright at the Hippocratic
call. *My God, it's Kyle Tatum!* she thought in her first
instant of clarity, shivering in a mixture of fear and
delight. *What could he possibly be doing here in the
middle of the night?*

The breeze from the air conditioner chilled her; for a
fleeting second she realized she'd fallen asleep after

many dips in her mosaic-tiled pool and still wore her mint-green string bikini. It was hardly the proper attire in which to greet an irate pilot at her door. Especially Kyle! It had been weeks since she'd last seen him at the Johnson Space Center, and he'd never been to her house. She hadn't thought he even knew where she lived! She wanted to look for a robe, but somebody, somewhere, needed her surgeon's hands. The doctor in her warred with the woman, and as usual, the doctor won.

Erin sidestepped the quilting frame that owned the front room, and unbolted the heavy oak door. It creaked on its clumsy, off-balance hinges as she stepped back to confront her nocturnal visitor.

The man on the porch had boot-black hair and the bronzed features of a native warrior from one of Frederic Remington's Old West paintings. Navy slacks caressed his taut thighs and a blue cotton shirt, rolled up at the sleeves, firmly outlined his broad chest. Dark hair beckoned from the unbuttoned vee at his neck.

He was not alone. Beside him stood Jeb Henson, another pilot-astronaut and the commander of an up-coming medical mission in Erin's field. He had a blond, boyish look that belied his not-quite forty years; he wore charm as proudly as the silver oak leaves Erin had once seen on his collar. Although he politely kept his eyes on Erin's face, it was obvious from his muted smile that he was embarrassed by her appearance and felt awkward intruding on her at three thirty-seven in the morning.

Kyle did not share his friend's response. As Erin stood in the doorway, his cobalt-blue eyes arrested her with an untamed look she had never seen in them before. They were stalking her, eyeing her sultry appearance with bold anticipation. They read the sleepy dew of her graceful rose-mauve lips, the dusky gray of her moonlit eyes. Erin's strawberry blond hair, usually artfully wrapped in a French braid to offset Houston's heat, now tumbled in slumberous disarray, threatening to abandon the last of its interlacings if she so much as shook her head.

Just when she thought he'd finished his visual feast, Kyle's potent gaze moved down lower. In a brief victory that all but cast her bikini on the floor, he took visual possession of her body, finally resting not at her breasts as most men would, but on the lanky smoothness of her legs. At five foot nine she had more golden skin from thigh to toe than many women, and the shapeliness of her limbs made the most of every inch.

Usually Erin was flattered by compliments on her appearance, but at the moment Kyle's blatant assessment violated her sense of decorum. He had come here, uninvited, waking her up with dire pleas of some medical problem. Yet his eyes flared with another message...and to her great embarrassment, her entire body seemed to be saluting in reply! Already her nipples were erect against the sheer fabric that covered her richly curved breasts. Kyle would know he'd brought them to full attention by his wordless command.

It was Jeb's silent presence that brought Erin to her senses and provided her tongue with a tart defense. "You said there was a medical emergency, gentlemen," she announced firmly, determined to conceal her response to Kyle's graphic appraisal.

"Forgive us, Dr. Ness," Jeb replied, now eager to state his business. "The simple truth is that we have a problem. A friend of ours has been injured, and we need a doctor...a NASA doctor... to help us."

Instantly she tossed aside her frivolous sensuality

and became Dr. Ness. "Let me get my bag. You can tell me his symptoms on the—"

"We don't need you to operate on him!" Kyle said testily. "We've had it up to our wazoos with doctors. What we need is a way to get him *away* from the damn—"

"What Kyle is so indelicately trying to say," Jeb Henson cut in, "is that we've been unable to get much information about Roger from the staff at Our Lady of Mercy Hospital."

"Roger? Roger Shaw?" Of all the names they could have mentioned, this one distressed her the most. Not because Roger had gorgeous chestnut hair and a heart-stopping smile. . . not even because he was the kindest person that Erin had ever met. Roger Shaw, emergency surgeon extraordinaire, was professionally everything Erin had ever wanted to be. Roger was the physician astronaut assigned to Jeb Henson's 61-J space shuttle flight coming up in late summer. He would be the first doctor to operate in space. . . albeit on a simian test subject rather than a human being.

"Yes, Roger," Jeb confirmed. "Now it's nothing big, but—"

"What happened?" she demanded.

"Dammit!" Kyle snapped with a dismissive gesture of his fist. "Would you just listen? The problem isn't medical, it's procedural. There's no chain of command over there!"

"Kyle, a man has been injured. I am a physician. I need to know his medical condition!"

"Erin, please," Jeb picked up smoothly, giving Kyle a glacial look that commanded him to silence. "Apparently Roger was driving home from a date on the other side of Houston. Some idiot ran a red light, lurched around the intersection a bit, and knocked up

Roger's Porsche. He called Kyle to come get him. Now he was hardly hurt at all—''

"How do you know that?"

"Because I know what hurt is, dammit!" Kyle burst out, his face getting darker. "Hell, lady, I've been shot down three times!"

"Then you ought to know how an injured person can behave in shock. Did he—"

"He wasn't in shock! He sat there making jokes. He didn't even want to see a doctor, for God's sake! But I insisted. You work at Our Lady of Mercy on the weekends, don't you?" He raked a hand through his hair.

Erin suspected he was becoming more agitated by the moment. The Kyle Tatum she knew would never have ogled her legs so blatantly, nor would he have been so rude.

"Look, Erin, they won't let me in to see him. It's a civilian hospital and they have no regard for my Naval rank. They just keep saying he's in surgery. But that's impossible!"

Erin could no longer remember why she'd ever been attracted to this brash pilot. How could she have imagined hurt in his eyes when she'd refused to go out with him!

"That was five and a half hours ago and they're still giving us the runaround. That damn Dr. Jefferson won't see us, and the rest of them won't give us any word at all. They've obviously screwed up somehow. They're out of line—"

"*They're* out of line?" Erin repeated, appalled at the unjust accusation of her colleagues. "I suspect the nurse on duty is just trying to teach you some manners. If you were half as rude to her as you've been to me you'll be lucky if she *ever* lets you see Roger! My God! Do you pilots think you own the whole damn world?"

"Roger's not a pilot!" Kyle exploded. Then his fury collapsed like a wave hitting the beach and dissolving under its own weight. His shoulders slumped before her while one tense hand raked through his hair. "Roger—" he breathed in a voice stripped of arrogance "—Roger...is my friend."

She got it then. For all the bravado and the quick angry words, Kyle Tatum was deathly afraid. Fighting the truth, he knew now that somehow Roger had fooled him, playing the clown while in pain and shock. Jeb Henson wore a more pleasant mask, but it was a shield for the same brand of fear.

Erin was surprised at her lack of perception. She'd let her woman's response to Kyle cripple her instincts as a doctor. She'd been trained to deal with rage and denial; she'd seen grief and fear in bereaved loved ones in every uniform it wore. Knowing NASA's pilots as she did, she should have remembered that charm and arrogance could both be dress blues for mourning.

As she marched silently to the phone past Kyle's anguished profile, she already knew what the outcome of her call would be. She knew her people; she trusted the staff at Our Lady of Mercy. There was only one reason that anyone on duty would have told these two men that Roger Shaw was still in surgery after five and a half hours; only one reason to let them believe that their friend was gravely, perhaps fatally, injured.

He was.

BY NOON THE NEXT DAY there wasn't a soul at NASA who didn't know that astronaut Roger Shaw was in a coma, his body attempting to cope with internal injuries that would more than likely prove to be fatal. Declaring his condition to Kyle Tatum the night before had been very difficult for Erin; his rigid courtesy an obvious cover for his feelings.

Erin knew her own feelings had been equally transparent. Her concern for Roger was shared by both Kyle and Jeb, so her few speechless moments of grief had not embarrassed her. And Jeb Henson would have to be blind to have missed the electrical storm that had swept her house when Kyle had appeared at the front door! For two years she had carefully guarded her response to this man; the cool mask of indifference had always remained securely in place at NASA. But last night he'd taken her by surprise.

When Erin went on duty at the hospital she found Kyle in front of Roger's door in Intensive Care. He was still dressed in blue, his body slouched in an orange plastic chair. Big brown hands cupped his skull as he leaned forward, head down, his elbows perched on his wide-spread knees. Erin briefly remembered the proud, demanding officer who'd ogled her so freely just the night before. The contrast would have made another woman weep. But Erin Ness was not a weeping woman.

She was a woman with vision, ambition and consummate surgical skill. She had come to Houston to go up in space, to fulfill a lifelong dream first spawned by John Glenn's triple orbit around the world not long after her eighth birthday. Climbing to the top of the heap at NASA had never been easy and was not always fun, and there were days when Erin asked herself if she wouldn't be happier devoting herself to surgery in a drier climate and a less volatile atmosphere. But she was not a quitter, and her childhood fantasy had yet to become real. Backing out now was simply not on her list of choices.

Unfortunately, Kyle Tatum was not on her list

either. She had learned very early in the game that professional women who wanted to succeed could not afford to date their colleagues, in medicine or in space. Boardroom decisions based on bedroom memories were unstable ones at best. This knowledge made it easy for Erin to deflect the eager group of admirers who had crowded her first weeks in Houston like senior students sniffing out incoming freshmen. Yet even then, in the crush of orientation and excitement and awe at rubbing shoulders with honest-to-goodness astronauts, she had realized that not one of her fleet of pilots could touch the hem of Kyle Tatum's oldest pair of jeans.

For several weeks she had sensed his eyes on her, but he had never joined the drooling pack that flanked Erin and her women friends. Only after her assignment took her to a department away from his own did Kyle approach her for a date. With the epitome of formal grace from another age, he'd invited her to dinner on a cruise...a Shakespearean play in Hermann Park...and, finally, to Houston's world-famous grand opera. After each rejection he would wait a week or two, then formally ask her out again, his poise never wavering no matter how he might be feeling.

And Erin was certain what he was feeling! The chemistry between them—refurbished so potently last night—must have been as obvious to him as it was to her, and all the more galling in the face of her courteous but unwavering resistance. Resistance! Where had that granite backbone been last night? From the moment his brazen eyes had swept hers, Erin had experienced an instant lift-off of her senses that had taken her by surprise. Her legs had stretched and trembled. The string bikini had all but come untied of its own volition! She couldn't help but wonder what the consequences might have been had Jeb not been there....

Of course, Kyle had been cooler toward her after that last rejection, and now, when he passed her in the hallways he gave her nothing more than a regulation smile. She was certain that he had ripped her page out of his little black book long ago. Only in his desperation to find out about Roger had he come to her, tucking his pilot's pride away long enough to seek help for his friend. And that had been her undoing.

In those early days she had told herself repeatedly that underneath the charm, Kyle Tatum was just as shallow as every other conceited pilot she'd met at NASA. Alternately she'd reminded herself that if he really was as traditional as he appeared, he was woefully unsuited for a modern woman like herself. Kyle undoubtedly preferred his women barefoot and pregnant, or at least in the kitchen full-time. Finally she'd tried to convince herself that the attraction between them was only physical anyway. Coupling all those defenses with the risk of career suicide inherent in dating a senior astronaut who someday might well be in a position to decide on her assignment to a mission, Erin had forced herself to keep a safe distance from Kyle Tatum.

But now as she stood in the hospital corridor, just a few yards away from his vulnerable eyes and thick black hair—mussed by his exhaustion and nervous hands—she couldn't remember why she'd ever pushed him away. At noon Jeb Henson had told her that Kyle had stayed at the hospital all night and refused to leave until Roger regained consciousness. It was unlikely that Roger ever would.

Silently Erin approached the grieving, solitary man before her. Only after she stood beside him for several

moments did Kyle look up; even then she didn't think
he recognized her right away.

"Erin. Hello...Erin," Kyle mumbled, rising to his
feet almost instinctively. His thirty-six-hour beard
smudged the trim lines of his virile face; his once-smart
shirt now looked wrinkled and old. "Do you have any
news?"

His eyes were so weary, so insistent on hope, that it
took Erin's best training not to make up something encouraging. "I'm sorry. No," she said, forcing herself
to tell him. She'd already checked Roger's chart, knew
that he was holding, almost steady, but had given Dr.
Jefferson no particular reason to hope. His head injuries were extensive, some organs were damaged, and
several of his vertebrae were cracked. "He's still alive,
Kyle. That's the best news we can offer."

Kyle slumped back down into the chair, the picture
of a man in despair. Erin didn't know how to reach
him and suddenly wasn't even sure that she should.
She was used to desperate strangers hunched over in
hospital halls and accustomed to loved ones using any
means to deal with grief and pain. But this man, she
realized, made her ache in a way that she had almost
forgotten, or perhaps had never known before.

"Is there...anything at all I can bring you? Something to eat, something to read—"

"News that he's getting better. That's the only thing
I need."

It was the first flare of feeling she'd seen in those
haunted eyes this evening, and his fervor paralyzed
Erin in midspeech. This was not the time to paw
through her bag of doctor's tricks to find a way to dislodge him, though it was clear he urgently needed food
and sleep. It would be foolish to drag this man from
his purpose...and unrealistic to try.

"I...I'll try to drop by later," she told him, feeling helpless and suddenly eager to escape. He offered no farewell as she left; gave no sign that he'd heard her tentative promise, much less that he cared.

Erin walked away, knowing that she could do more doctoring in the emergency room this evening than clucking over a man who was not yet ready to seek comfort. The only thing she could do for Kyle was to call Dr. Jefferson before she scrubbed and ask that Kyle be admitted to see Roger, no matter how briefly. Policy fluctuated in such cases; her recommendation could open the door.

It seemed like a longer shift than usual at Our Lady of Mercy. Weekends always brought heavy traffic to the emergency room, and tonight was no exception. Erin had been a surgeon long enough that she met few surprises on the operating table, only a few mysteries that she could no longer medically explain. But taking that knowledge and making it work...that was new each moment, a gift of life that she would never tire of giving...and never be too tired to give. She still took every death personally; under her skilled hands there were mercifully few.

Tonight there weren't any. By morning she had treated three children burned in a fire and stitched a badly wounded old man who'd been robbed and knifed; she'd delivered a fifteen-year-old's baby and brought down a junkie from his delirious trip. By the time she was relieved by the next shift she felt as if she'd been in surgery for three days straight, and yet, as always, she felt deeply satisfied knowing she'd made a difference in people's lives.

At times like this she often wondered what happened in the Emergency Room during the days she spent at NASA, where her surgeon's hands grappled with notepad and pencil instead of scalpel and human life. The difficulty of balancing both jobs was not unique to Erin; all the doctors at Johnson Space Center felt the strain of their commitments, knew the tug of classroom and lab research versus real-life surgery. She wondered how Roger Shaw resolved that dilemma, with his brilliant mind and masterful surgeon's hands. She had volunteered to fill in for Roger on the late-night shift, even though she knew she'd be exhausted. It was the only way she could think of to help him.

Tugging the pins out of her mandatory Operating Room hairdo, Erin's weary thoughts eventually forced her back to Roger's room in Intensive Care. Eight hours had passed since she'd left Kyle Tatum in the hallway, but when she returned he looked even more ensconced in place. He stood again when she approached him, a little less surprised to see her this time.

"Is there any change?" he asked by way of greeting, oblivious to her own exhaustion and blood-stained garb. It was a rhetorical question. Kyle Tatum knew what his friend's chances were, knew that not one iota of activity near Roger's room would have escaped his eye. He was an aviator, a test and fighter pilot, an astronaut; he was accustomed to the odds of life and death. Yet some inexplicable fraternal code bound him to that bedside.

Determined to find a way to soothe the proud yet humbled man before her, Erin asked, "Have they let you in to see him?"

He nodded earnestly. "Twice. It can make all the difference. He's got to know there's somebody waiting."

When Erin laid a hand on his shoulder in an instinctive gesture of comfort, the heat from his body seemed to scorch her fingers and she jerked her hand away, embarrassed at her own reaction. How could she have hoped that a platonic touch was possible between them?

"Does Roger have any family?" Erin quickly asked to regain her composure. "Is there anybody we should call?"

"His ex-wife wouldn't give a damn," Kyle declared bitterly. If he was at all disturbed by the undercurrent between them he was determined to ignore it. "His mother lives in Oregon. She's an invalid. I talked to her this morning." Compassion for the helpless woman lined his face. "I almost wish I hadn't. There's nothing she can do but pray and suffer."

That's about all any of us can do, Erin wanted to say. She processed a number of other well-meaning reassurances through her mind, discarding them all in the face of his pain.

Erin stood beside the silent, hurting pilot and queried softly, "Is there anything at all I can do for you, Kyle?"

"Nothing."

The word came out so harshly that it arrowed through her calm. To understand his grief was one thing; to be brushed aside like a buzzing gnat was something else altogether. Kyle had made his feelings clear: despite his physical attraction to her, Erin was merely an information source, a possible vehicle to Roger, no more and no less. Certainly not a source of comfort, another human being who wanted to ease the burning in his heart! She was, it seemed, in his way.

For an instant Erin stood next to Roger's door, listening to the predawn silence of the ward, the squish of cushioned white oxfords and patients restless in their sleep. She was exhausted, depressed and dirty; her back was sore and her feet felt like hot bricks.

Beside her sat Kyle Tatum, sleepless for two nights already and prepared to stay that way until his friend recovered. Compared to his vigil, her own weariness seemed petty. She wanted to reach out and hug him, draw some of the poison out of his heart into her own, but his dark and distant eyes forbade her. He would suffer, and he would suffer alone.

At last she turned and walked down the hallway, certain he would not even notice she was gone. Almost at once a nurse from the office stopped her, her voice low and urgent as she asked, "Is it true you're going to cover for Dr. Shaw tonight?"

Erin nodded.

"Any word on how he's doing?" She gestured toward Roger's door.

Erin shook her head, then started down the corridor as the nurse frowned and scurried off. Too tired to think past the moment, she almost didn't hear the velvet rasp that reached her as she touched the hallway door.

"Erin."

Kyle had spoken her name with a note of respect she hadn't heard lately. Slowly she turned to face him. Mute gratitude in his eyes told her that he understood why she was glad to make a sacrifice for Roger. For the very first time he seemed to sense her need to share the harness and yoke of his pain.

With infinite care he rose to speak. He plunged his hands down into his pockets as he apologized. "You...arranged for me to see Roger, didn't you?"

She nodded. There was nothing else to say.

"Thank you. That was...very kind."

Erin waited, certain he was not yet finished. She

ached for him; the simplest words of gratitude were such an effort in the face of his own helplessness. He was a man accustomed to taking charge in any situation, uncomfortable asking for favors or thanking those who gave them.

"You're going to work for him tonight." It was not a question. "You must be very tired."

She tried to summon a tiny smile. "Not as tired as you are, Kyle."

He shrugged his shoulders, as if it didn't matter, but the fatigue in his face made his skin almost gray. Erin waited, wordless, uncertain of whether he wanted her to go or stay. She knew he would not ask her and it was that knowledge, paradoxically, that made her want so very much to be with him.

"Kyle...would you...mind very much...if I just sat here with you for a while?" She met his eyes and whispered, "Roger is my friend, too."

For the first time in countless months, Kyle Tatum graced her with his sunshine-and-morning-dew smile. Weariness and despair seemed to slide off his shoulders, replaced by the magic that always strained to draw them together.

"No, Dr. Ness," he told her as the new dawn light seemed to fill up the entire hallway. "I wouldn't mind that at all."

CHAPTER TWO

WHEN KYLE GESTURED toward a pair of chairs by the wall, Erin felt as though he had just opened a car door for her as they'd started off on their first date. She had come back to Roger's room solely to check on his progress and to offer comfort to his friend. But now that she sat beside Kyle—so close that his knee brushed hers as he settled into the neighboring chair—she felt a trembling in her chest that had nothing to do with medicine or sympathy.

"Do you always work here on Friday nights?" Kyle asked, his eyes absorbing her uniform with appropriate sobriety. Despite his rumpled appearance, his characteristic officer's restraint was now back in place, and Erin knew she should have been grateful. Yet part of her missed that brazen visual assault he'd launched from her front porch. Her breasts swelled just a bit at the memory.

"Yes. I asked for this shift. It gives me the rest of the weekend without any commitments."

He offered her a cautious smile. "Busy social life, Erin?"

She flushed, remembering how many times she had turned him down. "Actually I spend most of it reading. Even with only one day a week in surgery, it's almost impossible to keep up with everything new in emergency medicine and work full time at NASA."

He nodded as though they shared a common bond.

"I have the same problem. Not reading so much as air time. When I was test flying my senses were keen as a razor blade. I could fly anything upside down or backward. Now I'm lucky if I get out of the simulators long enough to fly a T-38 once a week."

It wasn't the first time Erin had heard this complaint from a pilot. The T-38 had been the standard training jet at NASA since its inception and now contributed to maintaining flying proficiency only in the most general sense of the term. Most of the aviators longed for the speed and power of a more complex and contemporary flying machine.

Suddenly she realized that Kyle was staring at her. She'd completely forgotten his last sentence... dropped the conversational ball. But not because she wasn't listening. His eyes—those beautiful, passionate, sea-blue eyes—had settled on hers and had just asked a question of their own. *Why, Erin? Why did you always turn me down?*

She couldn't answer. Even if he'd asked her with words she probably couldn't have told him at the moment. Suddenly she couldn't remember.

"Did you know I've been teaching Roger how to fly?" Kyle announced abruptly, his eyes moving past her to a nurse in the hall.

"No," she managed to respond. "He never mentioned it."

Kyle smiled, returning his gaze to her face. "He's not very good at it yet. But he will be. Roger can do just about anything he sets his mind to."

Erin didn't want to remind him that Roger would probably never fly again. He would probably never even regain consciousness. But this was a time for hope and camaraderie; Kyle could deal with reality later.

Abruptly he stood up, pacing toward the far wall and then back to stand before her with his hands in his pockets. "What really burns me about being alone here," he confessed, "is that I don't think the guys would give up so easily if he were Navy. If this were a base hospital overseas there'd be a dozen guys filling up this hallway."

"Maybe it's different when men are at war," Erin offered.

"Maybe. But still. . . it bothers me, sometimes, how we keep our distance from the civilians. Before I came to NASA I didn't have a single friend who wasn't Navy. But now that I've flown with these guys. . . served on a crew. . . it just seems like we ought to act like a squadron while we're together, no matter what branch of the government we come from."

His use of flier's logic gave Erin new insight, but she decided to listen while he talked. He needed to get his feelings off his chest, and *she* needed to watch the way the muscles in his neck rippled while he talked. She needed to imagine her fingers in his hair. . . .

"Take Roger, for instance. I didn't like him much at first. He just seemed *too* friendly. Super Surgeon. . . Jolly Roger, we called him. Everybody's pal. On top of being a doctor, he was a sandcrab—" He stopped at her puzzled look. "A civilian, you know."

He looked embarrassed as he realized that Erin was a doctor and a civilian, too. He didn't need to explain his resistance to doctors; all the pilots considered the flight surgeon their greatest enemy, the guy who could get them grounded. But his prejudice against civilians surprised Erin and made her a little uncomfortable.

"So what made you change your mind about Roger?" she asked.

"Well, not too long after I got here, I started having

chest pains. What timing! I'd survived combat and test flying and being married to Vivian, and as soon as I got my orders for Houston, I started getting pains that wouldn't quit. It didn't help any that my family has a history of heart trouble.''

"And you'd already figured out that an astronaut can't have so much as an ingrown toenail on his record and still command a mission," Erin contributed, eager to keep him talking.

"Precisely. I was scared to death I'd lose control in the T-38 and they'd pick it up on the ground. Tatum's got heart trouble. Chuck the astro career—you get the picture."

Erin got the picture. He was a true member of his breed. Never mind *going down* in a plane because of a medical problem or smashing yourself to smithereens. Just make sure nobody clipped your wings!

"So one day Roger told me he needed a ride, but the minute he got in the car he turned doctor on me and started asking about my chest. He said he'd report my medical condition to the NASA brass and the Navy unless I let him examine me."

Erin shook her head. "A brave man, Dr. Roger Shaw."

"And stupid. I nearly took his head off. I wanted to know how he found out, how much he knew, what kind of blackmail he had in mind. Damn crazy thing about Roger, he honest to God just wanted to help. He said he knew what NASA meant to me because he had the same dream. He couldn't turn me in because he was an astronaut, but he couldn't ignore my symptoms because he was a doctor."

"Roger really is special." Erin reached out to touch his arm. "You have good taste in friends."

Instinctively he covered her fingers with his own;

new flames seared them both and bound them together. In a runaway toboggan rush of feelings, Erin realized that Kyle had never touched her before. If he had, she would never have found the strength to turn him down so many times.

Then Kyle met her eyes, his own a puzzle of unreadable emotions. She watched him take control of his desire for her and store it somewhere out of view. Then he gently released her hand and took a step or two back before he forced himself to continue.

"Turned out that all I had was heartburn," he murmured, his voice not quite steady. "Excitement and pressure from this powerhouse place. I was more relaxed in Vietnam! He started me on some over-the-counter antacid and that was the end of it."

Carefully reading his mood, Erin suggested, "Sometimes the body knows best. Mine, for instance, is telling me that breakfast is in order. Would you mind walking me down to the cafeteria?" Before he could protest she told him, "They can call me anywhere in the building if there's the slightest hint of a change in room 106A."

She gave him a moment to adjust to the idea, even though she knew he was just about ready. Surely he was hungry! Besides, he needed to do something to stop thinking about Roger.

Kyle didn't say much on the way to the cafeteria. The newborn tension between them lingered despite his restraint. He could tuck his desire for Erin under his cap, but he couldn't pretend it wasn't there.

"This looks like a mess hall," Kyle observed as they toured the plastic trays, plastic forks and virtually plastic food. "You'd think they'd provide a more uplifting atmosphere in a hospital."

"Well," Erin began, stifling a sudden domestic urge

to cook for him, "there is a little outdoor patio for the staff with a few benches and trees. I don't use it much because it's usually so steamy outside, but this time of day a little breeze might save us."

"That would be great." His genuine smile revealed a pair of dimples that added a spirit of playfulness to his classically contoured face.

Erin wasn't at all sure what she might be able to get him to eat, so she gathered up a little of everything that looked remotely tempting. Too quickly for her to protest, Kyle paid the cashier, picked up her tray and motioned for her to lead him to the patio. Not for the first time it occurred to her that what had started out as a gesture of solace had ended up feeling like a date.

"You're not much on the weather in this part of Texas, are you, Erin?" Kyle questioned as he opened the outside door for her.

"Nope. In fact, it's my personal opinion that Houston has without question the most disgusting weather on the face of the earth."

Kyle laughed. It was the first time she'd ever heard him do it, and the joy in his voice warmed her.

"Surely you don't *like* this oily swampland, Kyle. It reminds me of a nightmare, or a grade B Japanese monster movie."

Again he laughed, more heartily this time, and Erin suspected she might actually have claimed a portion of his mind from Roger. "Hey, lady, I don't disagree with your assessment. It's just that I've been in places so much worse, without air conditioning or swimming pools. . .or hope. . . ." He paused, letting his memories of war settle in the air between them. "Anyway, the insect repellent works on Houston's bugs and you don't even need it indoors. You're even safe to eat fresh fruits and vegetables! Where are you from, anyway?"

"Southern Arizona. Hot and dry in the daytime, cold and dry at night. It's this awful humidity that gets to me. It's like having a mask over my face."

"You must really want to be an astronaut to put up with Houston." His eyes studied her as she peeled an orange.

"To put up with Houston, the work load, the absence of a social life, and the interminable waiting to go up in space. Two years already, and I haven't even been assigned to a flight crew yet. I'm not even part of the research team for Roger's crew, even though I probably know more about his work than anybody else at NASA." It occurred to her fleetingly that if Roger didn't recover in time to carry out the mission, her knowledge could be vital to the success of 61-J. She handed Kyle a section of the orange, then lay the rest of it on a napkin in front of him.

Kyle toyed with the fruit. His tone was troubled as he counseled, "Take it from me, Erin, being assigned to a mission wouldn't help. It just turns the screws tighter as you get closer and closer, waiting for something to go wrong."

"What could go wrong? I understand your mission has been fairly smooth sailing." Erin recalled that it involved some kind of laser-tracking research for the proposed antiballistic satellite system, the "Star Wars" defense frequently heralded in the news. "Not that I know that much about it—"

"And you won't," he stopped her gently, biting into the orange. "At least from me. It's a military project with international diplomatic ramifications, Erin, and there are some areas that still haven't been cleared for public knowledge."

Erin wanted to tell him she wasn't public, she was NASA...and presumably worthy of a little more trust. But this wasn't a time for self-indulgent diatribes. He was eating, smiling, talking about something other than Roger. That was all that mattered at the moment.

It was, for Houston, a beautiful day. It wasn't oppressively hot just yet; wispy zephyrs rustled the sailplane leaves of the pecan trees. It seemed like a perfect day for a picnic at a park or a sandy beach. She imagined herself stretched out on a blanket next to a plate brimming with cold fried chicken and potato salad. Beside her, Kyle would—

She stopped her daydream abruptly as she realized that he was studying her face. He gave her a slow, sleepy grin that hinted that his own thoughts had not been too far from her own. Erin tried to give him a smile that was nothing but chaste and proper, but the smile got away from her and showered him with affection. Even though Kyle's face was now impassive, she was sure that his eyes returned the depth of her feelings. But after a moment he looked away, rising from the bench as he began to collect his orange peels.

"This has been very nice, Erin," he told her as though it were time for a good-night kiss at the front door. "But I have to get back to Roger. The doctor said I could see him again about eight."

Maybe I didn't succeed here after all, she told herself. *He needs to go home. He needs to get some sleep. He needs to start accepting the possibility of Roger's death.* "Seeing him is very important to you, isn't it, Kyle?"

"It's important to *him*," Kyle countered earnestly, sitting down again. "I don't know whether you're one of those doctors who believe unconscious people can hear things, Erin, but I know they can. Some buried part of Roger knows I'm here waiting for him. As long as he knows I won't give up on him, I don't believe he'll give up on himself."

For a moment Erin was silent. While it was possible, even likely, that Roger could sense Kyle's presence, placing too much value on their moments together could only add to Kyle's guilt if Roger failed to recover. "Don't you think you could. . .get some rest in between visits? I really think you'd be more use to Roger."

"No, I can't get some rest. He has to know I'm *not* resting. He has to know he's a damned inconvenience, just like you got me to eat because my misery was an inconvenience to you."

"Kyle! That's not—"

"I thought you understood, Erin. I have to stay."

She sighed deeply as the barest hint of a breeze lifted a lock of her hair. How many other things had she misunderstood? So much of their communication seemed to lie in the unspoken. At times she was absolutely certain that she could read his mind. . .and his heart. And yet. . . she could have been completely off base. She respected him. . .hurt for him. . . wanted him. But did she really understand anything about a man like Kyle Tatum? "I understand that you owe a debt to Roger, Kyle, but—"

"I don't owe it just to Roger. I'd do this for any guy I picked up off the street and brought in here. I owe it to Murphy the Medic."

Erin raised her eyebrows questioningly.

"Look, Erin," he declared with sudden urgency, "you've got to understand about Murphy so you can stop worrying about me. Murphy was this scrawny kid out of Iowa—Ioway, he called it—face all acne scarred. The third time I got shot down—just south of Hanoi—this kid was the first guy I saw when the rescue helo dropped me on the deck. I don't think he'd ever seen so much blood—he was shaking worse than I was. I mean, it was my third tour in combat and I was ready to die every day. But I knew I was running out of chances, and I'd never been hit this bad.''

Erin saw fatal injuries daily, but still the thought of Kyle bloodied in combat made her heart ache. To see his proud and regal body damaged—

"I asked him his name and he said his unit called him Murphy the Medic, because he was a medical corpsman. I asked him if he'd ever seen a man die before... I really felt like he needed some preparation.''

Erin could hardly breathe, and it wasn't even hot in the courtyard.

"'Lieutenant, sir,' he said to me, 'I'm nineteen years old and I never been over the state line till I went to boot camp. I ain't never seen a man die and I sure as hell ain't gonna start with you.' ''

Despite the tension of his words, Kyle tried to smile. It wasn't the same smile that had warmed her blood just moments ago, but it touched her just the same. "I laughed. There I was. I'd nearly bought the farm, and this kid's greatest fear was that *he* was about to watch me die. It was better to laugh than to give up altogether. So I said to him, 'Murphy the Medic, if you get me home to my wife in one piece, I'll fly you personally to Pearl Harbor and have my mother cook you the finest meal you've ever had in your life. I'll even fix you up on a date with my sister.' ''

Kyle took her hand, kneading her fingers with unconscious intimacy. She was sure she'd still feel the heat on her knuckles hours from now. "I don't remember anything after that, Erin. But when I came to three days later, they told me that Murphy had refused to leave my side since he first brought me in. And he talked to me the whole damn time... pumping me for details on my pretty sister... telling me he'd never been to Hawaii. . . hollering that he was too damn tired to stay up forever while I slept the war away. What kind of an example was I setting for the enlisted men? To this day, Erin, I don't know how much I heard while I was out and how much they told me later. But I am absolutely certain that Murphy the Medic kept me alive. Some damn fool kid with a backwoods education who didn't know me from Adam. Not the flight surgeon, not the damn ventilator. He *willed* me not to die, Erin. I've got to pass it on.''

For several moments the silence was eerie. There was nothing she could say except, *Thank God for Murphy the Medic!* For three whole days Kyle needed to stay with Roger, and she would make no further effort to sway him from his course.

"Did he ever get to meet your sister?"

Kyle laughed again, then reached out to touch Erin's cheek. Somehow they'd left the hospital behind; they were on a deserted island where they didn't need to fear the impact of every intimate gesture or meaningful look.

"I don't have a sister," he admitted, his fingers wrapping tiny curls in the ends of Erin's strawberry blond hair. "But my father arranged with an admiral friend of his for Murphy to have a date with his daughter—a virtual miracle in Murphy's eyes. It cost my dad a whole wardroomful of saved-up favors.''

This time Erin laughed with him, feeling instant kinship with Kyle's father. "I bet your father didn't mind."

"Hell, no. He would have given up his command to get me back alive, even though it would have killed him at that time.''

"At that time?" Erin asked, instinctively knowing they were on tender ground.

Abruptly Kyle released her hair as though he'd just noticed it in his fingers. "My father is...just about ready to retire. Physically. He knows he should and he'll leave with honors, but it's still...very hard for him to imagine not being on active duty."

Erin could appreciate his father's feelings. She could never understand quitting a career to have babies, a pattern she'd seen in so many of her childhood friends. Some of them were happy, true enough, but for Erin Ness....

She didn't have time to dwell on her thoughts because Kyle was checking his computerized watch, obviously eager to return to Roger. "I know you need some rest right now, Erin. If you've...got a few spare minutes when you come back on duty, maybe you could...drop by Roger's room."

It was a question he would not have asked her a few hours ago, and the fact that he did so now assured her that she had not imagined those special moments of intimacy.

"You can count on it, Kyle." Her eyes found his and sealed the promise. Fatigue still marred his dark brown face, but there was a gentling there now, a sense of camaraderie that lifted the tired edges of his mouth. She would not be leaving him as alone as he had been before.

Without a word he raised one hand and laid the palm flat against her cheek. His fingers splayed across her ear in silent speech... a bouquet of roses and thank-yous. Some part of Erin longed to ask if his wartime wife was as real as his mythical sister, but before she could speak he had vanished, leaving her face bare and aching in the new morning sun.

LATE SUNDAY NIGHT, his vigil completed, Kyle Tatum returned to his room at Bachelor Officers' Quarters and slept for almost sixteen hours. It was midafternoon before he awakened, still feeling muzzy and totally depleted. Nevertheless he quickly made the bed, took a shower and started to dress to return to the hospital.

B.O.Q. wasn't a bad place to live, considering all the other holes in the earth he'd had to call home. He had privacy, at least within the cubicle of four khaki-colored walls. He had enough to eat, and he had companionship—though he could never pretend that the nightly gathering at the Officers' Club was any substitute for a wife and children. The Navy provided good accommodations; he couldn't really complain. But he would have preferred coming home at night to a sea nymph in a mint-green bikini, string bows at the ready, with a smile like sunrise on the ocean and a heart that understood him almost before he spoke.

It was not unlike the vision of domestic perfection he'd had a lifetime ago when he first met Vivian...a fantasy that had never materialized and had only added to his other wartime nightmares.

Vivian had crudely challenged his lifelong beliefs that women should be cherished and protected and loyal to their menfolk, understanding that the Navy comes before *everything*. After six months of marriage on a sexual merry-go-round, the ride began to slow down. Reluctantly he realized that he'd changed all he could change and still be Kyle Tatum. Vivian hadn't really changed at all. Slowly, he'd begun to reclaim his values.

After that it was all a blur. "If you loved me, Kyle, you'd this...if you loved me, Kyle, you'd that...." He'd almost welcomed the news that his squadron was going into combat. Some of the men had transplanted their wives to Japan, but Vivian had eagerly made plans to stay stateside near her folks. Kyle was relieved to be free of her harping, but it hurt him that she had never once asked him to take her along.

He couldn't imagine Erin Ness flitting off to mom and dad if her man was in danger. She'd probably cart her medical bag right into the foray, reviving hapless soldiers with her dazzling smile.

He could see that smile as though it were painted in a picture on his wall. It was the first thing about Erin that had captured his attention when she'd arrived at NASA, proud and determined and—under all that ambitious carriage—just a little bit scared. He hadn't planned on getting involved with an astronaut. He wasn't even sure that women should be allowed to *be* astronauts! Space was a profession that could destroy even the best of *men*. Between his chivalrous, albeit traditional, upbringing and his devastating marriage to Vivian, his instincts now, more than ever, steered him away from career women.

But when it came to Erin, his instincts had let him down. He'd fallen for her so hard that it had embarrassed him, even though only his closest friends had been able to read the signs. Encouraged by the hunger he kept reading in her eyes, he'd given her more chances to turn him down than he'd ever given any woman. When at last he had given up on her, it was only with the greatest reluctance...and no small amount of lingering hope. He'd never yet managed to walk past her in the hall without his pulse jumping.

His reverie was broken by a knock on the door. "It's just me," Jeb's voice reached him reassuringly.

Kyle didn't bother to reach for a shirt before he let Jeb in. "Has there been any—"

"No change. I called about an hour ago. They told me Dr. Ness had left orders to notify her immediately if they had any news."

Kyle nodded, his face a mixture of pleasure and relief as he continued dressing. He had been too foggy
by the time he left last night to know for sure what
he'd said to Erin, but obviously she had followed
through on her promise to keep an eye on Roger.

"I . . . got the impression that Erin spent most of the
weekend with you at the hospital." Jeb's tone was noncommittal as he sat down in the regulation wooden chair
by Kyle's desk. The two men had been friends for a long
time. Jeb had already gone up in space before Kyle was
sent to Houston, but their paths had crossed many
times before in the Navy. They'd even flown together in
combat. In public they always behaved like Naval officers, but alone they were just old friends.

"She did," Kyle replied, buttoning up his shirt.
More than once over the weekend he'd thought of Erin
Ness as an unexpected miracle in the midst of Roger's
tragedy. At his darkest moment she had lifted Kyle
from despair and filled him with new hope. She had
listened to his jagged speeches and profound moments
of exhausted silence; touched him when he needed to
be touched and left him alone when he needed to re-
treat. Except for surgery and a brief stint of sleep, she
had not left his side for two days.

"Why, uh . . . why do you suppose she did that?"
Jeb asked.

Kyle stared at him blankly; he was still pretty tired.
"I'm not following you."

Jeb crossed his ankle over his knee and sighed.
"Why do you suppose she spent the weekend there at
the hospital with you? She's a very busy lady."

Kyle faced his friend. "I asked her to stay with me.
Besides, I think she's as upset about Roger as I am."

"I think it'd be safe to say she's got a vested interest
in the outcome of his accident."

Kyle's eyes darkened. He knew perfectly well that if Roger couldn't go on 61-J, Erin was as good a candidate as any to replace him. She'd dropped more than one hint to that effect over the weekend. She also knew that Jeb would have a big say in the replacement decision, and if anybody could sway Jeb's vote, it would be Kyle Tatum.

But that's not why she gave me all those special hours, his heart hollered in rebuttal. *After two years, the seed that's lain dormant has finally had a chance to take root. Don't rip the new shoot out of the ground before it's even had time to grow.*

"What is it you're trying to say, Jeb?" he demanded, pushing all logic from his mind. "I asked Erin to spend some time with me and she did. She was a tremendous comfort."

"Oh, I'll bet she was."

"Jeb—"

"Look, Kyle, you've asked her to spend time with you before. Several times, in fact. As I recall, it never did you the slightest bit of good until Roger got hurt."

He could not refute Jeb's very accurate memory. "Okay. I struck out with Erin before. Miracle of miracles, she seems to have noticed me at last. Ironic under the circumstances, but I'm not about to look a gift horse in the mouth." He could have added that Erin was the only antidote he had to his current sorrow, but he was too proud to confess that, even to Jeb.

"It's only a matter of time before we decide to replace Roger," Jeb declared, ignoring Kyle's explanation. "Erin must realize that. She—"

"You can't replace him yet! It's only been three days, Henson. It's not right—"

"I didn't say it was right," Jeb countered calmly. "I said it was only a matter of time."

For several minutes the two men glared at each other in silence. Jeb tugged the hem of his trousers and said nothing while Kyle battled the claw of unrest in his stomach.

"Tell me what you came here to say, Jeb."

Jeb shook his head. "I'm not sure what I came here to say. I like Erin. I've told you before that I think she's far too ambitious to ever make you happy, Kyle, but I respect her work. I know Roger does, too. I think it's great that she's been so supportive this weekend, but... I think you might just want to take a moment to ask yourself why."

"Why what?"

Jeb leaned forward and dropped his words like bullets into a pistol chamber. "Why is this woman suddenly so damned interested in you and Roger?"

By Saturday it seemed to Erin that her hospital weekend with Kyle had been a dream. Despite the undeniable magic that had drawn them together... despite the empathy nurtured in those empty hallways... despite the tender promise of their not-quite-platonic goodbye, almost seven days had passed without a word from the pilot who had touched her heart.

She reasoned that Kyle had been too busy to call her. She even tried to convince herself that maybe she only wanted him as a friend. But just as babies come when they will, her newborn, unscheduled longing now cried at birth with new life of its own.

If Kyle had merely been a friend in crisis, Erin would have called to see if she could be of help. If he had been another man she'd met and longed to see again, she might have summoned up her courage to ask him home for dinner, tossing her never-date-your-colleagues rule out the window. But she stumbled between these two positions, so she couldn't reach out to him at all. Adrift in a stormy sea, she couldn't reach the lifeboat.

Normally Erin relished a quiet night at home after a strenuous week. Once a caretaker's house on an old sorghum plantation, her gingerbread cottage was a delightful collection of nooks and crannies and lovely wood trim, the perfect backdrop for her knickknacks and quilts. The surrounding half acre was a rambling nest of untended roses and native wild flowers that she was always too busy to keep up. But she didn't care. She loved the cocoon of privacy that sheltered her from the rumble of traffic between NASA and Heron Bay Naval Air Station.

Tonight she would have welcomed at least one pilot's car from Heron Bay. She wasn't really at home by choice—she'd cancelled a friendly date and turned Roger's shift over to a friend in hopes that she'd hear from Kyle. Somehow his week-long silence robbed the private evening of its pleasure.

Dressed in her customary off-duty wardrobe—this evening a floral lavender bikini—Erin lay curled up on her couch with a stack of NASA briefs on her lap. In the last week she'd read everything she could get from the files on Roger's research for 61-J. The top brass had decided that Roger would be in no condition to complete the mission whether he lived or not, and Erin had been one of three physician-astronauts approached as a possible replacement.

She had mixed feelings about the assignment. Personally, she didn't like the idea of replacing Roger. Despite the obvious medical signs that his recovery was quite unlikely, Erin refused to give up hope. Every night she checked into his room, hoping to find some sign of

improvement that everyone else had missed. She'd
been a doctor long enough to know that sometimes
comatose patients come back step by step or all at
once; and sometimes they just quietly die. There was
still no particular reason to lay odds on which path
Roger would take.

Professionally, of course, Erin was ecstatic about
the chance to be assigned to 61-J. She was tired of doing legwork for other doctors and tired of waiting for
everything she wanted in life. Like any astronaut, she
wanted to go into space as soon as possible; and like
any emergency-medicine specialist, she was extremely
interested in the applied surgery that would take place
on 61-J. This would lay the groundwork for the emergency medical-care system on the permanent space station that NASA planned to set up within the decade.

But she refused to allow herself too much hope this
early in the game. Her competition was fierce. Dave
Porter had been at NASA longer than Erin, and had
an excellent record. Cameron Michaels had come to
Houston the same year she had and was a first-rate
surgeon, but he was conceited and not always easy to
get along with. Every likely candidate with more
seniority was already assigned to an upcoming mission
and could not be moved without disrupting schedules
all the way down the line.

For the hundredth time Erin reviewed the reasons
she deserved the assignment. There was no finer surgeon at NASA, although there were others who were
just as good. Her technical record was flawless; she'd
bent over backward to keep her professional re-
lationships cordial and clean. She had earned her
reputation as a workaholic, and she knew anyone who
took over for Roger would have to put his personal life
on hold to pull everything together in time. Finally—a

subtle point which she could never mention in an interview—she was absolutely devoted to Roger Shaw, with an almost naive kind of hero worship, and she would do everything in her power to carry out the mission the way he would have done it.

She pushed aside the fear that nudged her shell of confidence. She'd never known a single astronaut who didn't end up crawling the walls from stress long before the launch date. In Erin's case—taking over in midstream—the pressure would be magnified. The risk of failure would be far greater... the desire to succeed more intense. It was enough that this mission would be the apex of her career, the dream she'd fought and slaved for in her endless struggle to prove her worth as woman, physician and astronaut. But if her first space flight was 61-J, she couldn't just be good enough for Erin Ness. She had to be good enough for Dr. Roger Shaw... or at least good enough for his memory.

Erin picked up a set of photos from the floor and studied them with care. The first shot was a handshake between Roger and the chimp he would have operated on during the mission. Dozens of vital tests would be made to prepare mankind for his first emergency surgery in space, whenever that might be. The problems of operating in zero gravity were endless—starting with how to keep the patient, the surgeon and the instruments from floating around the cabin, and ending with the effects on blood clotting, transfusions, infection and anesthesia. Roger's replacement would try to pluck this data out of a hoard of instruments and a single surgical procedure on this unsuspecting chimpanzee.

He had insisted on establishing a rapport with his patient, a Hippocratic notion that his other crew members found absurd and Erin found delightful. He'd renamed the hairy fellow Quinto, Spanish for fifth, and dubbed him the fifth crew member on the mission. In each picture he looked at Roger with patent adoration, his toothy grin for the cameras sassy and gay. He wore a mini NASA jump suit, complete with his name and the 61-J arm patch. Roger looked proud enough to start passing out cigars.

"You can't die on us, Roger," Erin said to the attractive man in the photo. "Even if somebody else goes up on the shuttle, 61-J is still your mission and you can take all the credit for its success. You'll never have to doubt that it was worth your time and energy as a surgeon. Someday a whole space world of people will owe their lives to you and this little guy."

It occurred to her that she was beginning to act like Kyle...talking to a man who was not only unconscious but not even there. She wondered if the speech she just made might give Roger a boost as he lay silently in bed, but she discarded it as sentimental. After all, Kyle really meant something to Roger. Erin was just a friendly acquaintance.

She dug a little deeper into her pile of NASA newsletters until she came to her collection of astronaut biographies. She was sure she'd read them all at one time or another, but there were one or two she might like to look at again.

It wasn't Roger's bio but Kyle Tatum's that ended up in her hands a moment later. He was dressed in his Navy dress blues in the photo, looking grave but incredibly handsome. Under the photo were listed his hometown, flight background and military honors. There were many of the latter. But next to his name and age came the single word that she knew she had really been seeking when she'd plucked this sheet from her pile: divorced.

He didn't belong to Vivian anymore.

Erin wondered what would cause a passionately loyal man like Kyle to abandon a lady he'd promised to love for a lifetime. Surely *he* had left *her*...no woman in her right mind would give up Kyle Tatum! He'd asked Murphy to send him home to his wife, but it was his mother's hospitality he'd offered with such pride. Something about that mismatch bothered Erin. Maybe the marriage was already in trouble when Kyle was wounded. It occurred to her hurtfully that Vivian should have been the one willing him to live, not an unlikely hero named Murphy the Medic.

Erin suspected that the comfort she'd offered Kyle was small compared to Murphy's. And now she wondered if it had been worth it. When she'd tried to ease his hours of painful waiting, she had never imagined how much of Kyle's anguish would end up in her own heart. Yet somewhere in the intensive hours they had spent together, with secrets shared and wounds well tended, new feelings had been awakened in Erin. Kyle had warmed and then melted all of her rational defenses, and she had been so worried about his feelings that she'd forgotten to guard her own. She had learned to wait for his sunlight smile, and only now—alone at midnight—did she realize that he had left her in darkness.

As THE REST OF NASA began to accept Roger's death as inevitable, Kyle's determination to see his friend through this crisis seemed to grow even more intense. He'd gone back to work, but he still checked into room 106A twice a day and took a few moments to talk to Roger. He had never seen the slightest sign that Roger knew he was there, and this Sunday afternoon had been no different.

Kyle wondered if Erin ever checked on his friend, but he couldn't bring himself to ask the nurses. Mercifully he had not run into her at all last week. Keeping away from that special lady was one of the hardest things he'd ever done in his life; to meet her face to face and maintain a safe distance might well be impossible.

Yet if he were honestly facing a choice between betraying Roger—by indirectly helping Erin take his place on the mission—and denying himself Erin, there was no debate. A fallen comrade had to take precedence over a woman—any woman—and especially one about whom he had no objectivity whatsoever. He could have asked her about Jeb's fears, but what would that have gained him? She'd hate him for suspecting her of such guile, and he would probably believe anything she told him anyway.

Jeb had never mentioned Erin again since the first time he had planted his seed of suspicion, but Kyle could not forget his friend's clear logic. After his diligent but utterly fruitless pursuit of Erin in her early days in Houston, how could he explain her sudden interest in him? Even her intense concern for Roger seemed suspect when one considered the superficial nature of their professional relationship. That, plus her blunt confession of expertise in Roger's field, were giving Kyle reason for serious concern.

Several facts remained irrefutable. Erin was a top contender for Roger's place on 61-J; Jeb had a major role in that decision and had already been approached by more than one close friend on behalf of someone in the running; and after a two-year perfect record of *never* dating anyone in Houston with whom she worked, Erin Ness gave every visible sign of being ready and willing to explore any kind of relationship Kyle might have wanted.

Yet after last weekend the hospital seemed, to Kyle, unaccountably bare without her. Over and over again his thoughts boomeranged back to their special time together right here in these dreary halls. How impossible that it was all a con! Yet how could he take the risk of betraying a friend who lay so very near death? It was a wartime code that he could never shake, a standard of combat loyalty that he could not violate until either Roger recovered or Kyle had proof that Erin's interest in him was genuine. If she were chosen for 61-J and it was through her own merits, he'd be happy for her. But if he learned she had used him to get the inside track on Roger's position, he could never forgive himself. And if she *weren't* chosen, and she still wanted him, then he could be sure of her feelings. He desperately hoped he wouldn't see her again until the decision was made.

That hope was crushed just moments later. Kyle's senses told him that Erin had rounded the corner even before he heard her footsteps and glanced up at the sunlight in her eyes. Mutual understanding drew them together as she approached him, and suddenly he was certain that if Erin Ness had been a salesclerk or a waitress she would have wanted him just the same.

"Hi." She greeted him, a thousand promises in the single word. Her smile reached out to touch his heart. She looked a bit uncertain, but so glad to see him that she couldn't seem to restrain her joy. "You look so much better. Do you feel a bit more rested?"

He nodded as he rose to meet her, his own smile suddenly matching her own. The magic was still there! It hadn't been a mirage conjured up by his own longing. *You're wrong, Jeb,* his heart thundered. *Thank God!* "You look pretty good yourself," he told her, as though her white doctor's coat were a lace and chiffon evening gown. "Then again, you always look great to me."

As his hands came up to cup her face, her eyes glistened with hope. No, it was more than hope. It was relief—naked relief that he still wanted her. It had occurred to him once or twice that she might have been puzzled by his failure to contact her after their special weekend, but he'd never imagined she cared enough to be genuinely wounded by his silence. Now her eyes told him a different story. How cruelly he'd misjudged her! He would have to ease that pain. Starting right now.

"I'm glad you're here," he whispered. "You're not working again, are you?"

She shook her head. "Not really. I just had a patient from Friday night I wanted to check on. Dr. Jefferson takes over after my shift, but. . . it's kind of hard for me to let go on the really grave cases."

He nodded, admiring her concern. "There's been no change with Roger," he told her.

"I know." She dismissed the information quickly and changed the subject. "Did you hear that they've decided to assign another surgeon to 61-J?"

He didn't like the question. He didn't like the enthusiasm that bubbled so obviously beneath the surface. *Was I wrong?* he asked himself.

Slowly his hands slid off her face. Apprehension leaked into his heart. "Yes. I heard that."

"They're considering me to replace Roger, Kyle. I can't tell you what an honor it is."

Is that why there's magic in her eyes today? he asked himself. He struggled for words but found none.

"I've always looked up to him," she continued with spirit. "I've studied everything he's ever done, and I know that if anybody can carry out Roger's wishes on this mission, it's me. I feel it. Like fate. I'd do my best for him—"

"You don't have to convince me, Erin," he cut her off. "Save your speech for the interview committee."

She took a step back and stared at him, a bit confused by his tone. "Have you eaten today, Kyle?" she asked gently.

"No."

She smiled again. "Great. I've got an idea. Let's zip over to my place and let me fix up something that isn't reconstituted. Ever since I saw you looking at that plastic food in the cafeteria I've wanted to cook for you." Hesitation washed across her face, as though she was afraid she'd gone too far.

Dammit, what is she thinking? What does she want from me? "I . . . I wouldn't want you to go to any trouble for me, Erin," he said out loud. "I'm really not hungry."

"Hey, I have to cook for myself anyway."

"Erin—"

"Besides, it would really help me to bounce some ideas off somebody who's already been assigned to a mission. You might be able to give me some pointers as to what they're looking for. I've got copies of every brief that could remotely relate to 61-J, but I never like to leave any stone unturned."

His eyes darkened. "And I guess I'm an unturned stone. . . ."

She looked a little baffled by his attitude, but she clung to her smile. "We don't have to talk about the mission if you don't want to, Kyle. Let's just get something to eat and relax a little bit." She linked her arm with his in anticipation of the walk toward the parking lot, but Kyle could not bring himself to move. Roger still lay just fifteen feet away.

"I'm. . . sorry, Erin." He had to push the words out one by one. "I won't be able to accept your kind offer."

She released his arm, looking puzzled, but she took it in her stride. "Well—no problem. It was just an idea. If you'd like to take a rain check for some other night this week—"

He shook his head. His eyes were anguished, but his mouth was firm. He was a Naval officer. He would do his duty.

"I don't think another night would be any better, Erin. My schedule is very full."

For several moments she stared at him while pale scarlet flushed her ivory skin. She could conceal neither her surprise nor her humiliation. He hadn't just turned her down. Despite his strained courtesy, he'd all but slapped her in the face!

Dammit, Jeb, Kyle thought, *would she look like that if all she wanted was the mission?*

"I. . . won't. . . keep you," she forced out, her composure temporarily destroyed. In a moment she recovered, her voice tense but clear as she moved away. "I'll see you around some time."

"Sure. Thanks for everything," he announced in a voice his own mother would not have known.

Then he stood perfectly still as the woman he ached for marched proudly down the hallway. He knew he'd battered her feelings, but he didn't know if it was her professional dream or a private one that had taken the blow. Either way it made him sick to hurt her; it made him crazy to deny himself.

He slammed one fist into his palm and silently swore an oath he'd learned at sea. Then he turned back to the wall and whispered, "This one's for you, Roger. This one's for you."

CHAPTER THREE

FOR THE NEXT TWO WEEKS Erin rode an emotional roller coaster. The highs were filled with interviews and conferences and unofficial chats with Jeb Henson and the rest of the 61-J crew. The lows were filled with thoughts of Kyle.

None of it made sense! Every one of her usual instincts told her that the chemistry between herself and Kyle Tatum had always been perfectly in tune. During that first meal at the hospital they had reached a level of empathy that some friends don't attain in a dozen years. Even their shared silences were perfect. The yearning and peace, together in delicate balance, surrounded them like a halo whenever they were in the same room.

So how had she so misjudged him? A courteous man, he was obviously embarrassed by having to turn down a colleague he could now only view as overly aggressive, especially considering his traditional background. And he'd had to reject her not once but twice, patiently waiting for her to get the hint and leave him alone. How could she have imagined that glow in his eyes just before she'd asked him home for dinner... misread the way he'd touched her face? A thousand times she'd tried to explain it, and a thousand more times she'd told herself it didn't matter. But the days had snowballed into weeks and still she ached to see him, still yearned for his touch, and desperately hoped that their paths would never cross again.

"Rinny, what's wrong with you today?" the dark-haired girl across the table whispered, concern clouding her angelic face as they sat together in NASA's cafeteria. "You haven't said a word since I got here. If you're really too busy to see me..."

"Don't be silly, Katie," Erin countered brusquely, remembering that she'd invited her younger sister's friend to lunch to cheer her up. Katie's husband had only recently been transferred to Heron Bay, and his pregnant wife needed a woman friend to tease and gossip with and share news about the baby. At first Erin hadn't had much patience with what she considered idle patter, but after a month or two she'd come to value the compassion and unconditional affection of this innocent, sterling woman who was a distant link to her own family. "When I don't have time for my friends it's time to jump off this Ferris wheel," she told Katie with a grin. "How's the baby-to-be?"

Having struck a subject that always made Katie glow, Erin was awarded a seven-minute treatise on the status of the decorating options on the nursery. The crisis seemed to center on whether jungle animals or Winnie the Pooh would make a better theme.

"I'm so sure it's a girl, I want to go ahead with pink gingham for the cradle skirt, but Billy says I'm jumping the gun and we ought to go with yellow or white."

"Billy's right," Erin agreed, wondering what on earth Katie would do when her young husband went to sea for the first time this summer. "Babies are never what you expect them to be. Besides, the quilt I'm making is mint and kelly green."

Katie's eyes lit up like a child who'd just been allowed to open a gift the day before Christmas. "You're making a quilt for the baby, Rinny? With all you have to do?"

Erin smiled, the look on Katie's face worth all the hours of stitches she'd have to put in. "I certainly am. My grandmother spent an entire summer when I was ten teaching me to quilt, and it doesn't look like I'll ever get to use the skill for a baby quilt of my own."

"Rinny! Don't say that! Of course you'll have a baby. You're not too old at all!"

Erin shook her head. She was not at all troubled by the fact that she hovered on the precipice of thirty. "Not too old, Katie. Just too busy. Until I fly a mission it's hard to think about settling down."

"That's just because you haven't met the right person, Erin," Katie declared with sincerity that was hard to disregard. "I know you're not like me, and having a career is really important to you, but that doesn't mean you can't love somebody forever, too."

Erin couldn't argue with that. A month ago she would have said it didn't matter. Dating had never been as important to her as it was to most of her friends, and she'd never understood why some of them had tossed their careers out the window—sometimes just by neglect—when some handsome man came calling. Yet on this sweltering afternoon in early May, when the biggest break of her whole career beckoned to her from a tantalizing distance, her excitement remained on hold, anesthetized by Kyle's defection. It was puzzling. It was irritating. And worst of all, it hurt like hell.

"Rinny," Katie's voice reached her gently, "this is me. I've known you since you were the neighborhood tomboy. I even let you perform your first surgery on my doll."

Erin had to chuckle.

"Don't shut me out. Something's bothering you. Let me help." She gave Erin that sweet, supportive smile that always made Erin feel like she was back in Tucson, where everybody was proud of Rinny Ness even if she fell flat on her face. "Or at least let me listen."

Erin sighed and stretched her hands out nervously on the table. "It's not that big a deal. I just did something really stupid that I can't get out of my mind."

Katie tipped her head, waiting.

Erin lifted her hands in defeat. "Somehow I misinterpreted the friendly interest of a fellow astronaut. A pilot." She didn't really want to go on, but she had Katie's full attention. "He had to turn me down rather pointedly. I embarrassed him and I embarrassed myself."

Katie looked stunned. "He didn't want to go out with you? Erin, what man in his right mind would turn you down? You're beautiful! You're talented! You're—"

"Hey, *I'm* not the one who needs a sales pitch! Save it for Kyle. Maybe I'm getting my just deserts. I've been turning men down for so many years I guess I forgot what it was like to be on the losing end. Kyle is the only one I've really wanted in an awfully long time."

"Kyle?" Katie repeated gently. "That's a dignified name."

"He's a dignified man. But entirely too formal and traditional for me anyway. We're terribly ill-matched."

Katie shook her head slowly at the rationalization, then asked earnestly, "What's his rank?"

"His rank?" Erin echoed. "I don't know." She shrugged. She knew perfectly well that Navy people put great stock in such things, which was one good reason to be glad that Kyle was no longer interested in her. Military pomp and circumstance held no attraction for Erin.

Katie shook her head. "You don't *know*? Erin, if you care about him you ought to care about his rank, especially if he's a career officer. My Navy wife's handbook says that a woman's sensitivity to such things can make or break her husband's career."

Katie's naiveté rarely surprised Erin any more, but this time she couldn't summon up one single syllable of retort. She stared blankly as Katie finished her lecture.

"There are subtle clues that help you determine rank, but most of the time all you have to do is look at the shoulder board on dress uniforms and the collar insignia on khakis. Now if your pilot is—"

"Katie!" Erin interrupted. "In the first place the pilots assigned to NASA only wear their uniforms on special occasions, a fact for which I am supremely grateful. God knows there's enough military chauvinism around here as it is! Secondly, all I know about uniforms is that Kyle looks absolutely stunning in his. Especially the one he wears in the summer. It's white with navy and gold accents and—"

"Coming this way," Katie whispered.

It took Erin a second to follow her clue. A man in the uniform Erin had described was approaching their table, a man who charged her pulse by his very presence. The Navy summer dress whites he wore were the perfect contrast to his dark bronze skin; the gold wings he wore proclaimed that he was a pilot. *Her* pilot.

"Excuse me. Could you . . . spare me just a moment, Erin?"

His tone was neither hard nor pleading, and at first she couldn't bear to meet his eyes. Instead she looked at Katie.

"Kyle Tatum, I'd like you to meet a friend of mine from back home, Katie Matthews. Her husband's also a pilot stationed at Heron Bay."

It wasn't a bad stall. Her voice didn't even reveal her inner trembling. Then again, Kyle didn't seem to be studying her with any particular interest. Taking her lead, his focus was all on Katie. In an instant he read her sparkling youth and protruding abdomen, then greeted her like she was a queen he'd waited all his life to meet.

"How nice to meet you, Katie Matthews! It's a privilege to meet a friend of Erin's." His eyes conveyed friendship, then acknowledged her tummy. "I see you're on the way to becoming a mother. Your husband must be very proud."

Erin was surprised by his opening lines, but Katie took them in her stride. She was entranced with Kyle. "Yes, sir, Commander," she emphasized his rank for Erin's benefit. "He's very happy. He's hoping this will be the first of many."

Erin clipped off her rejoinder, having made her "wait and see how much work the first one is" speech already... perhaps too many times.

But Kyle nodded in blithe agreement. "My mother wanted a dozen children, but she almost died just having me. I always felt especially treasured."

Katie bloomed. "I think every baby should be treasured, sir. Some people just discard them willy-nilly, or raise them in their spare time, like a garden flower. But to me there's nothing more important, no dream more special—" She broke off, suddenly embarrassed. "I'm sorry. Rinny says I get carried away."

"Rinny's right." He winked at Katie but kept his eyes from Erin's face. "And I think it's great. I wouldn't have much use for a woman who wasn't enchanted with her own children. If you weren't so happily married I'd be tempted to come calling.''

Erin could hardly believe the conversation. Not only were the two of them ignoring her, but they sounded like a couple out of a 1930s movie! Katie, of course, was still terribly young and had always been delightfully guileless. But Kyle talked like a man who'd never left Peoria. She'd always known he was old-fashioned, but his fascination for babies was just...just...

Charming, really. Just because she couldn't see fitting bottles and diaper pails into her own busy life didn't mean it wasn't exciting to see someone else who was thrilled to be expecting. She'd delivered enough unwanted infants to appreciate the sentiment her two companions voiced so freely. Children should be treasured. To her surprise the echoed adage suddenly made her sad. Grown-ups were difficult enough to fit into her busy life. She would never have time for a baby.

Never one to dwell on what she could not have, Erin rose with dignity and cleared her tray off the table.

''Nice to see you, Kyle,'' she tossed out as though he meant no more to her than a friendly checker in the local grocery. ''Catch you later, Katie. Thanks for coming over. Give me a call in a few days, okay?'' She gave her a warm smile.

It was not a bad exit, she decided as she stacked her tray. But she wasted no time leaving the lunch room, seeking the privacy of the nearest elevator.

''Erin! Hold up a minute. Please.''

Erin stopped and sighed deeply three steps from her escape hatch. She didn't like this part of the script, the part where he apologized for turning her down, hoped he hadn't offended her, maybe even tried to make up for being honest by pretending he might like to come to dinner some other time. But she was not to be spared. He followed her into the elevator.

Erin kept her eyes on the floor numbers above her, hoping she could avoid his omniscient gaze. But he took her shoulders gently and turned her till she faced him, his eyes searching for some intimate secret hidden in her face.

Kyle looked like he was hiding more than one private thought himself. His eyes were that same smoky-blue shade she remembered from the night he came to her house, full of passion... or anger. His fingertips seared her shoulders with the same white-coal heat she felt whenever he touched her. *Dammit, Erin, you've got to get over him,* she ordered her heart, summoning up a cloak of anger in a last ditch effort at self-protection.

"I'm in a hurry," she stated coldly. "Make it quick."

Her subterfuge was useless. His eyes read her pain and confusion.

"I didn't stop by just to meet young Katie," he admitted. "I wanted to ask if I might... cash in that rain check for a home-cooked dinner some night." To fill her stunned silence he tacked on, "I don't want you to go to any trouble for me. We can keep it as casual as you like."

A slow, deep rage—genuine this time—tugged at Erin. She didn't need this! She had already learned her lesson! "You made it exceedingly clear that you were too busy to come to dinner, Kyle. I hope *I* made it clear that I won't pursue the matter further."

He dropped his hands from her shoulders, but he refused to release her eyes. "My schedule has changed. This week I have all the time in the world."

The declaration stood between them, a challenge or

a promise to be formed in Erin's hands. But it was too late; it couldn't be that easy. Stifling her feelings, she told him tersely, "As it happens, I'm very busy right now. I don't see how I can fit you in."

It was not easy to look as though she were angry when her eyes were full of hurt. Kyle refused to let her off the hook; he never looked away. When her resistance finally wilted, her eyes dropped to his buttons as she waited for his next words. Suddenly she wanted to know more about the rows of ribbons on his chest—each one a brief, brave piece of his personal history. There must be some military reason why he was in uniform today, but her knowledge of such things was too limited to guess what it might be. She decided that Katie was right—if you cared about a Navy pilot, you ought to care about the Navy. At least a little bit.

"I'm really sorry I had to turn you down before, Erin," he whispered from a place all too close to her head. "My reasons...had nothing to do with the way I feel about you. I'm not sure I can explain—"

"Well, I can," she said, finally meeting his gaze, "so let's not play any games here. The weekend Roger got hurt, you needed somebody and I happened to be there. It was sort of like the way a soldier curls up with a local woman when he's in combat overseas." She was running out of resistance. His eyes were so full of anguish and self-reproach. What was he thinking? Had these last two weeks been as hard on him as they'd been on her? If he really cared for her, *why* had he turned her away so...terminally? "You already said thank-you, Kyle. Now let it be."

"I don't want to let it be, Erin," he growled, along with an unspoken promise too primal for words. As the elevator settled on Erin's floor, his massive hand reached over to rest against her throat. Her pulse thundered against his palm. She knew that someone would see them; there were most likely people on the other side of the door. Yet she was helpless against his magnetic touch.

Without a word Kyle slid his hand up across her trembling chin until he pillowed her ear with the heel of his hand; his fingertips lifted the satiny red-gold hair at the back of her neck. Splinters of flame charred the length of her spine; both breasts swelled in invitation. When she was powerless to speak, he repeated in a husky growl, "I don't want to let it be."

"YOU'RE LOOKING MIGHTY CHIPPER, Kyle. Glad to see you've decided to join us again."

Kyle raised his mug to his buddies with a smile. Happy hour was a Navy tradition that no pilot ever missed without a good reason, but this was Kyle's first night at the Officers' Club in almost a month. "I decided I'm going to have to carry on even though Roger's still out of commission." He knew by the look on more than one face at the table that his friends already considered Roger dead. Almost everyone did. Except for Erin, whom one of the nurses said still checked into room 106A every evening, after Kyle had gone.

Actually, it was the same nurse who was responsible for his reunion with Erin that afternoon. Over the weeks he'd gotten to know most of Roger's nurses pretty well, so he was not surprised when today's pre-dawn conversation had turned to Dr. Shaw's working relationship with Dr. Ness. But he had been amazed to learn that Erin had never stopped her daily visits to Roger, even though no one on the interview committee seemed to know about it.

"Dr. Ness talks to him just as much as you do,

Commander," the night nurse had told him. "Ever since they started talking about replacing Dr. Shaw on the shuttle, she's gone in there every night and brought him up to date. She keeps asking him what she should do. Once I heard her tell him that she felt guilty at first even thinking about replacing somebody as special as him, but now she was sure that she should be the one to go up so she could give him all the credit. She's afraid that Dr. Michaels would try to hog the glory for Dr. Shaw's research if they were to choose him. She's not as worried about Dr. Porter."

Kyle had listened to the nurse with shame and disbelief as she unveiled a new vision of Erin's interest in 61-J. This was the woman he thought might be using him to get to Jeb?

"One night she told him she'd even gone to check on that chimp—the one Dr. Shaw was going to operate on—just to make sure they were treating him right. It's funny, Commander," the nurse had finished with affection in her voice, "I never heard Dr. Ness talk that way to Dr. Shaw before the accident. Sometimes she acts like she doesn't need anybody, but I always thought she sort of...well, looked up to him. Like a kid to a teacher. She'd never let him know how much she really thinks of him. No wonder his accident has hit her so hard."

Kyle had thanked the nurse profusely and floored his red Saab all the way to NASA. For three weeks he'd been hanging by a thread, thrashing about in search of anything that would free him from this hell of his own devising. He'd never expected a total stranger to hold the key to his deliverance.

It occurred to him belatedly that neither he nor Erin had mentioned Roger in the hall today. Just as well. If he'd told her the truth about his earlier suspicions, she probably would have abandoned him on the spot. As it was he'd had to rush off when another officer had arrived, angry because Kyle was fifteen minutes late to meet a visiting admiral. It was a nearly unforgivable breach of Naval etiquette, and something that Kyle could hardly ever remember doing before. The simple truth was that from the moment he'd first laid eyes on Erin and her delightfully pregnant young friend, he'd completely forgotten his appointment.

"I don't know what they're going to do about it," Alan Clayburn was saying when Kyle mentally rejoined the conversation. Alan was the commander of Kyle's shuttle crew and, like Jeb, had flown with him before in the small circle of the Navy. He scratched his carrot-red head as he declared thoughtfully, "The Russians are acting like nobody has ever done any surveillance in space before."

Of course their mission encompassed a bit more than surveillance from space. It would explore the possibility of launching antiballistic missiles from orbit, effectively eliminating the possibility that Russian nuclear weapons could ever reach the United States. They might leave the Soviet missile silos, but they'd be destroyed over Russian air space. At the moment it was a long-range dream, but one that seemed to Kyle more than worth the effort, considering the consequences.

"I can't say I'm very happy with the way those White House talks are going," Kyle added to Alan's concerns. "I've never seen so much civilian interference in a mission before."

"This is a civilian organization, Kyle," Jeb retorted, reminding Kyle that Jeb was the senior astronaut in the bar. "When you've been here a little longer you'll realize that as long as you're at NASA you've only got one foot in the Navy."

"And only one wing in the air!" Kyle complained. "If I don't go up in something more substantial than a T-38 soon I'm going to put in for a transfer."

"Sure you are!" Alan chuckled. "You're going to walk right out of NASA six months before your first shuttle launch!"

They all laughed at the absurdity of Kyle's suggestion, then filled their mugs again from the pitcher of beer on the table.

"I'm not so sure I was kidding," Kyle added more somberly. "I'd really like to get back to test flying."

Jeb's copilot, Mark Calloway, refused to take him seriously. Then again, Mark Calloway refused to take anything seriously. He was a short, wiry man who always wore a grin. "Time enough for that when you're done here," he told Kyle impishly. "Which might be sooner than you think, if the Russians have their way!"

Suddenly it occurred to Kyle that for the first time in years, he had another factor to consider when he asked for new orders. Putting his feelings about NASA aside, he had a very strong reason for wanting to stay in Houston at the moment. How long that might be the case was anybody's guess; he'd wanted Erin for two years without the slightest encouragement, but now that she actually seemed to return his feelings, anything could happen.

"So why are you all smiles this evening?" Alan asked him. "Got a pleasant night lined up you want to share with your old pals?" Alan was a good friend, and if they'd been alone he might have told him about Erin. But Jeb, always alert, was watching him from across the table.

"Oh, I'm just getting a bit of home cooking tomorrow night. You know that's always enough to make a single man smile."

Alan laughed. "You never smile like that when you come to our house, Kyle, even though you insist that Leslie is a damn fine cook."

This time everybody laughed but Jeb. He was sitting across from Kyle, his back against the massive gold wings that owned one entire wall of the bar. He frowned as he declared, "You're seeing Erin again, aren't you?" He wasn't asking a question—his announcement bore a lash of disapproval.

Nobody else at the table seemed to notice. But Mark Calloway, who surely knew that Erin was a top candidate to replace his former crewmate, tossed out with uncertain humor, "Erin Ness? I thought she never dated pilots."

"That's the rumor," Alan answered, his laughing eyes on Kyle. "But who listens to rumors?"

Kyle answered his grin with one of his own. "Personally, I've given up rumors for life. More trouble than they're worth."

He lifted his mug of beer and tried not to look at Jeb. It was a wasted effort.

"The decision will be announced on Friday, Kyle," Jeb revealed in a voice too low for the others to hear. "Can't you just wait—"

"No." He knew that Jeb's interest was genuine and his advice was wise. But it was time to follow his heart instead of his head. He'd already come too damn close to losing Erin Ness. His voice was hoarse as he declared quietly, "She's expecting me tomorrow night, Jeb. I won't let her down again."

CHAPTER FOUR

BY THURSDAY NIGHT Erin felt like a jellyfish beached by ebb tide. While she was sure that Kyle would indeed arrive for dinner, beyond that she allowed herself no expectations. Their last parting had been poignant and openly sensual, but misreading a similar mood had cost her dearly before.

For the past few days schoolgirl jitters had sapped her of time and efficiency and a good night's sleep. She'd replanned the meal a dozen times, debating between her finest dishes...too fancy, too common, too many last-minute touches. Her spaghetti was great but so ungraceful...and gourmet cooking was unforgiving to the less-than-perfect cook. She finally decided to go with something tried and true that *everybody* liked...roast beef with mashed potatoes and gravy, and a vegetable salad—the latter in honor of Kyle's avowed love of fresh produce. She'd even stayed up late the night before baking a batch of whole-wheat rolls and two cherry pies from scratch. It was the sort of meal her grandmother would have offered her best beau as a sampler quilt of things to come. While Erin was hardly planning to offer a showcase of her domestic talents to Kyle, he was, at heart, a very old-fashioned man who would probably like an old-fashioned meal when he came calling.

The only trouble was that cooking and quilting were the only old-fashioned things about Erin. It took no genius to perceive that Kyle's perception of men's and women's roles emanated from a galaxy different from her own. But tonight she would not allow any nagging doubts to interfere with this glorious second chance. They would be together, they would rekindle the magic they'd found in those dark, somehow intimate hours at the hospital, and they would—wouldn't they?— begin to forge a relationship that would last for more than a weekend.

"This is not a smart thing to do, Erin," she reminded her image in the mirror for the fifty-first time since he'd invited himself to dinner. "You want him too much to think clearly. He thinks he wants your legs and your smile. What he really wants is some sweet petunia like Katie who's regulation-issue Navy wife material. You don't stand a chance, Erin Elizabeth. Not for the Navy, not for the wife, not for the sweet petunia."

She smudged on another layer of gray-blue eye shadow and dabbed on a trace of perfume. Her hair was wrapped loosely around two painted combs that matched the bright candy-pink of her shoulder-tied ruffled sundress; she'd arranged ringlets cascading here and there almost as an afterthought. *Afterthought!* She laughed at the word. This evening, right down to her pink-painted toenails, had been planned like a shuttle launch. Her appearance was feminine, but not too bold. The house was clean and graced with tiny vases full of flowers...nothing ostentatious, just warm and colorful. She'd tossed her best blue throw cover over the old couch and dusted the picture of two children that hung above it. She was just pulling down the cover of her rolltop desk to hide the mess when the doorbell rang at precisely six fifty-nine. It jarred her

like a locomotive's whistle; she couldn't believe she'd
ever heard the sound before.

"Be calm, Dr. Ness," she told the radiant, trembling woman in the mirror. "Even if it kills you,
follow his lead."

It wasn't a hard lead to follow. She opened the door
to a smiling Kyle Tatum in the most deliberately casual
outfit she'd ever seen him wear. Designer-cut jeans of
new black denim wrapped around his thighs. A bright
red Mexican *guayabera* shirt, Houston's borrowed
solution to the heat and humidity, flagged his chest
and accentuated his dark hair and blue eyes. It seemed
appropriate, somehow, that the color would clash so
vibrantly with her own choice. He was dark and regal
and grinning just like Erin wanted to but thought she
shouldn't. She gave up the game and just grinned
back.

"You're an incredibly beautiful woman, Erin," he
told her. It was heady stuff.

"You're not an unattractive specimen yourself,
Commander."

He smiled at her playful use of his title, but made no
comment.

She stepped back to let him enter, noticing for the
first time the package he carried. It was the size of a
large book, wrapped in frogs and goldfish. He crossed
the threshold and placed it in her hands.

"I somehow didn't think you'd be much on flowers," he teased her. "They're so... traditional, after
all."

She could have told him that flowers would have
been lovely, but she decided that it might sound less
than gracious since he'd brought her something else.
"If you're trying to be original maybe I should get

some medicinal spirits handy. It's probably moon rocks or a tarantula."

"Not quite. Despite my efforts at creative whimsy, I did try to get something you'd have some use for."

She shook her head. "You didn't have to bring me anything, Kyle. I really wanted to cook for you." She hadn't intended to relax so quickly, but it was hard to ignore his playful charm.

Yet now he replied on a more serious note, "I know that. And I thank you."

His solemnity surprised her. But the change in mood brought them yet closer. The air grew sultry. From a point that seemed too close for speech he whispered, "I think this is the part where you're supposed to have a necklace with a broken catch or a zipper you need some help with. Some excuse for me to nibble on your neck."

Her deep breath swelled her ribs and breasts against the tight pink bodice. His lips were close enough to touch hers. "I guess I forgot my line," she murmured. "Maybe the director should think of another lead-in."

They forced a laugh together. Then right on cue, the bow on Erin's left shoulder slipped down her arm, and their laughter shook with new communion. Instinctively Erin tried to push the errant strap back in place, but Kyle stopped her with his huge brown hand. "Please, Doctor. Allow me."

With slow, provocative mischief, he moved yet closer, lifting the strap and then pulling it open with a single tug. "I've always wanted to pull your strings," he growled with the velvet purr of a tiger. "First that damn green bikini. Now this . . . confectionery thing."

He braced his hands on her shoulders, smiling inches from her mouth. With ponderous, deliberate movement, he bent to kiss the skin the strap had covered...a moist, warm kiss, near the hollow of her throat. Sensual hunger seized her stomach, but Kyle retied the bow precisely and released her. It promptly fell off her shoulder again.

"I think it was tighter the first time," Erin pointed out.

He laughed, the vibration quaking inside her own throat. "What powers of scientific observation. I can see why you're such a successful surgeon."

Still holding the package, she reached for the strap again, sure his little game had ended. To her surprise he stopped her with a single shake of his dark-maned head. "I did it on purpose, Erin. Leave it."

They stood close enough to breathe as one, with only the box between them. His heated gaze swept from her lips to her eyes and back again; then in a rush he took her.

It was only a kiss, their bodies still separate, but she felt his name being tatooed on her heart. Like a match tossed into hay Erin burst into flames. Kyle's touch was more willful than she had imagined; his heat fierce and potent, his taste warm and sweet. His tongue circled her lips before plunging within them, triumphantly claiming them as his. His need was her own, his victory hers; his passion enflamed her.

He broke away with the same force with which he'd started, then kissed her again in a gentle farewell. She stared at him, hungry...aching for more.

His eyes were clear skies of desire. He breathed heavily, in search of steady rhythm. "Erin," he started once, then started over. "Erin..." There was new magic in her name. "Now that we've...set the tone for the evening...it might be a good idea to...get on with dinner...before we skip it altogether and get started on dessert."

She wasn't sure what he'd said but she knew what he meant. That searing moment had had to come between them; now that it had, anything else that happened this evening would be all right. Without pretense she stepped back a moment to get herself together, then noticed the crushed package mangled by her own hands.

"Why don't you come sit in the kitchen while I finish up?" she suggested. "I've just got to mash the potatoes and then we can eat."

"Are the potatoes real?" he asked behind her, mischief in his voice.

"I take full credit for whatever you eat here, Kyle Tatum," she teased him, grateful for the change in tempo. "And it took a hell of a lot of time to put together, so I expect some up front humble gratitude on your part."

"Yes, ma'am. Humble pie coming right up."

"No. That's coming after dinner. Cherry, in fact."

He grinned with delight. "Real cherries or the kind that grow in a can?"

"Real, my fresh-fruit-and-vegetable friend. I had them imported from Arizona."

The banter continued as she finished preparing the meal. Kyle sat at the table and fingered her hand-quilted brown-and-yellow napkins. "Are these... handmade, Erin?"

"You betcha."

"By your own little hand?"

"Don't you recognize my stitches?"

He didn't react, and she went on, "Never mind. Surgeon's joke. Yes, I made them. I've made every quilt in the house, not that I'd ever need them here without an air conditioner."

"That's nice." He sounded wistful. "My mother used to sew shirts and things for me when I was a kid."

She could have told him that shirts and things, even with collars, were novice tasks compared to hand-pieced quilting. The time alone was beyond any modern comprehension, and the folk art of quilt design was hundreds of years old.

"No little shirts for me. The only baby quilt I'm making is for Katie."

Kyle picked up his fork and poked his fingers absently. "You're allergic to babies, Erin?"

"Of course not. I deliver one or two a week. At least I did when I was in the Emergency Room full-time."

His blitheness dimmed a little. "That's not exactly what I meant."

Sensing he was going to ask the question she'd answered on a dozen dates since her first prom at seventeen, she told him, "I like babies, Kyle. I just don't have time for any. I rather doubt that I ever will."

Erin placed the gravy boat on a trivet and sat down, glowing with expectation. She had served him a feast. She unrolled her napkin and waited.

"That...could change...someday, couldn't it, Erin?"

She didn't want to talk about children over dinner. But his joyous response to Katie's pregnancy underlined the gentle plea in his voice and the question in his eyes. She waited, groping, then tried to be honest.

"Kyle, I've devoted my entire adult life to my career. I've lived with fatigue and survived by sheer will to get where I am. Now...I suppose that someday I might get tired of that. Someday I might welcome the patter of little feet. But quite frankly I doubt it. All I'm sure of right now is that the focus of my life is to get into space. Once I get there I may be able to look at things from a different perspective."

She regretted the accidental pun, and by the look on

Kyle's face, he did too. She suspected he regretted ever asking the question.

"Let's not be formal. Just eat to your heart's content." She passed him the meat, then the glorious mixture of seven kinds of vegetables.

"I'll do that, ma'am." A smile was back on his face, albeit a less vigorous one, and Erin decided to relax and turn the topic to less complicated things.

"Did you want to be an astronaut when you were little, Kyle?"

"Nope. I wanted to be a pilot."

Erin laughed. "Silly question. Does your dad fly, too?"

"Sillier question. He was born a Navy pilot. Me, too—they might as well have named me Admiral Anthony Kyle Tatum III right at birth, Erin."

"Foregone conclusion? Don't you even have to work for it?"

His jaw tensed. "Of course I have to work for it. I get no special favors because of my family. But barring some unseen tragedy, I'll live up to my father's expectations."

Erin ladled some gravy on her potatoes. "That's really important to you."

"Of course it's important to me. Isn't family important to you?"

She shrugged. "Of course. But I never felt I had to be anybody in particular to please my father. He would have been just as happy if I'd stayed in Tucson and raised babies."

"Heaven forbid."

She couldn't tell by his tone if he were teasing. She decided to pretend that he was. "'Erin Elizabeth,' he always said to me, 'Just follow your dreams, sweetheart. Pick out your favorite mountain and don't stop climbing until you reach the top.' ''

He nodded, looking strangely touched by her declaration. "Are your parents still in Tucson?"

"Both of them were killed a few years ago."

Kyle was silent for a moment, then said softly, "I'm sorry, Erin. That must have been very tough for you."

"It was, Kyle, but I've worked through it now. I have wonderful memories of both of them."

He smiled. "Did they always call you Erin Elizabeth?"

"Only when they were trying to get my attention. The rest of the time they just called me 'Rinny.' ''

"Well then, tell me, Erin Elizabeth," he asked with a grin, "is 61-J the mountain you're trying to climb? Are all your dreams really tied up in this mission?"

She was surprised to find she had to consider the question; her hesitation bothered her. "I thought they were when I first got here, Kyle. And I guess they would be...I'm sure they would be if they sent me into orbit tomorrow. But I've already spent so much of my life researching and waiting, exhausted and overworked. Some days at NASA I just wonder what I'm doing. I see more books and machines than patients."

It was a long speech. One look at Kyle's sober face and she regretted it.

"Then there are days when I'd sell my soul to fly in space," she finished on a brighter note.

His eyes met hers with probing caution. "I guess things would...really come together for you if you were chosen to replace Roger on 61-J."

She took a deep breath, unable to disguise her anticipation. "I'd give my right arm for that assignment, Kyle."

He stared at her for a long time, then put down his fork. "It would be hard to do surgery without your right arm," he answered flatly. She couldn't tell whether or not he was making a joke.

"Maybe my appendix, then," she suggested in what she hoped was the same vein. "After all, I suspect that's what I'll end up taking out of the chimp."

"You say that like you think you're a shoo-in for the job." Now there was no doubt about the tension in his voice. Erin wasn't sure what to say, so she opted for the truth.

"Some days I'm absolutely sure that they'll pick me, Kyle. I honestly don't think there's a better surgeon at the center, and I've got enough time and training here to fill in the rest. I'm willing to work around the clock to get this mission off the ground in six months."

Kyle helped himself to more salad. "You ought to go into advertising." Again his tone left her feeling uneasy. Maybe his sense of humor was more wry than she had thought.

"I didn't mean to toot my own horn, Kyle. But you did ask why I thought I had a chance, and I don't think they'd have called me back so many times if somebody on the committee didn't think I could make the grade."

"Ah. You think you have a...mentor backing you? I guess that could really make the difference if you're neck and neck with somebody else."

She shrugged, feeling the need to change the subject. "I don't have a mentor, now that you mention it, but I sure could use one. The only person—"

"Who's on the committee?" he interrupted precipitously.

"Well, there's Dodson and Rafner, of course, and the flight crew. Paul Stevenson is an anesthesiologist. Tall, somber fellow—"

"I know Paul," he said very quietly.

"And then Mark Calloway is the copilot." She liked Mark; he was well on his way to dispelling many of Erin's stereotypes about pilots. "And of course, Jeb is in charge. He seems...a little distant with me. All I really know about him is that he's your friend."

There was no mistaking the darkness in his eyes now. "Let me tell you something else about Jeb Henson you may not know," Kyle declared almost grimly. "He's scrupulously fair and objective. Friendship has no influence on his professional decisions whatsoever. His willingness to replace Roger so quickly should have told you that."

"That must have been very difficult for Jeb. Personally, I mean." She remembered Jeb's face the night he'd come to her house. He might be fair and objective, but Roger still mattered to him as a friend.

For a moment Kyle seemed to leave her, his face growing dark and tense. She didn't know just where his thoughts had taken him, but suddenly she wanted him back at her side. She reached across the table and took his hand. His eyes lifted to hers with new warmth; he seemed to relax. For a moment he just kneaded her fingers and said nothing. Deciding not to dwell on the past, Erin continued to lead the conversation.

"Jeb isn't quite as passionate about the Navy as you are, is he, Kyle?"

He laughed, his good humor apparently restored. "No, ma'am. He came in from the outside. Officers' Candidate School."

"And you," she deduced, "must be a Naval Academy graduate."

He laughed even harder. "Is it hot in Houston in September?"

She started to clear the table, feeling steamy enough in late spring without Kyle's knees nudging hers under the table. "I don't know, Kyle. I keep trying to understand you pilots, but there are some discrepancies that confuse me."

"Such as?" He handed her his plate.

"Well, for all the gung-ho Navy and Air Force stuff I hear, I've seen a lot of the astronauts leave the service to stay at NASA once their seven-year military assignment is over. It makes me wonder if they're really all that sincere."

She reached for the mashed potatoes, but he got there before her, slipping his hand beneath her fingers. The gesture warmed and surprised her. So did the look in his eyes.

"I'll just answer that for me. Space is super and I'm all for it, but going up as a passenger or even a civilian pilot wouldn't mean a thing to me. I'm a Naval aviator, Erin, an officer and a gentleman, and until you know what that means you won't even begin to know the real Kyle Tatum." He drew her fingers to his lips.

She leaned down and kissed him, just once, unable to think of anything to say. She cared for him very much and desperately hoped she'd get to know him better. But she couldn't say she had the slightest idea what to do with a Naval aviator, an "officer and a gentleman." She had enough trouble balancing her career with men who looked at women as equal partners in the twentieth century.

"Are you ready for some pie?" she suggested.

He released her hand and stood by the table. "I'm full, Rinny. It was marvelous. Your gravy is almost as good as my mother's."

"Almost?" she cried in mock dismay, loving his use of her family nickname.

"Have mercy, lady. It would break her heart if I said I liked it better."

"It'll break my heart if you don't say you like it just as much."

"That's a hard one, Erin. Can you think of a way to sway my vote?"

Accepting his challenge, she put down the bowl and walked around the table, cockily slipping her hands around his weight-room shoulders. "I can do things for you your mother can't."

His arms stole around her, his fingers chilling her uncovered back. "Might I ask for a demonstration?"

With faultless timing the pink strap he'd tied so loosely slipped again, and they both burst into laughter. The shoulder beckoned; Kyle bent his head. He ravaged her bare skin with mock fierceness, his lips caressing the first swell of the top of her breast.

Then he stopped and read her desire. He pulled her close enough for a kiss, then claimed her lips with his own.

He meant it to be a casual kiss, but it staggered Erin just the same. Every time he touched her, tiny explosions went off inside her body. She clutched his shirt and leaned against him, savoring the taste of him.

"This isn't bad for a preview," he breathed against her throat a few moments later. "I like it just as much."

"As much as what?" she asked, forgetting the cause of this casual embrace.

"The gravy, Rinny. Your bribery is very effective."

She chuckled into his shoulder, embarrassed in a very pleasant sort of way. "You sure you don't want any pie yet?"

"No, ma'am. Later, yes. Why don't we take a walk?"

"A walk?" It seemed an odd suggestion on a night that could drown in its own sweat. But Kyle seemed determined.

"I always like a walk after dinner. Even on deck. On a starry night a homesick sailor can pretend he's strolling with his girl."

She liked the sound of that. She liked the sound of his voice, the sound of his breathing.... "You've convinced me."

"I knew I would."

Just a trace of cocky pilot showed through his amorous grin as he took her hand and led her toward the back door. "You better open this up or I'll think you don't want it," he teased her, grabbing Erin's package and handing it to her as they went outside.

The scent of lilac was rich, dramatic, more potent than Erin's best perfume. Her old-fashioned pool, cracked here and there and framed by springtime bluebonnets and buttercups, was always lit by a soft underwater light. Kyle heightened the mood by his nearness. She could feel his warmth beside her as she opened his present.

"I'm suspicious of Navy fliers bearing gifts," she told him. "It's probably something strapless."

"Why, Erin Elizabeth!" he chastised her, smiling. "How can you even suggest such a thing? Although, come to think of it, an outfit of yours did inspire my selection."

He continued to grin contentedly when she opened the gift. It was a yellow inflatable air mattress for the swimming pool.

"Kyle, what a nice idea! Shall we try it out tonight?" It was hot and muggy and the cool water beckoned. He glanced from Erin to the pool, considering her invitation. Then he answered slowly, "I don't have a pair of swim trunks with me, Erin."

Electrodes bounced between them as he waited for her reply. She wanted to tell him it didn't matter. She could think of no finer way to end this evening than playing porpoise around his magnificent, naked body. Yet she'd rushed him before and it didn't seem quite right; he'd probably been raised with the notion that nice girls didn't kiss until the third date. There would be another time. If it worked out between them... there would be lots of other times.

"Bring one along next time you come," Erin told him, sweeping the mood away. "How did you know I had a pool?"

"You've got to be kidding," he retorted, picking up her "maybe later" cue. "Aside from your midnight attire and your obsession about Houston's heat, you always smell like chlorine. I didn't figure it was something you used to scrub for surgery."

"Chlorine?" she moaned, her favorite perfume now wasted. "That's the most unromantic thing a man has ever said to me."

"That's a first. I've never been called unromantic before. Hopelessly traditional, overprotective and sentimental, yes. And a few choice things I wouldn't repeat before a lady. But unromantic—"

"All right, I take it back. You're devilishly romantic, irresistible, sexy—"

"Good girl. Keep going."

"That's a dangerous thing to call me."

"Would it be dangerous to ask you why?"

They were having fun in the verbal repartee, and Erin wasn't going to spoil it with a women's lib lecture. "Would it be dangerous to get on with our walk?

My limit outside the air conditioner this time of year is about a half an hour.''

"Probably less if your engine overheats."

"Who says my engine's even started?"

"Saucy wench," he teased her, taking a mock bite out of her right ear. "I'll get you hot enough to beg for mercy. Then we'll see who's proud."

Kyle put an arm around her shoulder, tucking her against his chest. With natural comfort she slipped her arm around him, loving the feel of him nudging the side of her breast. They walked past the pool toward the free-growing garden, making no pretense at serious talk.

It was a clear, dark night. Stars glistened in the sky.

"Even when I was little I liked astronomy," Erin told him. "I'd sit out in the backyard—or lie down on the grass and look up—and try to find the North Star."

"You think we could find it better lying down or standing up?" His lips were tugging on a loose strand of her hair. The thrill of his nearness chased down her legs and back to her stomach, rehearsing for whatever came next. She struggled to conceal her arousal.

"I'm afraid NASA's formal classes have sapped some of the magic of stargazing out of a view like this," she suggested, waiting for him to respond with an innuendo in his spirit of playfulness.

Kyle turned her body around instead, his chin on her head as his chest braced her back. His arm touched her breasts on the way to her shoulder and pushed off the tied strap again.

"So you think the night is short on magic, Rinny?" he questioned, his voice low and lost in her hair. His fingers grazed the fine skin of her shoulder, the motion causing friction between his elbow and her breast. His free arm swept around her midriff. The warmth trapped her breath. Without warning, her nipples grew rigid, causing paralysis deep in her throat.

"What do you think would excite you? A trip to the moon? Or just around the Earth a few times? Shall I take you into orbit?"

Erin didn't translate his double entendres. She didn't speak at all. The heel of the hand on her shoulder was edging perilously close to her now pulsing breast. The hand on her waist was not moving, but four fingers stretched below her navel. His thumb touched the center of her ribcage. *Breathe, Erin,* she ordered herself. *Be calm.*

"You told me at dinner you'd do anything at all to circle the globe, Doctor." His low rasp thrilled her. "What exactly did you have in mind?"

Erin didn't know what she had in mind. Thinking was getting low on her list of priorities. She hadn't known what to expect tonight; she hadn't decided that making love this soon was the right thing to do. He was still bombarding her with kamikaze messages. Some were easy enough to listen to: *I want you so badly. Let's make love tonight.* But there were those hidden ones she struggled to recollect. *I'm an officer and a gentleman. My reasons for turning you down had nothing to do with my feelings for you.... Would you ever have time for a baby?*

With all his questions clattering in her brain, it was hard to hear her own voice. At times she felt like she'd been waiting for Kyle forever, and yet tomorrow she might decide it had been too soon.

He rubbed her stomach in a slow circle, then slid his hand under the pink fabric and over the side of her breast, hovering a millimeter from her nipple.

To hell with this logic. I want him.

"You're the pilot in command of this spacecraft," she managed to whisper. "You know the territory. I'll ride along wherever you want to go."

It was the moment when his hand should have seized her yearning nipple; he should have turned her in his arms and kissed her. Firecracker passion should have sizzled between them. But his hands, so strategically balanced, stopped moving. He whispered one word.

"Anywhere?"

There was something in his voice that told her—with the tiniest pinprick of warning—that her playful words had displeased him. She had no hint as to why. They'd been verbally romping since they left the table, and she knew he'd enjoyed the implied foreplay between them. Now he was launching a challenge...designed to test her. Designed to hurt?

Her body stiffened. She didn't plan it that way; his hands just didn't feel quite the same on her skin. Yet when he released her, ever so reluctantly, she felt naked, abandoned, bereaved. Her upthrust nipples, slow to get the message, remained at attention. Waiting.

"Thanks for dinner, Erin. I have to go."

His words were bad enough, but the sight of his hands in his pockets—that nervous gesture she was learning to dread—told her that he was in turmoil. Her own body was a jumble of feelings at odds with her heart. Something was wrong. She was lost and still wanting. His face was a mask.

"Want to walk me to my car?" he asked in a quiet voice.

Numbly she nodded. He took her hand as they ambled through the garden, but his touch was light and noncommittal. When they reached his red Saab he turned to face her, his eyes midnight-blue and troubled as he searched her face.

"I really appreciate all the effort you went to, Erin. It was really special."

"It was my pleasure," she told him coolly, struggling to conceal her bewilderment. *Trust him, Erin. He has his reasons. Maybe it's just too soon.* She tried to smile in the dim light of the porch.

"I'm sorry I have to go."

He didn't need to say it; he certainly didn't need to say it with such genuine regret. She wanted to offer him a piece of pie, but something in his eyes stopped her.

He leaned down to kiss her, his mouth chaste but warm. She said nothing as he stood there, eyes on her, then met her lips with his again. This time his mouth was hard, demanding. It ordered, begged and yearned for her compliance. She reached for him, unthinking, her hands upon his face.

Something was happening between them...new peace bathed Erin's soul. It was the kiss she'd been expecting in the garden—kindling and white-hot coals and sparks and flame all in one.

When at last he pulled away, he did not try to conceal his longing. But incredibly, he took her hands and moved them from his face. Gently, regretfully...but remove them he did. His eyes plundered hers for meaning, asking a question she could not read. If he'd told her he'd changed his mind and asked to stay, she would have said yes no matter what it cost her. But it wasn't the question he was asking. Some other query lay in his mind.

"I'll call you soon, Rinny," he promised, his voice a knot of desire. "There's just something I've got to be sure of before I can stay."

CHAPTER FIVE

ALL THROUGH THAT SLEEPLESS NIGHT, Erin retraced her evening with Kyle, trying to make sense of what had happened. Everything had been joyous, sensual, utterly perfect from the moment he'd arrived. They'd talked about families and NASA and Roger; 61-J and chlorine and the true pilot's Navy. They'd bickered, but it had been mainly in jest. The overall feeling, even when he left, was one of mutual pleasure and growing commitment. They were both on the brink of falling in love.

Love. It was an unsettling word, one that spoke of a relationship that went beyond sweet nights in bed and bright sunshine every morning...one that could turn her life inside out and spill her ambitions into the sea. Several years had passed since Erin had last succumbed to such a feeling. She hadn't really fought love...it just hadn't called to her from the hearts or faces of the men she'd known in Houston. Except for one. Now it prowled at the edge of her senses, like an aircraft circling a runway waiting to be waved away or beckoned in. But it seemed to her that Kyle, not Erin Ness, was manning the control tower.

Concentrating on work that morning was a challenge. Blood clotting in space suddenly seemed meaningless to Erin; her disinterest truly shocked her. But the few strands of her thinking that weren't wrapped up in Kyle were stretched out in taut readiness for news about the mission. Rumors had started to ricochet all over the center that Roger's replacement would be announced this morning.

She had accomplished very little by eleven when her reverie was broken by the beep of her phone.

"Dr. Ness? They want you upstairs," a secretary's voice informed her with just a hint of amusement. No further clarifications were necessary. Today there was only one 'they' in the center; there was only one reason 'they' wanted to see her.

Erin scrambled up the stairs like a pony heading for the barn at feeding time, her heart thudding in anticipation. This was it. Everything would start or finish in this instant. How many people had they called in before her? Would they smile when she walked in or stare at her with "we regret to inform you" stamped on their foreheads?

She stopped in front of the door to smooth back her hair. She tried to calm her pulse as well, but the effort was wasted.

They sat in a semicircle around the conference table: Arthur Rafner, Carl Dodson, Jeb, Mark and Paul... wearing poker faces all around. A jet landing at the base sounded like a volcano erupting in the awesome silence.

The men sat perfectly still until the noise receded. Numbly Erin lowered herself into a chair. Her eyes went first to Jeb, then to the other crew members, then back to the big brass in charge. Carl Dodson opened his mouth to speak, then stopped to look at Jeb, the man Kyle insisted was objective no matter whom it hurt. "Commander?" he asked with mock formality. "Would you like to do the honors?"

Jeb stood up, looking every bit the Naval officer he was despite his casual civilian clothes. He walked around the table until he was only an arm's length away from Erin. His eyes told her nothing. Slowly he held out his right hand in a fraternal gesture. "Welcome aboard, Dr. Ness. We're proud to have you on 61-J."

Erin lost the next twenty minutes. She knew that she had babbled in delight, then earnestly promised to achieve the loftiest goals of 61-J. Her stammering enthusiasm had entertained Mark and embarrassed Paul. Jeb showed no emotion at all, but promised to go over the details of her assignment with her during lunch. After all the backslapping was over, she was told to tie up all the loose ends of her current assignment and get ready to meet the press at five o'clock. By Monday morning her body and soul would belong to mission 61-J.

Erin was euphoric but silent as she walked beside Jeb toward his office. She had the distinct impression that he wasn't altogether happy with the group's choice, but it didn't seem like the right time to ask him. He *was* the commander, her immediate link to the upper echelons. He was also Kyle's friend.

"I'd like to lay some groundwork here, Erin," he announced briskly when they were settled in his office—the heart of mission 61-J. "The schedule we've laid out is very optimistic, in that we're hoping we won't have to postpone the mission in spite of this snafu." His eyes revealed no memory that his comatose friend Roger was the "snafu." "But the bottom line is, the next five months will take everything you've got. You're going to have to master everything we already know and figure out most of what we still don't have a handle on. You've got to pull together everything that was in Roger's mind, his notes and his briefs and then take all that knowledge one step further to perform the surgery. Right now you're excited, grateful to every one of us for choosing you. But I warn you, Doctor, before we launch *Odyssey*, you may wish to God we'd never even heard your name.''

Erin met his eyes with all the gravity his words required. ''I won't let you down, Jeb. I intend to give this mission everything I've got. I've waited for it half a lifetime, and I won't let anything stand in my way.''

He nodded slowly, his eyes unreadable. ''May I remind you of those words from time to time if it becomes necessary?''

Before Erin could answer his question, a quick knock at the door heralded the entry of a tall, dark man in aviator's greens. Even before he spoke, even before she saw his face, some part of Erin twisted, leaped, burned at the knowledge that he was near.

For a moment Kyle's eyes met hers with surprise and warmth and latent longing. They seemed to physically caress her. ''Erin,'' he whispered, his voice hoarse and low.

Her relief that he still wanted her was enormous, but her fear that Jeb would find out how things were between them was even greater. After the noble speech she'd given him just moments ago, she could not afford to have him think that only half her heart would really belong to 61-J. The other half was already committed.

''Kyle,'' she said simply, her voice cool and calm. She hoped he would understand her discretion.

He did not. Wariness clouded his cerulean eyes. ''Excuse me, Jeb,'' he declared, his tone more strained than friendly. ''I don't mean to interrupt anything here but I came to ask if the 61-J assignment has been announced before I went down to see Erin.'' An observer would have assumed he was discussing a woman who was not in the room.

Jeb's face was immobile. "The assignment has been announced."

Kyle breathed deeply. "And who is Roger's replacement?"

He stated the obvious. "Erin Ness."

Kyle turned to Erin as though she had just walked in the door. His smile was stiff as he asked her, "Would you like to have lunch with me, Erin?"

She hesitated, not at all certain what was going on in his mind. Jeb said nothing, but she knew he'd already ordered sandwiches and coffee for both of them. "I...believe I'll be tied up through lunch going over the mission, Kyle."

"I see." His tone was cold. "Perhaps you'd like to celebrate this hearty news with me this evening on the *Obsession*. They serve a terrific meal at sea where it's nice and cool at night." The actual words were gracious; almost exactly as the first time he'd asked her out. But the look in his eyes matched his brittle voice. It wasn't an invitation—it was a dare.

She didn't know what was bothering Kyle but she couldn't find out now. She had to get him out of here before he spoiled Jeb's critical early impression of her. She told him the truth. "Some other time, perhaps, Kyle. I'm working this evening."

"Tomorrow night, then."

Erin shook her head. "I'm sorry. I'm working then, too." It was her turn to cover for Roger.

The look on Kyle's face said he didn't believe a word, and she wondered why. Every time she saw him some new facet of his personality unfolded to her, and up till now each layer had made her ache for him a little bit more. But now, at the very pinnacle of her success, he was tugging on her skirts, trying to pull her down. What was going on inside this man who'd called her Rinny with such warmth in his voice just a few hours ago? Had he moved to Antarctica overnight?

"I see," Kyle declared. He stood perfectly still, like the calm dead center of a tornado. She could feel the black cloud of fury hovering above him, and it frightened her.

"No, I don't think you do," she retorted. Jeb's presence suddenly seemed less important than making things right with Kyle. "In addition to my own shift, I'm still cov—"

He cut her off briskly, his eyes meeting Jeb's for the first time. "Maybe I should take you out for dinner instead, Henson. You won this round. There ought to be some place in Houston that serves fresh crow." He left with the quickest of nods, the aftershock of his tension making Erin quake.

She glanced at Jeb, but his neutral eyes told her nothing. She struggled for composure, remembering her new role and her professional duty. This was her very first hour as a member of Jeb's crew! She'd just promised that nothing would stop her from doing her best. She couldn't go running after Kyle like a heartsick schoolgirl! But she was full of hurt and panic. Whatever was wrong, she had to confront it. She had to confront him, this instant, before he disappeared into some cell of the honeycomblike building or the airfield. Or worse yet, onto the foreign shores of Heron Bay Naval Air Station for three unendurable days.

But the look on Jeb's face stopped her before she could move an inch. It was so cold, so full of... disapproval? Disgust? She wasn't sure, but she didn't dare try to leave the room. Instead she asked boldly, "May

I ask you a question, Jeb? Assuming the answer is not classified information.''

"Shoot. My orders are to share with you everything I know about this mission." No warmth graced his words.

"I'd like to know if my...selection was unanimous."

For several moments he studied her coldly. There was no mistaking his discomfort. "Yes. It was unanimous. Why do you ask? It doesn't matter now. You're in."

She swallowed and faced him squarely. "It matters that I'm going to be working with you so closely for the next five months and you...give me the impression that you very much wish somebody else was sitting in this chair. Anybody else! What have I done to you, Jeb?" *And what on earth have I done to Kyle?*

His face was a closed mask. "Nothing. You were my first choice because of your surgical record, Doctor, and for no other reason. Do your job and we'll get along just fine."

Concentration was almost impossible with memories of Kyle's dark accusations whipping Erin's heart, but almost two hours passed before she was free to leave her new commander. Instantly she bolted up the stairs to Kyle's office. The door stood ajar, and she noticed two photos of fighter jets and an Anthony Kyle Tatum III flight award as she marched uninvited into the room.

Kyle looked up quickly, surprised to see her, and his eyes deepened to a shade of blue close to that of the Blue Angels Phantom in the autographed poster on the wall behind him. "Did I forget to bid you farewell?" he barked. "My mistake. Goodbye. I have a lot of work to do."

"And *we* have a lot of work to do on our relationship if you think you can sweet-talk me Thursday evening and chuck me into the dumpster by Friday noon," Erin snapped back, her fear veiled in indignation. "Whatever you're upset about—"

"What makes you think we have a 'relationship,' in shoddy repair or otherwise?" His frigid tone underlined the cruelty of his words. "We just work together, in the loosest sense of the word, and if you think I've been 'sweet-talking' you, Dr. Ness, then either you've never seen me chasing a lady or you've just been without a man for one hell of a long time."

For several moments Erin raged in silence. Was this the man who'd held her in his arms last night? Who'd promised to make her sizzle and then left her alone to burn? For every sweet moment she'd ever given him, he had paid her back with icy withdrawal. He'd never been able to explain his reasons, either! Erin had gone the extra mile on this one, turned the other cheek. But Kyle was obviously unwilling to heal this breach of his own devising, and she refused to beg. She had just been assigned to the mission she'd dreamed of all her life, and her crew commander had already made it clear that she'd have no time for play or personal crises. She had no more heart for Kyle's mercurial games.

"I'm sorry if I misinterpreted any inadvertent form of interest you may have accidentally bestowed upon me from your lofty perch, Commander. I won't be troubling you any further with my interest or my time."

"I don't know why you'd bother," Kyle seethed at her proud, retreating back, "now that you've got what you wanted all along."

This time Erin whipped back to face him, sudden insight giving her new hope. "Is that what this is all about? You're jealous that I'm going to be working so closely with Jeb?"

"Jealous?" His vice guffawed the word. "I'd have to have a smidgen of affection for you to be jealous, Doctor, and believe me, I'd never look twice at a woman who'd sell herself to steal my best friend's place on 61-J."

He'd said it now; the words hung between them, waiting for confirmation. Hurt and disbelief burned Erin's cheeks, but not a twitched eyebrow gave away Kyle's feelings.

"You know, Erin, the pathetic thing is, it wouldn't have done you any good. Hell, you could have slept with me, with Jeb, taken on the entire crew! Henson just doesn't play favorites. He works hard and he plays hard, but he never mixes the two. The final decision wasn't his anyway. So you shined my boots with your ego for nothing. How's it make you feel?" He glared at her from what seemed like a great distance. "You got the assignment on your own, Erin. I never did one damn thing to help you. As a matter of fact, I was hoping they'd pick somebody else! Anyway, I hope you've learned something from this whole damn mess."

Tattered inside in a way she knew could never be repaired, Erin tugged on her own uniform of hauty indifference. She righted her spine and met his eyes with her own gray-ice stare.

"What I have learned, Commander, is the way an 'officer and a gentleman' court-martials and discards his friends. Now I can truthfully say that I do know the *real* Kyle Tatum."

BY SATURDAY NIGHT Erin had been congratulated no less than six dozen times by co-workers, reporters and patients who eavesdropped on the news as it swept ahead of her like wildfire. She'd called her friends and tried to sound happy, then she'd called Katie and told her the truth. She'd waited for this mission for nearly twenty years, and now that she'd finally attained it, her euphoria had lasted less than twenty minutes before Kyle Tatum had torn it to shreds. It was at the top of the list of things for which she'd never forgive him.

A dozen comments over the last few weeks now made sense to her...his hesitation Thursday night abundantly clear. His accusations, implied but never spoken, had always been waiting just beyond those sensuous lips as they nibbled on her hair. *Is it me you want or just my nod toward you as surgeon for 61-J? Is all this magic a mirage? What motivation could possibly be strong enough for you to break a two-year perfect record of never dating a man who works for NASA?*

What would never endure close speculation, however, was how Erin had deluded herself into believing there was something *special* evolving between her and this arrogant, artificial space cowboy. It was like going to sleep with the sweetest of daydreams, only to wake up engulfed in a monstrous nightmare. Kyle thought she had used him, and yet Erin was certain that *she* had been the one betrayed. He would never understand it, never believe that she was innocent of his accusation...just as he would never comprehend the core of Erin Ness herself. Proud of her achievements, tender in her love... trying to harmonize her feminine grace and professional courage. Clearly, Kyle had found such a union unbelievable.

Erin was almost glad she was working an extra shift this weekend. In spite of the mound of briefs and manuals she'd brought home at Jeb's direction, her concentration was so shredded by tumultuous thoughts of Kyle that effective research was impossible. Her mood was not brightened when the doorbell rang less than an hour before she was due back at Our Lady. She was in no condition to greet another reporter, especially dressed as she was in nothing more than a strapless apricot maillot. But when the doorbell repeated its imperious summons, she stretched out her sun-warmed legs and strolled toward the front of the house. In a last-minute concession to modesty, she grabbed a discarded cotton blouse and slipped it on. Even unbuttoned, it provided a certain amount of concealment for her brimming bodice.

When Erin opened the door, she was surprised to see her uninvited guest. Kyle Tatum stood on the porch, a study in contrition—hands in his pockets, his eyebrows asking permission to enter her home. He was clad in white trousers and an open-weave shirt in a stunning shade of teal. The color enhanced the power of his eyes and his gorgeous copper skin.

Mentally comparing his manner with his first arrival there—three weeks or a lifetime ago—Erin was determined to hold her own, bare legs and all. Coolly she gestured for him to enter, leaving the door open. She was not about to ask him to sit down.

"May I help you, Commander?" she questioned, her voice too brittle.

"I think I may owe you an apology, Erin."

"We're in complete agreement."

Erin knew why he was here. He was a man to whom honor was important, and honor required righting a wrong. She'd expected him, sooner or later, regret on his face, cap in his hand. She was almost glad he'd come so soon: she was still angry enough to be unforgiving. And she knew, with the rational side of her heart, that anger would be her best shield. She'd given her best to this roller-coaster ride, and it was time to forget the amusement-park jockey who'd so freely tossed her out of the train at the highest point of the trestle. Mission 61-J would be her lover now.

When he lifted a hand to touch her face, Erin jerked her head out of his reach. *It won't work this time, Kyle,* her fierce eyes told him. *I know all your tricks.* "If you're going to apologize, get on with it, Commander," she said aloud. "Otherwise go home. I have to leave for work in less than thirty minutes."

Her sharpness seemed to surprise him. He pushed the door shut before he faced her. "If I misjudged you, Erin, I'm sorry. I—"

"*If* you misjudged me! That's your idea of an apology?"

His eyes darkened. "Look, Rinny, I'm trying to—"

"Rinny is a family name. You have no right to use it."

Her words slapped him in the face, and he shook his head as if from the impact. "I said I was sorry, Erin. I came here to straighten everything out. I don't know why you—"

"Did it ever occur to you that maybe I'm not interested in how sorry you are? That it doesn't help how I feel one iota?" If he thought a few sweet words of humility could brush away the damage, then he had something to learn about Erin Ness. "It's too late to straighten *anything* out, Kyle. It's all over between us."

He jammed his fists in his pockets. "Look, Erin," he declared with rising feeling, "I know you have a right to be angry. I said some lousy things to you yesterday—"

"You said I'd sell my body to any man who could help boost my career!"

He could not meet her eyes; his tone was low and husky. "I was afraid you were using me," he confessed in a near whisper. "I felt like I was betraying Roger. I'd wanted you for so long, Erin, and you'd never given me the time of day before. Suddenly you were dying to be with me. There had to be a reason. Please tell me what it is."

Erin stared at him in disbelief. "You still don't know?"

"I need to hear you say it."

She shook her head. "Any man who would write me off on the flimsy evidence you had doesn't deserve to hear what you're asking for, Kyle."

"Dammit, Erin, I had my reasons! I can give you a dozen things you said and did that made me come to that conclusion."

"So I'm still guilty? Next you'll be accusing me of secretly drugging Roger to keep him unconscious! Why did you bother to come here at all?"

He took his hands out of his pockets long enough to run them through his hair. She didn't need any more clues to know that his outward calm disguised genuine distress. "I'm here because I can't bear the idea of hurting...the Erin I think you are...with the words I said to...the Erin I was afraid you might be. I was already suspicious before I got the news of your selection through the grapevine. When you didn't even bother to come tell me about it yourself, I knew I didn't rate very high on your hit parade. But I wanted to confront you anyway, to be absolutely sure. When you turned me down three times in a row, I figured—"

"You figured wrong. I didn't come see you because I was with Jeb and the committee from the time I got the news until the time you showed up in his office. And even if I hadn't been busy, I would have shown more discretion. I certainly expected *you* to! What did you expect me to say when you asked me out in front of Jeb? You know how I feel about dating NASA people! It's bad enough that I was willing to break the rules for you without throwing our affair in my new mission commander's face after I'd just promised him that I belonged one hundred percent to 61-J! Besides, you weren't asking me for a date. You were...jabbing me with a sword!'' Before he could reply, she tacked on, ''But just for the record, Kyle, I did have to work last night...and this evening as well. I'm still covering for another doctor who happens to be in a coma.''

That leveled him. He could not meet her eyes. In fury she razored him yet further. ''Of course, I don't need to fill in for Roger any more now that I've got the mission, do I? After all, my only motivation was to pick up brownie points with you and Jeb.''

He actually was speechless. No suave retort seemed to come to his lips. For an instant Erin reveled in his misery, glad to pay him back for all the pain he'd caused her. ''I'm going to be way too busy now to indulge your tantrums, Kyle. Even if I needed a man to keep me happy, it sure as hell wouldn't be one who's a millstone around my professional neck. There are plenty of spine-tingling male choices out there who appreciate me and won't impede my upward mobility.'' She gloried in the brilliance of her punch line. ''Now if I don't hurry, I'm going to be late to work. See yourself out, will you?''

Holding on to her anger for self-protection, Erin made a fine dramatic exit before her eyes grew red and damp. She fought the insistent moisture. *Damn you, Kyle Tatum—you've made me cry! No man has done that since med school!* She stalked through her bedroom door and slammed it shut behind her.

Before she had time to wipe her tears, Kyle flung it open and marched into her room.

"It appears I have yet more to learn about officers and gentlemen," she said to him in genuine surprise, her voice thick and unclear.

"Don't play the ingenue with me, Erin, and stop throwing my wings in my face. We're past the junior prom stage here. You made it damn clear the other night that you wanted me to spend the night in this room. It's way too late to disinvite me."

"That's where you're wrong, Kyle."

"You deny that you wanted me to make love to you when I came to dinner?" His voice was incredulous. "That's hardly going to win you points for honesty, Erin."

She moved a little closer to her dresser, knowing he'd won that round. The bed, covered in a pastel-flowered quilt, suddenly filled up the whole room. Erin couldn't deny that she'd wanted to share it with him; still did, in the private coves of her heart. But it was a risk she was no longer willing to take. She didn't know him anymore; overnight they'd grown too far apart.

"All right, Kyle. If honesty is what you want, I'll give you some. I did want you Thursday night. I've wanted you off and on since the first time you ever asked me out; I've wanted you unceasingly since the night you came here because of Roger. I wanted you enough to ignore some very basic differences in the way we look at the world... enough to ignore the fact that getting involved with you might sooner or later injure my career." She turned back to face him, gaining strength through her logical recitation. "Well, it happened sooner rather than later, and it brought me to my senses. It's not going to happen again."

"Erin—"

"Now hear me out, Kyle. There's no excuse for what you said to me yesterday . . . and no excuse for the way it poisoned my joy and my work. I can't have that kind of emotional chaos in my life and pull off this mission. There couldn't be a worse time for me to get involved with anybody . . . especially a man who has no faith in me whatsoever."

Kyle stood still for a moment, his proud leonine head all but bowed before her. He did not refute her words. "I'm sorry, Rinny. I know I let you down. I'll make it up to you. I promise."

The tender sweep of his husky voice brushed her senses. She could almost feel his biceps against her breasts as his arms enfolded her. She fought the mirage; she couldn't let it happen.

"I think it's too late for that, Kyle. This . . . relationship is too much like a hollow whiffle ball for my taste," she told him. "It looks solid from a distance, but up close it's just got too many holes to survive a good hit."

"Every batter gets three strikes before he's out, Erin, no matter what condition the ball's in." His voice had completely changed now—gentle, enticing, the flip side of that strained arrogance he had shown when he'd first arrived at her door. In a flash of understanding she remembered how he'd behaved when Roger was injured, waspish to cover the pain of the sting. No wonder he'd been too testy to soothe her with his apologies this evening. Under all the flippant bravado, Kyle Tatum knew how grievously he'd wounded her, and he really didn't want their shaky affair to collapse totally.

"The ball game's over, Kyle," she said a little more gently. "I wish it weren't, but it is. I really do have to get dressed now."

In a single step he was at her side, his hands capturing her face. With gentle insistence he lifted her chin. Reluctantly she met his smoky gaze. "If you've really got to go to work, Erin, we need to make our peace now. Please don't make me wait till sunup to hear you say you forgive me."

He looked...different, somehow. Tired. Maybe even scared. She forced herself not to notice.

"All right. You are forgiven. But I still have to go to work. So please get out of my bedroom. Good night."

The tension seemed to ease a little as his fingertips caressed her face. They were just as gentle as she remembered them. "I'm sorry I broke into your room like this, Erin. I just...had to resolve things with you this evening."

She was starting to feel shabby. He *was* trying to apologize, and she wasn't making it very easy for him. "It's okay, Kyle. We're still friends. We all do idiotic things every once in a while."

He looked relieved, but his dark eyes were still cautious. One thumb swept across her lips in a sweet, nervous gesture. "I can...wait outside while you change if you like. Then I'll drive you on over to the hospital."

"I'm perfectly capable of driving myself, Kyle," she told him, deliberately moving away from the invitation for his kiss. She was no longer angry. She was in trouble. He was assuming—no doubt about it—that they would pick up where they left off Thursday night. *How I wish we could, Kyle. But it really is too late.*

He read her eyes and her tight, proud shoulders. He did not try to reclaim her face. Carefully, he suggested, "Maybe I should just come back tomorrow after you get some sleep. When's a good time to call?"

The moment had come. She tugged on the ends of

her cotton blouse, hunting for a pocket, a strap, anything to play with. She tried not to look at his thighs. She had to tell him. She had to be strong.

"There...isn't any need for you to call me, Kyle. I don't think it's in my best interests to continue seeing you socially."

For a full sixty seconds his eyes drilled her face. He didn't believe it. The planes of his cheeks grew hard as the muscles tensed beneath his smooth brown skin.

"We've finished the 'Hell hath no fury' scene, Erin. This is the part where we kiss and make up. What time do you want me to call you?"

She knotted the ends of her unbuttoned blouse and sucked on her bottom lip. His eyes were boring into hers now, waiting, watching. She remembered how he'd pinned her like this near the elevator the last time they'd had a fight; melted her anger, rekindled her need. If he did it again could she resist him this time? Would his irresistible blend of tenderness and strength be her downfall once again?

"I don't want you to call me, Kyle. I'll let you know if there's any word on Roger, of course, but other than that I don't plan to go out of my way to see you again." She didn't think her announcement could possibly hurt Kyle any more than it hurt her to say it, but the shock on his face told her she was wrong.

He stepped back from her, looking like a man who'd just been told his sweetheart has died. He stared at Erin for an endless parade of minutes. Never, never, had she seen him look like this. Not even in the hospital that first lonely night, waiting for Roger to die. He hadn't tossed Roger away with his own two hands; this time he could blame no one but himself. When at last he spoke, his voice was as strained as she'd ever heard it, hushed and hurt and awesomely still.

"I won't...beg you, Erin, but I wish you'd reconsider. Don't make your decision based on just this one fight."

She stepped toward him, wrestling with the need to touch his face. She had to make him understand. "It's not just what you accused me of in your office, Kyle. Or even how it affected my first glorious day on an honest-to-God space mission. You've hurt me several times in the past few weeks, more deeply than I think you know. You've ignored my basic rights as a person and as a professional. You've wooed me when it suited you and cast me aside on the slightest suspicion. I'm tired of it. I don't need this in my life. I've got too many other things to do."

Still he watched her, pain unhidden on his face. "And have I...given you nothing to...offset those troubled moments?"

She closed her eyes; she could not answer. She prayed he wouldn't touch her. "I just don't think it's going to work, Kyle." Her tone was muted. "I'm sorry. I can't tell you how much I wanted to be with you. But I think we're just too different to be comfortable dating."

"Dating?" he repeated, bulldogging the word. "*Dating?* Erin, that's not what we've been doing." He moved closer; she couldn't seem to push him away. "Don't you understand? We've got to go over these rough spots in the beginning. A few scraped knees and bruises are par for the course when people start falling in love."

Erin's eyes flashed open. He was near enough to kiss her, but he kept his hands at his sides. He waited—oh, how poignantly he waited—while she searched for a way to refute his words. "I...wasn't sure that...what we were doing...could be...called...falling in love." He hadn't used the term lightly, so neither could Erin. She didn't want to love him; she wanted to go to work. She wanted to get back to constructive fatigue, running on the hamster wheel of success. She didn't want to lose herself in this tender, turbulent man.

Kyle didn't move, didn't touch her, gave no hint that he realized they stood inches from her bed. But his power engulfed her just the same. In a husky breath that all but demolished her defenses he whispered, "I sure had the impression that we were... both heading in that... general direction." He paused, his lips waiting for hers. "Weren't we... Rinny?"

For a thousand years she tried to deny it, struggling for conscious breath. But there was no logic to what she was feeling. For weeks this man had peppered her emotions with yes, no and maybe, and now, in his silence, he was demanding her final answer. He was a proud man who would never beg her; if she said no tonight, he would not ask her again.

Dynamite went off somewhere in her head. Tears swam in the gray pools of her eyes and then, uncontrollably, lapped over their banks. She closed her eyes against the moist confession, too battered now for words. Without a sound Kyle bent even closer, touching her moist cheek with the tip of his tongue. On one side, then the other, he kissed away her tears.

"Oh, Kyle," she crumpled against his warm, thudding chest, "I can't let you go."

His arms came around her so fiercely that he almost crushed her, but she didn't care. "My God, babe," he whispered, in a voice so haunted it pierced her soul. She tried to hug him yet closer to ease his still-bleeding wounds. She couldn't tell where hers began and his stopped; they were one and the same.

He rocked her, rubbed her back, clenched two fists in her hair. There was an anguish in him she had never seen before, and the knowledge that she was the cause of it wounded her even as it gave her power. She had hurt him and now she struggled to cleanse his leftover pain.

He pulled back to see her face, his eyes demanding reassurance. She found the words he needed. "We've. . . both been moving in that direction, Kyle. Don't you ever doubt it."

His mouth took hers with sure possession. There was no maybe in his touch, no hesitation in the tongue that circled her lips in rough impatience before it plunged inside her waiting sweetness. Her arms embraced his shoulders, lifting her breasts to swell against his massive chest. Their bodies crushed together as their spirits joined, promise radiating in the kiss that left her quivering when finally he pulled away.

Kyle took off her blouse as though the fabric were a threat to their closeness, then slid his hands over her shoulders, warm palms resting on the bare skin he had exposed. He kissed both of her temples, both ears, both eyes, then hugged her so closely that there was nowhere to kiss but the top of her head. He ran his long fingers through her hair, tugging just enough to titillate her scalp, then bent to kiss her searching lips, begging forgiveness all over again.

"My chest feels like somebody left a loaded dumpster on top of it." He nuzzled her neck as he spoke. "I can't breathe. Do you think you could fix me up, Doctor?"

Despite his effort at humor, Erin knew he was hurting with leftover fear. Ignoring the knowledge that somebody else needed her medical skills, she unbuttoned his shirt and put both hands inside.

"What you need is a little hand-to-heart resuscitation," she told him, kissing the pulse at his throat as she rubbed his crisp dark hair. "A little massage from a trained professional should make you feel better."

He purred like a tiger, his hands still gripping her shoulders as she continued her sensual caress. "I always obey the doctor's orders, Erin. How long do you think I should stay in bed?"

She tugged his shirttail out of his waistband and slid her hands all the way around him. His bare chest melded with her nearly naked bodice, the apricot fabric now fighting her full breasts and threatening to release them altogether. "I think you should check in at noon tomorrow and spend the rest of the weekend under a doctor's personal supervision." Deliberately she rubbed her breasts against him.

He groaned from a secret place deep in his throat, then kissed her again with a wild kind of frenzy. His eyes were dark, sizzling with newly awakened need as he broke free of her lips. "You're absolutely sure you have to go to work?" he asked her, the anguish in his voice begging her to rearrange reality.

Unable to speak, she nodded. There had never been a moment in her life when she'd wanted less to go on duty, but it was Saturday night and the Emergency Room would be full of fragile lives depending on her care. Desperately she struggled to remember her obligations.

But Kyle kissed her again, this time his mouth an undulating current that swept her into its tide and let her drift just far enough to feel the undertow before he tugged her back. His hands traveled hotly down the back of her low-cut suit, resting at last on the base of her spine where two fingertips tucked just inside the lowest edge of the fabric.

"If you really have to go," he whispered to the

space below her ear, "then it would be wise for us not to start anything we don't have time to finish."

She hugged him tighter, her teeth closing gently around the corded muscle of his left shoulder. He opened his mouth against her neck and stroked it with his tongue, silencing any sensible retort she might have offered. In mischievous foreplay the hand that edged her suit brushed ever so lightly over and over the same fingerlength of spine.

The rush of hunger arched from her vertebrae to her loins, and she knew the time for sensible decisions had very nearly passed. Fully aroused, she forced herself to release his powerful shoulders to rest her hands lovingly on his face.

"You're...going to have to help me here, Kyle," she struggled to tell him, battling for air. There was no way she could hide her desire. "If it were anything but E.R. duty...."

The need in his eyes belying his chastened schoolboy grin, he slowly moved his hands from their unerring position and stuffed them back in his ever-waiting pockets. She was surprised that he released her so quickly, but she knew he gloried in her blatant disappointment. That he shared the feeling was evident by the taut outline of his stiff manhood, unconcealed by his close-fitting slacks.

"I'll call you around noon," he promised, without moving a foot from her side.

"You're leaving?" she asked, then had to laugh at her mournful tone.

Kyle chuckled gently, then hugged her again in a gesture of mutual sympathy. "It's your commitment here, Erin. You call it."

She tried to smile. His nonchalance helped; some of the fire in her limbs was already cooling.

"There's really no choice to make, Kyle, or believe me, I'd choose to stay with you." She looked at her watch. "As it is I'm going to have to fly to get there on time."

"No problem," he said, grinning. "I've got my T-38 parked right outside."

They laughed together, knowing that at the moment they'd think anything was funny. It was Erin who finally forced herself to remember her duty. With a tender smile he could not misinterpret, she told him, "Please get the hell out of here."

He bowed saucily, his cheeks dimpling, but he still stood rooted to the floor. "Before I go, ma'am... there is just one quick thing I'd like to do... with your permission."

Delirious with the magic between them, she responded to his mood and curtsied deeply. "Your wish is my command, Commander."

His grin was one of untarnished victory as he moved forward to untie a make-believe bow in the nonexistent pink strap over her naked left shoulder, stretching out the imaginary ends until they touched the shoulder blade in her back and the upper curve of the breast that had throbbed for him the night he'd come to dinner. Then without rushing, he slipped his right hand inside the strapless maillot, weaving a slow, sensual trail around the soft circle of her breast. For several moments his fingers lingered, promising release from the sweet anguish he induced deep within her. When at last his fingertips claimed the stiff center of her areola, teasing the turgid peak with tiny flicks, Erin cried out her hunger and collapsed against his chest.

His free hand swept her against him, bracing her head as he kissed her once more. The palm of his hand crushed her nipple, then pressed it in circles as she begged him to stop-go-and-stay.

When at last he abandoned her breast, it was only to slide both hands down her bared lower back, crushing her just once against his hardness.

When at last he released her, he shook his head and met her eyes. "I've wanted to do that for forty-eight hours."

"It's okay," she murmured, ready to burst with joy and frustration. "I had the same fantasy. And I think I'd rather feel like this than...the way I felt the last time you went home."

He nodded, his lips curving a tender smile. "Me, too."

"Good night, then, special friend. I've really got to go."

Again he nodded, mouthing the word "good night." But in a final farewell gesture, he bent his head so his lips could grasp her half-covered nipple, wetting the supercharged center of her breast. She gasped in disbelief at his power and chutzpah. He stroked the fabric with his tongue just once before he retreated and left her aching for more.

KYLE WAS IN AN INCOMPARABLY GOOD MOOD by the time he reached his room at B.O.Q. His hunger for Erin was unabated, but knowing he'd left her equally aroused gave him a sense of kinship and expectation. They hadn't solved all their problems, of course, but he had no doubt now that they would. She had all but admitted that she loved him, and in the last hour, somehow, hearing her say that had become very important to him. *If I needed a man...* she'd said in her anger. Hell, she needed him. He'd make sure she needed him! He'd call her at noon and pursue her till midnight, compounding her passion till she was ready to beg. Then he'd fulfill her most frenzied daydreams; he'd make her realize that Kyle Tatum was the heart and soul of her existence. He'd never give her a chance to leave him again.

It occurred to him, briefly, that Erin was free to change her mind by morning. But he dissolved the thought. He had to learn to trust her. Besides, he'd have to make sure that he conquered her heart, not just her body. He could have seduced her, even in her anger, but it would have been sex, not lovemaking, and only for a night.

I'd rather not have her at all than like that, he told himself. The first time he made love with Erin would *not* be the last. It would be slow and well seasoned; she would simmer all day. He would tempt her, arouse her, force her to admit that he was all she wanted. He would wine her and dine her and melt her with flowers. He would give her every romantic tidbit of his own romantic soul whether she wanted it or not. He'd make her feel like a woman, make her cry for him as a man. He'd take all day to court her as he should have from the start. When they finally came together, it would be like a wedding night. A new beginning...a fresh start.

He was enjoying the memory of the look on her face as he'd bid her breast farewell when the telephone started to ring. He didn't take time to analyze the peace-shattering order: at midnight on a Navy base it could only mean bad news. The only thing worse was a pair of officers in dress blues coming up a young wife's front walk in the middle of the night during wartime.

"Commander Tatum here," he barked into the phone, his voice hard and calm as befitted an officer.

But his hand pressed nervously against his stomach, where a swelling balloon of fear told him that the first words he'd hear would end his twenty-nine day wait for news of a change in Roger.

CHAPTER SIX

"KYLE, HE'S AWAKE! He talked to me! He even remembered my name!"

Erin never got out any more details—Kyle's delirious hoops of rejoicing smothered her efforts at technical explanations. Almost as excited as he was, she finally gave up rational conversation and just told him to meet her at Roger's room.

"You can see him for a few minutes, Kyle. If I'm not here when you get here—"

"On my way. T-38 parked right out front."

Erin estimated the trip from the base to Our Lady of Mercy to be roughly fifteen or twenty minutes. Kyle drove it in twelve and a half. She heard him coming half a corridor away and rushed to tame his celebration—or at least his noise—before he disturbed the whole ward.

"Kyle—" she started, just before he grabbed her in his arms and swung her in a series of mad, joyful circles.

"He did it, Rinny! I knew he would. He showed everybody. I told you! I told you all! Murphy the Medic would be so proud."

By now his voice was an ecstatic hush, common sense and her nonverbal prompting helping to lower his tone. He kissed her half a dozen times in a spirit of euphoria rather than passion. Erin was too happy to care how it looked. But Roger was waiting, still terribly frail despite the miraculous breakthrough, and Kyle needed a doctor's sage directions before he bounded off the walls of the patient's room.

"Kyle, I know you're dying to go in there. But first I need to . . . play doctor here for just a minute."

He grinned, wild delight still circling his face. "I'd be happy to play doctor with you, Doctor. Just name the time and place—"

Gently she touched his face, remembering the first time she'd stood in this hall longing to embrace Roger Shaw's proud but unabashedly loyal friend. "I'm serious, Kyle."

He sobered, tensing in response to her change of tone. "I know he's not out of the woods yet, Erin. I know there's a hundred vital signs to check and technical jargon to record. But this *is* the turning point. This *does* mean there's really a . . . good chance that someday he'll be the old Roger, doesn't it?"

He looked so eager she could hardly have refuted his hopeful logic. Fortunately his assessment was correct. She kissed him lightly, hoping any nearby nurse would understand. "Yes. He's turned the corner, and there's every reason to believe now that with time—a *lot* of time—he'll be the way you remember him. But right now, Kyle, he's terribly weak. Even a smile will tire him, so don't be disappointed if he barely speaks to you." She touched his arm. "You're not going in there for you as much as you are for *him*. He needs to see that his buddy is very pleased to see him alive but not too surprised. You must never for a minute give him the feeling that you ever doubted he'd make it."

Kyle grinned. "Hell, lady, *I* never did!" He smoothed a loose strand of hair back from her face. "Don't worry about me, Erin. I know the drill. Three minutes tops, Officers' Club chat. May we go now?"

Wordlessly she squeezed his hand, then followed him into the room. She took a silent post at the door as Kyle moved to the foot of Roger's bed. He didn't say a word at first, just stood there, watching the man who was still swathed in bandages, with tubes in his nose and arm. Several minutes passed before Roger shifted in the Stryker frame and saw him. Relief washed over his pale face, lighting up the dormant laugh lines by his eyes. For a moment Kyle's face was beyond description, tight and raw with the joy of the moment. Then he forced himself to look relaxed, his dimples heralding a smile.

"Some people will do anything to get out of a little honest work," was Kyle's opening line. "Just like a doctor to think of a hospital as a place to go on vacation."

"Trick I learned from you," Roger forced himself to banter. "Only I didn't have any help from the enemy. I had to get shot down all by myself."

"Some guys have all the luck."

Roger swallowed hard. "What took you so long to get here? They have to fish you out of some satin bed or barroom brawl?"

"Very funny, sandcrab," was Kyle's rejoinder, his cheerful tone reflecting the joy he was feeling. "As it happens, Dr. Ness here can vouch for my good behavior this entire evening."

Roger struggled to grin a second time. "I'll bet she can vouch for more than that. I'll be damned if I'll ever go through this hell again to set you up with a woman, Tatum. From now on you're on your own."

"No jealous tantrums now, Roge," he chided, moving closer to the head of the bed. "As it happens I think Erin is planning to go out with you at least once as part of your recovery therapy. You'll have to pay her extra, of course, but your insurance'll cover anything the doctor recommends.''

This time Roger tried to extend his smile to Erin, but she could tell he was exhausted by the few lighthearted minutes of fraternal repartee. Hating to interfere, Erin willed Kyle to read the moment, and without so much as a glance in her direction, he did.

"I've checked all these folks out, Roge, and they're really top rate. Otherwise I would have had you moved even if I'd had to smuggle you out in a suitcase." This time Roger didn't even try to smile. "So be a good patient and it might even help you be a better doctor. Lord knows this hospital needs them. Erin has better places to spend her Saturday nights."

Right on cue the loudspeaker, voice quiet but firm, intruded on the moment. "Dr. Ness to Emergency... code blue...code blue...Dr. Ness."

Erin did not need a second prompting. Somewhere a heart had stopped beating...some nameless soul could not afford a moment's dawdling. But as she bolted from the room she smiled as Kyle reached out his strong hand to seize Roger's weak one. Man to man, Kyle met his friend's eyes with all the feeling he was far too "pilot" to ever express in words.

It was precisely twelve o'clock when the phone rang by her bed. It could have started ringing at dawn as far as Erin was concerned. Sleep had been out of the question after the events of last night.

"Good morning, Kyle," she drawled seductively into the phone.

"Good afternoon, Rinny," he answered in the same tone. "Are you still in bed?"

"More or less."

"Good. I'll be right over."

Erin laughed. "And here I thought you were a man of subtle finesse."

"Even I have my limits, lady, and believe me, you pressed them last night." Without waiting for her response he changed the subject. "You want to have a picnic on the beach?"

"Well..." Normally she avoided the outdoors in the daytime this time of year, but the beach just might be passable if the wind would keep blowing. Obviously it was Kyle's first choice of activities. "Sounds good. Let me see what I've got around here to—"

"Never mind. Your thoughtful escort will take care of that. You just slip into one of those not-quite-topless swimsuits you treasure that leave so little to the imagination. I'll be there in about an hour."

Kyle arrived fifty-eight minutes later with a picnic basket in his hand and wearing a pair of bright-red swim trunks. The sight of his rounded buttocks and long, muscular legs, exposed so blatantly to her sight for the very first time, was almost more than Erin could handle. The red T-shirt he wore firmly outlined his massive chest. Erin had covered her own modest blue one-piece floral suit with a pair of shorts and a halter top. After Kyle's earlier comments, she was not about to expose herself on a public beach.

He stood on the porch and looked her over. He grinned. She stood in the doorway and looked him over. His grin widened.

"Come here," he ordered in a low rasp.

She went. His arms surrounded her in a flaming welcome that left her sizzling. He kissed her just once, but that one time raked her senses over the coals of his desire and left her aching to pull his hands over her breasts. Somehow she managed to restrain the urge.

"Let's go," he suggested against her throat. "Quickly."

She could have told him she would have been just as happy to stay, but she knew he had other ideas for the afternoon. She refused to do a single thing to mar this incredibly perfect day.

It turned out to be a sweltering afternoon even at the beach. Houston never seemed satisfied with blistering temperatures; it always felt the need to add a dose of rain-forest humidity. As a newcomer to the area, she had been surprised to learn that the dust-dry cattle country Texas was famous for lay hundreds of miles to the west. Houston, less than an hour from the Louisiana border, wallowed in the Gulf of Mexico like a muddy alligator in a subtropical swamp. Even in May, when the rest of the country celebrated springtime, it was already hellishly hot in southeastern Texas.

"This is a terrible place to live," Erin complained after her third dip in the sea. "I wish NASA could set up headquarters somewhere more agreeable."

"It's going to," Kyle answered with a smile. "The Air Force will be taking us into space from Vandenburg on the coast of California in a year or two. The weather there is practically flawless."

Erin looked surprised. "You've been there? Don't tell me you subjected yourself to an *Air Force* base." The rivalry between the services was the source of constant joking at the center; she was curious to see how deep the feeling ran in Kyle.

"Of course not," Kyle teased. "I couldn't live surrounded by junior birdmen. But I was stationed at Point Mugu, just down the coast...a *Naval* Air Station where, incidentally, our people will be retrieving the solid rocket boosters for the Vandenburg launches.

Same old tale...the Navy always has to clean up after the Air Force.''

Erin laughed. "And the Army, too, no doubt."

"Of course. The other branches try hard, but they're just newcomers to American defense. The American Navy is over two hundred years old." He was laying it on pretty thick just to tease her, but there was no denying the pride in his voice.

"What's for lunch?" she asked, deciding not to dwell on the Navy. "Hardtack and saltwater?"

"Chinese takeout and beer. Somehow it seemed just right."

Erin laughed. "Today anything would seem just right. I'm starving."

They ate in companionable silence. The sea gulls tried to join them, and Kyle talked to them as though each was an old friend. When a pelican swooped down for a bit of noodle, Kyle looked jubilant. "Those old guys usually won't come so close. He must know you're a life giver and won't hurt him."

Erin chuckled at the massive bird and then at Kyle. "I wouldn't hurt him anyway."

Kyle returned her smile, then locked his elbows around his knees and stared at the ocean. "Vivian always hated birds," he declared soberly. "When I was stationed at Mugu we lived in a little house off the base where the swallows came to nest every spring. They were noisy and messy and generally irritating, but I could never bring myself to knock down the nests once the chicks had hatched." He closed up one of the containers and met Erin's eyes. "That's how I knew she was gone when I came home from Nam, even before I walked into the house. I mean—aside from the fact that she made no effort to meet me at the base.

There were almost thirty mud nests under the eaves on the porch and the sound of baby swallows everywhere." He looked away and stretched out his lanky legs. "I guess it was the time of year for babies. Vivian had one too, not long after I got back."

Erin froze from the inside out. A baby! My God! A baby! How tender he'd been with pregnant Katie! How clearly he adored children! How could he have gone this long without telling her something like this? But all she could ask was, "You have a child, Kyle?"

He couldn't conceal the bitterness in his voice. "Not unless my wife had a thirteen-month pregnancy. Odd, actually, that she managed to get pregnant while I was gone when she always refused to consider motherhood when I was there. 'Not yet, Kyle,' she'd tell me. 'We need more time alone together first.' Sometimes it was her career, sometimes it was the war, sometimes she didn't make up any excuses at all. She certainly didn't have any excuses to offer when I showed up to have a chat with the baby's father...a junior officer who'd served under me at Mugu. Vietnam draftee who left just as soon as his time was up." He smiled grimly. "Just couldn't wait to get home to *my* wife."

Erin didn't know what to say. Silently she reached out to touch his face, trying to erase the memory from his mind. For several minutes they sat on the sand together, listening to the sea gulls and the waves beating against the shore. The ocean breeze softened the glare of the sun. "She still hurts you, Kyle, after all this time," Erin finally whispered, snuggling closer to him. "I hope I can change that."

He put his arm around her and pulled her down on the beach towel. "Rinny, Vivian doesn't hurt me anymore. There's no part of her I want...no part of our life together that I miss." He started to rub his palm up and down the side of her arm. "What does still trouble me is the. . .lack of wisdom I showed with her right from the start. I was very young and ludicrously in love, but I was still an officer who'd been raised to act with restraint. She made me look like a fool, and she made me compromise a lot of my values. I was confusing lust with genuine caring." He slipped his arm around to her back and continued the subtle fondling. "I still feel a bit ill when I think of some of the things I was willing to give up just to have her in my bed. I'm not sure my father has ever really forgiven me."

"Forgiven *you*?" Erin questioned, hurting for him. "*She's* the one who was unfaithful!"

"And I'm the one who married her—secretly— bringing disgrace to the family. I let him down, Rinny. I let myself down. I won't ever do anything that foolish again."

He kissed her gently before she could ask whether his mother held it against him, too.

He smiled, as if the suggestion were silly. *It would almost be worth motherhood to raise a son like this,* Erin told herself, trying not to think about the way his fingertips were sliding under her straps so very near the side of her breast. "I could commit an ax murder with seventeen witnesses, and my mother would still stake her life on my innocence. I don't mean to imply that she's gullible or slow—she's as sharp as a tack. But I've never known a woman capable of more giving, worthy of more trust. Nowadays I run all potential marital candidates by her for approval before I allow my heart full rein."

Erin brushed his lips with her own. "Are there. . .many candidates for this exalted position?"

He laughed and shook his head. "A few strays here

and there before I came to Houston and none whatsoever in the past two years. I've had my eye on this beauty who would never give me the time of day." He pulled her closer and kissed her with such intimacy that she all but forgot they were on a public beach. The hand on her back never violated the rules of propriety, but its implied caress was too clearly etched in her memory to ignore.

Drawing back to a safer distance, Kyle declared with new solemnity, "I told you my father is retiring in July."

"Yes."

He was still close enough to tempt her. "There'll be a formal change-of-command ceremony. Very few civilians will be invited." He kissed her again, his lips sweet and beguiling. "I'd like you to come."

Erin's eyes opened in surprise. She had no interest in military events of any kind, and she wasn't at all sure what his father's retirement had to do with what they'd been discussing. But the look on Kyle's face made it clear that the ceremony was terribly important to him, and that made it important to her.

"I'd be delighted to go with you, Kyle, if you think it's...appropriate. I'm not sure your father would... consider me worthy of being included in such a select group."

Kyle grinned. "My father will be ecstatic. I've never asked to bring a lady to anything like this. You'll probably trip over the red carpet my mother will roll out."

She wondered if his mother's enthusiasm had anything to do with his earlier comments about her role as Kyle's marriage censor, but she pushed the thought out of her mind. They were enjoying each other now, and she refused to worry about unlikely scenarios in the future that might impede their joy.

"I'm not sure I've done anything to deserve the red-carpet treatment," she whispered provocatively against his throat.

"I'll make sure you do before we go," he countered, sweeping her against him with a kiss that left her without the sense of decency that a public beach demanded.

"Kyle," she gasped, breathlessly pulling away from his tantalizing hands. "Don't you...feel the lure of the sea calling you?"

He leaned back on his elbows to watch her, his tanned, muscled body looking even more virile in that position. "Trying to get rid of me, are you?"

She tried to look away but she could not. She'd been determined not to let him think she was too forward today, but it just wasn't like Erin not to be up front with the truth. "Under the circumstances, Kyle—" she gestured toward the several dozen people around them "—I think a moment's separation might be wise."

He was not offended. A predatory look flitted across his eyes, the glint that precedes the hunt. "I'll be back in a while. Anything I can do for you before I go?" His eyes darkened. "Or after I get back?"

"Get out of here," she growled, her cheeks putting on their own natural rouge. Had she no resistance to this man whatsoever? What would she be like when he *really* tried to seduce her?

It was her last thought as she watched his bright-red trunks tower above her. She could not keep her eyes from his perfectly rounded male buttocks as he sauntered toward the water, sensual confidence and expectation almost blatant in his stride.

WHEN ERIN WOKE UP the sun had moved three hours to the west, and she was almost alone on the beach. A makeshift umbrella of towels shielded her from the sun, saving her from the excruciating sunburn she'd earned more than once by falling asleep on the beach. The token gesture of Kyle's thoughtfulness pleased her, but his absence was troubling. It was so late! Where could he be?

She scanned the sandy space around her but saw only a couple with two small children. The father was in his thirties, tall and virile like Kyle, wearing red swim trunks like—

She looked again. It *was* Kyle! But why was he loping around the beach with a toddler on his back? The little girl was shrieking in delight, pointing at her brother who was half-buried in the sand. Suddenly both Kyle and his pig-tailed passenger fell to the sand and started mercilessly tickling the little boy. Then without warning both children turned on Kyle and attacked him in a juvenile version of wrestling that Erin and her sister had always called Big Bear and Little Fish. The children screamed in mock terror as Kyle threatened them, chased them, and playfully batted them about. Only when the little girl was trapped beneath his arms and the boy was clenched between his knees did he extract a desperate cry of "uncle" from each child before he let them go.

Suddenly he looked up at Erin and smiled in a way that told her he'd been checking on her all afternoon. He showed no embarrassment at his playful romping, just delight that she had finally awakened. Over the children's protests he said goodbye and promised to play the next time they met. Then he knelt beside the woman on the beach towel, whose back was turned to Erin. He touched her shoulder and gave her a smile. A surge of unexpected jealousy almost strangled Erin until the woman turned to wave at her.

She was probably sixty years old and plain as Job's turkey, but looked friendly enough. It wasn't hard to see why Kyle had stopped to chat.

"Friends of yours?" Erin asked as Kyle trotted up to her, taking a moment to pull her into his arms for a kiss.

"They are now. The kids' parents are getting divorced and grandma's filling in the gap. She doesn't have the energy to give them everything they need, so I decided to chase them around a bit."

"I'm glad you found something to do while I was sleeping. I didn't mean to zonk out on you, Kyle. But I've had a rough few days and been up all night—"

He silenced her with a kiss. "No apologies necessary. I'm glad you finally got some rest. Besides, I had a good time playing with the kids." As he knelt to pick up the basket, there was a sobriety in his face that surprised her. "I still don't have any children of my own, Erin. I borrow other people's whenever I can."

She really didn't know what to say to that, so she gave him a quick kiss instead. His response was warm, as always, but she had the uneasy feeling that it wasn't really the answer he'd been seeking.

But it was the only answer she could safely give.

IT WAS ALMOST DINNER TIME when they reached her house. Kyle walked her to the door and kissed her very soundly.

"It's been a splendid day, Rinny. Thank you."

Erin didn't know what to say. She couldn't believe he was going to leave without staying a little while. "Are you—" She stopped, trying to sound more serene. "When will I see you again?"

He grinned at her discomfiture. "When would you like to see me again?"

"I . . . well, I was . . . just wondering."

"Nothing ventured, nothing gained," he declared. It took her a minute to get his point; still she hesitated. Being overly eager with Kyle had always been a mistake.

Kyle sighed. He stepped a little closer and kissed her behind the ear, lingering long enough to stroke the sensitive area with his warm, searching tongue. "Would it really be that hard, Rinny?" His voice was a low purr. "Can't you just come right out and ask me to stay?"

"Stay," she breathed against him. "Please."

He kissed her on the mouth this time, his lips hard and hungry, his invitation less subtle than before. One hand pressed her waist against his body. His growing need was evident. "I promised Roger I'd go see him again tonight. Give me an hour and a half to go back to the base to change and slip over to the hospital. You doll up or rest, whichever you prefer. Dinner and dancing on the shore?"

Euphoric, Erin would have agreed to anything. "An hour and a half. And Kyle—" she said, stopping him with an impish grin.

"Hmmm?"

"Try not to be late this time."

HE CAME BACK EARLY, dressed in a light summer suit of powder-blue that made him look suave and very gentlemanly. He carried a lovely corsage of pink baby tea roses and insisted on putting it on Erin himself. It was not an easy task since she was wearing a white gauze sundress that worked just as well on the shoulder or off. In the mood to tempt fate, she'd decided to go braless and had pulled the ruffles as low as she dared.

"That's cheating," he declared when he first saw her. "Come to think of it, you cheat a lot."

She promptly pulled the ruffles up to her chin. "Is this better?"

He stalked her slowly, a predatory grin lighting his face. "I'm hanging by a thread, Erin. Do you want to eat dinner tonight or not?"

It was one thing to respond to his invitation; it was another thing to seduce him in her living room before they'd even gone out on a real date. "That was the plan," she told him smartly, tugging the ruffles back off her shoulders before he fastened the corsage to her dress.

It wasn't a bad plan, either, at first. Kyle took her to a seafood restaurant in Heron Bay that had an outdoor deck for dancing that actually was a private pier poking into the sea. While they waited to order she listened attentively as he repeated every word Roger had spoken during both visits—his private one and the earlier one when Erin was there. He was glad to be alive and still too weak to realize that all of his dreams had folded in on him.

They ordered fresh lobster, which Kyle insisted would be excellent, but Erin suspected that red cardboard would have suited them just as well for all the interest they had in eating. The awareness between them, brand new and eons old, had been mounting in stages for three solid days. By the time they reached the outdoor dance floor, Erin was almost afraid to touch the flawlessly muscled man who held her in his arms. Hoping he would understand her reluctance to cling to him in public, she kept her distance when the music first started. But Kyle quickly put an end to that.

"I've never understood rock music, at least as an excuse for dancing," he told her, his point underlined by the sultry 1940s tune the band was playing. "Nothing melts a woman faster than a saxophone, don't you agree?''

You could melt a woman with a kazoo, Kyle Tatum, she could have told him, but suddenly she was loathe to speak. He had pulled her close against him, one hand on her back while the other pressed her palm against his chest.

It was starlight dark on the wooden deck, and darker still toward the edge of the wharf where Erin and Kyle slowly drifted, the music overpowered by their own heartbeats' duet.

His eyes on her face, Kyle slowly released the hand that braced his chest and traced his fingers along the ivory skin of her collarbone. For several endless moments his fingers stroked that silky promenade until the need they evoked was suddenly too great for Erin to bear. She dropped her eyes and leaned on his shoulder, her head shielding his hand from some imaginary passerby's view. But they were completely alone on the pier.

Ever so slowly the caressing hand continued its search, its home base expanding, ever lower, ever deeper, until it rested on the swelling curve beneath the snow-white gauze of her dress. Her breath caught in a hushed gasp just before his burning fingers could—

In desperation, Erin all but pushed him away. Was he blind? Was he stupid? Couldn't he see how terribly she was aroused, with a need he couldn't possibly fulfill in this public place? *Oh yes, Kyle. I'm an experienced woman, and a few hugs and kisses and your hand on my breast shouldn't take me to such quick and piercing frenzy. But it does, Kyle...it does. It's different with you. It's different from—*

"Rinny...I'm sorry. Please don't be angry with me. I'm just..."

She couldn't believe the torment on his face as he closed the space between them. He looked just like she felt, only frightened as well...frightened that he'd rushed her, misjudged their mutual hunger.

"Kyle," she whispered, afraid to hold him close, "I'm not angry. I'm not mad at you. I'm just...I'm just..." She couldn't quite say how she felt. If she got out the words he'd think she was grossly forward. She tried to breathe and couldn't. She tried to look away but she couldn't do that, either. Finally she just burst out, "You've been taking me to the edge and leaving me there for three whole days and I just can't take it any more. I've never wanted a man like this in my life. All I know is that I...I really don't think I can bear to have you start something again until you're ready to finish it."

She stared at him in the dark, knowing that big-band music must still fill the night behind them. But all she could hear was the echo of her words, the unspoken question hanging between them. Then Kyle's eyes told her everything she needed to know. His pain was no less potent, his need for her no less keen.

The tempting delicacy of fresh lobster was a faint memory against this compelling magic; the seaside ambience of this special place suddenly a ludicrous waste of time. Kyle didn't ask again what her pleasure was. Almost beyond audible speech he ordered, "Come on, Rinny. I'll race you home."

Through the mass of weekend drivers and freeway cloverleafs they did not speak, did not dare to risk the tiniest of preview touches in the darkness of the car. By the time they reached her house, the silence was saturated with desire. Erin could hardly endure the moments it took Kyle to come around to her door, yet she knew the gesture was important to him and she didn't want to overdo her eagerness.

With perfect courtesy he escorted her from the Saab to her front porch, then paused with maddening tact when she tried to welcome him into the house.

"I know you're very tired, Erin," he whispered in a voice thick with frustration. "If you feel the need to...be alone and get some rest right now, I would understand."

Erin almost gaped at him. Rest! Alone! Was he crazy?

"Did that speech I gave you at the restaurant give you the impression I was craving solitude this evening?" she sputtered, unable to maintain the simplest veil of dignity.

He smiled...carefully at first, then his dimples gave him away and he laughed out loud. "No, ma'am, it surely didn't. But just the same I thought I'd be chivalrous enough to give you room to back down now that you've had some time to cool off."

Fresh arousal flooded her body. He could have taken her without a single kiss, right there on the porch, and she would not have complained. "What makes you think I've cooled off?" she queried saucily. "It's hot enough in Houston even when you're not around."

They laughed again, together this time, starting to relax in the certainty that the time for misunderstandings and urgent interruptions was finally past. "I think a quick dip in the pool might help to...solve the problem," he suggested.

Erin could have thought of surer measures, but she decided to follow his lead. "Excellent suggestion, Commander. Would you care to join me?"

"It would be a pleasure, ma'am," he retorted gaily, then tried to look crestfallen in the glistening moonlight. "But once again, I must report my failure to come properly attired. I left my trunks back at the base."

Discarding the last remnant of restraint, Erin told him what she'd longed to say on Thursday night. "Pay it no mind, Commander. I don't think you'll be needing them."

The look he gave her was more potent than the deepest of kisses. But still he kept his distance, waiting to make love to her in his own style. "I don't think you will, either, Rinny, but humor me, if you will, and go slip into something a little more...stringy."

She laughed, giddy with anticipation. "The green one?"

"That's it. And don't make the knots too tight."

It was a simple enough gift to give him, this fantasy. She skipped off to her bedroom, confident of the reception she'd receive just minutes later in their private bed of water.

She was not disappointed, Kyle was waiting for her on the yellow air mattress, paddling restlessly around the pool. He was clad in nothing but a water-soaked pair of black briefs that almost covered the essentials and did nothing whatsoever to conceal his anticipation. His azure eyes traveled the length of her body as she approached the pool, devouring every inch of ivory skin and green nylon as though it concealed some priceless treasure.

"Come join me, Erin," he invited with silky promise. He patted the floating bed. "There's room for two up here."

Erin dove into the water in the deep end and dolphined playfully to Kyle's side. She flipped the yellow mattress almost before he saw her, but he circled back and dunked her in quick revenge.

"Now, now!" she chided in between splashes and giggles. "You invited me in here. The least you can do is show me a good time."

"You're absolutely right," he agreed as he turned her on her stomach, then dove and crested beneath her like a slow-moving whale. She loved the feel of his back between her legs. "I'll be the sundeck where her ladyship can tan to her heart's content."

For an instant she gripped his shoulders and rode along as he stroked the water with the slow, sure power of his arms. Then without warning he sank deep beneath her and turned over, rising face up this time until he balanced her lower body on his lean hips and thighs.

"Now I'm a tugboat." He grinned at her surprise. "Just think of me as an ocean barge."

By that time it was hard to think of anything *but* him. Though Erin tried to anchor her hands on his chest and muscled shoulders, the water-treading jumble of their legs could not conceal the spike of his hunger. Sculling for balance with one hand, he seized the end of the string-bow at her breasts with the other, spilling them loose in the water.

The tingling that chilled her took Erin by surprise, and she gasped and went under. The scrap of green floated off unheeded. Instantly Kyle lifted her higher, his hands braced on her ribcage, fingers stretching toward her breasts. By the time his hands had found their fullness, his mouth had staked a claim on her jawline, his lips chewing sultry tidbits of throat, neck and ear.

Electrified by his onslaught, Erin forgot to tread water. So did Kyle. They both tumbled under the waves they'd created, legs intertwining in an instinctive search for satisfaction and support. Quickly Kyle thrust her back to the surface. His fingers brazenly uplifted her fully swollen breasts, then closed around each pointed circle. Still joined pelvis to pelvis, he towed her to the shallow end and perched himself on the steps, pulling her onto his lap astride him.

The change in Kyle was sudden. As Erin's knees locked around him, she knew that the time for poolside play had ended. All day he'd been a stalking predator toying with his prey; now he was ready to slake his hunger. Erin was utterly at his mercy, too desperate for his touch to even breathe her deepest longings. She would do anything at all for her deliverance.

Kyle's eyes were as blue as the pool when they met hers, declaring his intentions. His fingers honed in on the very tips of her throbbing nipples, tugging and twisting one, then the other, in the most delicious kind of rhythmic agony. He found her mouth and commandeered it to his service, forcing it to yield to his tongue's savage thrust. Beyond all conscious knowledge she sensed his hands slide over her hips, slipping beneath the bows of green at her thighs. As his fingers searched the stitching, his words nuzzled her throat and seared the hollows of her ears.

"I didn't want to rush you, Erin. I wanted to wine you and dine you...bring you candy and send you flowers. I wanted to melt that cool and efficient heart—"

"Melt me tomorrow," she gasped, knowing they were both beyond romantic speeches. "Tonight make me burn."

Kyle needed no more urging. He took her at her word. Like a proud mythological god of the sea, he rose from the water, clutching her thighs to hold her in place against his hardness. When he could feel her ankles joined behind him, he changed his grip, stirruping his hands beneath the quintessential source of her womanhood. She buried her face in his chest.

He walked three or four paces to the edge of the tile, never releasing his tumultuous fingerhold on the most sensitive part of her body. Erin clung to his shoulders as he lowered her to the grass. The blades were cool and soft beneath her. Nearby crickets cheered her on. Trapping her thighs between his own, he knelt above her, his magnetic fingertips urging her to potent new levels of desire as they slid benath the very last piece of green nylon.

"Touch me, Erin," she heard him beg her from a newfound place in her heart. Appalled at her selfish disregard for his needs in the midst of his determined concern for her own, she slipped both hands inside his briefs and released his throbbing male hardness, kneading it until his primeval growl of desire filled her with fierce satisfaction. She felt his breath warm her thighs as his teeth ripped loose each string bow with sweet, savage pleasure. Then in a sunburst of desire, he rolled on one side to tug off his briefs and grab both her wrists away from his body.

Lost in his urgency, she felt one triumphant hand force her arms above her head until her fingers clawed the earth, the position lifting her breasts to him in flagrant invitation. He blanketed one with his free hand and lapped the other with a tantalizing sweep of his tongue. Then he straddled her writhing body with his own, tapping and teasing her closer and closer to total delirium until at last she cried out, shattering, as he thrust his need deep within her.

Not until she had safely reached orbit and circled the stars did he complete his own journey. He clung to her as they shared the sweet anguish, moaning her name again and again and again. Erin laced her fingers in his thick black hair and pulled his face yet closer to her own. She scattered kisses over his throat, breathing disconnected words of fledgling love.

She wasn't sure whether or not he heard her whispered confession, but his arms tightened around her just the same.

CHAPTER SEVEN

WHEN ERIN WOKE UP the next morning, there was a long, supple male body in her bed. His regal black hair was tousled, his eyes were closed and his arms spilled over the covers near her breast. Her longing to snuggle up closer was overwhelming; yet despite the incredible joy of their union the night before, she felt almost shy lying naked beside him in the crisp dawn air.

Kyle rolled onto his side as he opened his eyes, studying her with a sleepy mixture of surprise and delight. "I didn't dream this," he said simply.

"No." She tried to smile, but a moment's hesitation froze her. She felt like she was the one who had dreamed it.

"You don't. . .think you made a mistake, do you, Erin?" he asked almost formally, his eyes absorbing her confusion.

"Not unless you did, Kyle," she whispered.

This time he grinned, his pilot's pride securely back in place. "Erin Elizabeth, God knows I've made enough mistakes with you to last a lifetime, but fortunately, none of them were last night."

She laughed, delighted and relieved. "Would you listen to this guy? No ego problems here!"

Playfully he grabbed her, rolling his lean body on top of hers as he pinned her to the bed. "I didn't hear any complaints out of you, Rinny. If there's something you wanted that you didn't get—"

"I got everything I wanted," she admitted impishly, her fingertips tracing his eyebrows. "But...that was last night."

He needed no further urging. With a speed that bore no resemblance to the slow, sultry lovemaking that had carried them through the past few days, he thrust the blankets away so their skin could touch. Instantly his fingers trapped her nipples as he rubbed his pelvis against hers, and within moments she was begging for relief. Their union was swift and potent; the afterglow a bonding that would grow with each joining.

"This could get to be a habit," Kyle whispered a few moments later.

"I think it already is."

He grinned, then kissed her very gently. "I've wanted you for so long, Rinny. I kept thinking I'd given you up, but...I don't think I ever really made it."

"I'm glad you didn't. Right now I can't even remember why I chopped these past two years out of our time together."

"I can't, either, but since you've admitted it was your fault, I think you'll have to spend the next two years making it up to me."

She chuckled against his shoulder. "Starting right now?"

He kissed her throat once, provocatively, then graced her with a brilliant morning smile. "It's as good a time as any."

AN HOUR AND A HALF LATER Erin walked into her new office—Roger's office—feeling like somebody else. This was her vision, her moment, her supreme triumph...the reason she'd marched alone with her head held high for so many years. The fact that she finally had someone to share it with made it even sweeter.

Kyle had not been happy that she'd refused to ride to work with him; she still wanted to keep their relationship quiet around the center. But he had accepted her decision and honored her feelings, then kissed her with such fervor that she had very nearly changed her mind. Despite the fact that she was already two days behind in her research for 61-J, she had promised to meet him for dinner. She had tried to convince herself she didn't have the time, but logic didn't stand a chance against the passion in Kyle's blue eyes.

It occurred to Erin briefly that except for his apology on Saturday night, Kyle had never mentioned her mission during the rest of the weekend. Refusing to consider the implications of that, she hurried down to the shuttle simulator and slipped into her jump suit.

The rest of the crew was already there. Mark and Paul went out of their way to welcome her with warmth, but Jeb was very businesslike. "Good morning, Erin," he greeted her briskly. "Hope you're on your toes today. We've got a lot of ground to cover."

"I'm one hundred percent here," Erin answered truthfully before turning her attention to the flight trainer, a middle-aged taskmaster named Seth whom she'd worked with before.

"I presume you've been over all the paperwork on this, young lady?" he queried sternly. Her nod was affirmative, but she felt a little out of her depth. Thanks to Kyle, she hadn't gotten much done this weekend. First she'd been too angry, then she'd been too thrilled. She'd sandwiched in bits and pieces of the reading, enough to get by, but she hadn't examined Roger's cabin assignments as thoroughly as she'd intended to.

"This is just a run-through to give you a feel for

what's going on," Seth explained. "After we're done, go over it with Jeb and read Roger's notes again, and it'll make more sense. Okay?"

"Okay." While Erin had spent many hours in all the simulators at the center, she had never worked with an exact mock-up of *Odyssey* as it would be adapted for her flight. Even though the morning's work dealt only with housekeeping details—where she sat during take-off and landing, her responsibilities regarding meals, equipment organization and care, she was thrilled by the knowledge that today's practice was in preparation for the real thing.

Since Erin was trained to operate on people, not chimpanzees, she spent the afternoon gathering up everything in the third floor library pertaining to space research with apes and monkeys, adding the briefs to the pile of evening reading that she'd have to fit in before Kyle arrived. Even the most optimistic observer could have told her that she'd have to cram five or six hours of reading into half an hour, but Erin brushed off the unsettling thought with a smile.

Quinto was cute, but as a date he couldn't hold a candle to Kyle Tatum.

WHEN KYLE REACHED THE HOSPITAL after work that night, he found Roger waiting tensely, his eyes full of naked pain that medication could not ease. He had more color than before and fewer tubes in his body, but he still looked pretty grave.

"I...I think I must getting better, Tatum," he croaked in a voice that did little to conceal his anguish. "I'm well enough to realize what rotten shape I'm in."

"That's a good sign," Kyle replied soberly, wounded by the sight of Roger's pale skin and dull expression. "I think it's safe to say I've seen you looking better."

This time Roger didn't try to smile. He turned his dark brown eyes away from his friend and whispered, "I'm not going up, am I, Kyle?"

Kyle felt the ache inside him as though it were his own. How would he feel if he lost his own mission? Lost his chance to prove his worth, to honor his family, to do the Navy proud? "No, Roge," he answered as he gently as could. "Not this time."

For several moments Roger was silent. Then he asked, "Who have they picked to replace me?"

Kyle's silence answered the question.

"Damn, it's Erin, isn't it?" Roger whispered.

"Is she a bad choice? From your point of view?"

Roger shrugged. "Anybody's a bad choice from my point of view. It's my mission! They should have postponed it altogether."

Kyle couldn't argue that. "I told Jeb that. I did my best, Roge."

"I'm not blaming you. I'm not blaming anybody. I just feel like...like..." He didn't finish the sentence. After a long silence, he asked pointedly, "Did you and Erin get together before or after she was chosen?"

"A little of both, Roge," Kyle muttered awkwardly. "But I didn't...we didn't...make it official until I was sure."

A stranger would not have understood Kyle's apologetic explanation, but Roger had no trouble reading between the lines. "I thank you for that. Must have been damn hard."

Kyle did not deny it. "It wasn't easy. I almost lost her."

Roger strained to roll over, then moaned as though his back was in pain. "Well, at least it's someone who's special to you, buddy. Send Erin by when I'm feeling a little better and I'll try to give her some pointers. I always thought she was a cut above the rest.''

Kyle found a smile, relieved that Roger was taking it so well and exhibiting some interest in the world beyond his bed. "I'll do that. She's going to need all the help she can get trying to fill your shoes."

Roger grinned, then closed his eyes in silent exhaustion. "Size 13D. She's got a long way to go."

Kyle laughed. "Just so she doesn't end up with your figure. I kind of like the one she's got."

Roger lifted his thumb in wordless agreement, then struggled to turn on one side. Kyle edged to the door and watched him for a minute.

"Roge?" he whispered.

"Mmmm?"

"I'll be here every day. Rain or shine."

Without turning over Roger mumbled, "I'm counting on it, Murphy. Otherwise I'll have you busted down to medical corpsman."

There was a smile on Roger's pained face as Kyle left the room.

ERIN HAD BARELY ZIPPED through her notes on the day's training in the cabin simulator when Kyle arrived. Despite the latent hunger that still lurked in his blue eyes, he seemed a little sober as he walked in the front door, keeping a staid distance between them. "Roger knows you've replaced him," he said by way of greeting.

It wasn't exactly the way she'd hoped to start the evening, but she tried to follow his lead. "How is he taking it?"

"Like Roger Shaw. Nothing gets him down for long."

Erin was relieved. "I'm glad. I hate to think of him

depressed. He's alway been...such a ray of sunshine.''

"I didn't think you knew Roger very well."

She laughed. "I've always worshiped him from afar. My ultimate masculine hero."

Kyle tipped his head and took a step closer. "You wouldn't care to rephrase that, would you?"

Taking the hint, Erin suggested, "My ultimate doctor hero. A purely professional kind of respect."

He smiled. "That's better. Are you hungry?"

The question lingered between them, offering alternate meanings. "I wouldn't mind an hors d'oeuvre," Erin suggested. "Just to hold me...for a while."

"I'd be happy to hold you for a while," he said, laughing, one-upping her pun. He took her in his arms and swallowed her laughter in a gentle, teasing kiss that washed away the tension of the day. Then he pulled away and opened the front door. "After you, my lady. We're going back to the wharf and tonight we're going to eat!"

THEY HAD A LOVELY EVENING. The lobster was terrific and the dancing still romantic. They managed to finish the meal this time, but after a twenty-minute goodbye on the front porch, Erin gave up her plan for late-night reading and led Kyle wordlessly to her bed. He was still there when she left for work in the morning.

The next three weeks followed the same pattern. Erin worked hard all day, read constantly until Kyle finished with Roger, then gave herself up to the glories of a night in his arms. Often she'd wake up at three or four in the morning too tense and worried about her backlog of work to sleep. If Kyle was there she'd silently pad out to the living room to read. Sometimes he'd find her there in the morning asleep on the couch;

sometimes he'd wake up and join her in the early hours of dawn, sleepily distracting her until she ended up back in bed, mesmerized by his touch.

Weekends brought no relief from the stress. Although the hospital had assigned another surgeon to cover Roger's hours, Erin still worked Friday nights. She vowed repeatedly to take the weekend days for her research and just see Kyle on Saturday night, but it never seemed to work out that way. He was either coming or going or spending the night whenever she'd planned to work, and her longing to be with him often took precedence over her study schedule. He was always courteous about their time together, responding cheerfully to whatever requests she made for him to stay or go. Yet there was a silent tension in him at times that made her uneasy.

Sometimes it was in the morning as she was dressing for work; other times it was late evening after they'd just made love. He would stare at her, caressing her face with his eyes, asking her wordless questions that she was not ready to answer. One morning she couldn't stand it anymore.

"Why are you always looking at me like that?" she asked him. It was Monday and she was feeling rushed. One more study weekend down the drain! She'd loved being with him, but now she'd have to pay the piper. "As though you aren't really sure who I am."

He smiled almost sadly. "I'm *not* sure who you are. All this weekend you've been my Rinny. Now you're going to turn into Dr. Ness again and go to a world I'm not allowed to visit. I might as well work clear across town or out of state."

She looked at her hands. He hadn't brought this up since the first morning he'd left her house to go to work. She'd hoped that that would be the end of it. "I thought I made it clear to you that my professional life and my personal life are separate. Surely you can't complain about our private time together.''

''Why should I complain? I love coming when I'm whistled to and sharing my nights with monkey books.''

Erin's lips tightened. ''Look, Kyle, you knew how busy I would be when we first got involved. As it is I've spent way too much time with you—I'm a good two weeks behind in my reading.''

He sat up a little straighter in bed. Her handmade quilt did little to cover his dark, muscular form. ''I am deeply honored by the personal sacrifice you've exhibited by spending your free time with me.'' Sarcasm poisoned his voice. ''I can't believe I was gauche enough to expect more than a perfunctory hello from you during your working hours.''

''Kyle, that's not the point. It just isn't professional—''

''Do you have to be professional all the time? Dammit, are we a couple or aren't we? Do you realize you've never let me take you to the base...never let me introduce you to my friends? Forced me not to share you with people I really care about? By keeping our relationship a secret you make me feel like it's...dirty somehow. Like one of us is married and we're sneaking out on the sly. Is that the way you feel?''

''Of course not. I'm proud to be with you.''

''Damn hard to tell it.''

He got out of bed and started to dress. She watched him silently. This was the first disagreement they'd had since they'd really been together; she didn't like it at all.

''Kyle,'' she asked more gently. ''What is it exactly that you want from me?''

He turned to face her as he pulled on his slacks, his eyes reflecting such frustration that it truly shocked her. They'd had such a short time together—such a short, utterly glorious time. Why did he look so sad?

"For starters I'd like to be able to tell the whole damn world that you're my lady. I wouldn't mind moving in with you right now. After that—'' he stopped, his eyes even more grave. "I've never been one to waste too much time wishing for what I can't have."

Erin moved close enough to rest her head on his chest. He did not move. Slowly she slipped her arms around him, dropping a kiss in the coarse chest hair. After a moment she felt his hands in her hair.

She didn't think the time had come to tell the rest of the world how she felt about this man who had brought such joyous sunshine into her life. But she was sure that the time had come to tell him.

"You've got me, Kyle," she confessed in a low, shaky tone. "Lock, stock and barrel."

He pulled her a little closer and managed a wan smile. "That's nice to hear, sweetheart. I just wish I could carry my shiny new rifle in the parade."

ERIN HAD HARDLY SLIPPED into her office—late after trying to sort things out with Kyle—when Jeb Henson marched in behind her and closed the door. She wasn't in the mood to talk to anybody; her farewell to Kyle had not been particularly reassuring. Clearly he could not tolerate the secrecy of their arrangement indefinitely. He was trying to be patient with her, trying to understand her point of view. But he was pretty much an all-or-nothing kind of person when it came to love and loyalty—a trait that Erin admired very much. Yet it was his very devotion to her that made it so hard for him to understand why she didn't want their names to be linked at NASA.

There was no easy way to tell him that she didn't want her role as Kyle Tatum's lady to eclipse her position as an astronaut in her own right. He had been raised to believe that a woman's finest achievement was her faithful support of her man; it would be very difficult for him to accept a woman who thought otherwise.

"Good morning, Erin," Jeb greeted her in his most formal Navy officer's voice. "May we speak frankly?"

"Of course." Her apprehension grew as she sat down and motioned for him to do likewise. While Jeb had remained courteous with Erin for the past month, he had never particularly warmed up to her, and the look on his face right now was decidedly cool. She had planned to spend some time this morning watching the last-minute preparations for an upcoming shuttle launch, hoping to pick up some subtle clues for a successful mission. But the look on Jeb's face told her she could scrap the next hour entirely.

"Before I tell you what I came here to say, Erin, I'd like to clear the air about something," he began in a rather stilted tone.

She nodded, totally in the dark.

"When we were considering you for this position, I found it...somewhat incongruous that you suddenly found time to get involved with someone who was very close to me. I shared my suspicions with Kyle. I was wrong. I'd like to apologize to you now for any distress my actions may have caused you."

Erin could not reply. Kyle had never blamed Jeb for his earlier suspicions, and the whole incident had been laid to rest for weeks. Why was Jeb bringing it up now?

"Thank you for your honesty...and your apology, Jeb. But it's old business. Kyle and I have forgotten it."

With her last words she realized that she was admitting to her ongoing relationship with Kyle. And why not, she asked herself, suddenly remembering the hurt in his eyes. Her place at NASA was secure. Kyle was right. He had earned the right to public acknowledgment of the hold he had on her heart.

"Have you also forgotten your promise to let nothing stand in the way of your devotion to this mission?"

Again she was surprised. "Of course not. I'm working around the clock, Jeb. I'm running on six hours of sleep a night. I've responded to every suggestion or order given me by any flight trainer or crew member—"

"Then respond to another one, Erin." His voice was dark. "You've been on 61-J for a month. By the end of this week Dodson or Rafner or somebody is going to ask me how you're doing. Is she cutting it, Henson? Is she giving it her all? Was she the right choice to replace Roger?"

Nausea swept over her momentarily. Why did he speak with such doubt? "Are you...going to have trouble with your reply?" she forced herself to ask him.

"Yes," he snapped back without hesitation. "You do good work when you're here, Erin, but you're slowing us down. You don't do your homework. You think you can wing it on a fifteen-minute scan of material you should have studied for six hours the night before."

Erin was so stunned she could not reply. She stared at him in crushed dismay while his eyes met hers without regret. Finally she stood to face him. "I'm behind in my reading, Jeb, but not because I don't put in the hours. There's just so much to do! I'm working ten or twelve hours a day as it is—"

◦§ IT'S A ◦§
HARLEQUIN HONEYMOON
A SWEETHEART
OF A FREE OFFER!

FOUR NEW "HARLEQUIN SUPERROMANCES"–FREE!

Take a "Harlequin Honeymoon" with four exciting romances—yours FREE from Harlequin Reader Service. Each of these hot-off-the-presses novels brings you all the passion and tenderness of today's greatest love stories... your free passports to bright new worlds of love and foreign adventure!

But wait...there's <u>even more</u> to this great offer!

SPECIAL EXTRAS–FREE!

You'll get our free monthly newsletter, packed with news on your favorite writers, upcoming books, and more. Four times a year, you'll receive our members' magazine, Harlequin Romance Digest! <u>Best of all, you'll periodically receive our special-edition "Harlequin Bestsellers," yours to preview for ten days without charge</u>!

MONEY-SAVING HOME DELIVERY!

Join Harlequin Reader Service and enjoy the <u>convenience</u> of previewing four new books every month, delivered right to your home. Each book is yours for only $2.50— <u>25¢ less per book</u> than what you pay in stores! Great savings plus total convenience add up to a sweetheart of a deal for <u>you</u>!

START YOUR HARLEQUIN HONEYMOON TODAY– JUST COMPLETE, DETACH & MAIL YOUR FREE OFFER CARD!

HARLEQUIN READER SERVICE

◦§ FREE OFFER CARD §◦

PLACE HEART STICKER HERE

4 FREE BOOKS

PLUS AN EXTRA BONUS "MYSTERY GIFT"!

FREE HOME DELIVERY

☐ **YES!** Please send me my four HARLEQUIN SUPERROMANCES books, free, along with my free Mystery Gift! Then send me four new HARLEQUIN SUPERROMANCES ™. books every month, as they come off the presses, and bill me at just $2.50 per book (25¢ less than retail), with no extra charges for shipping and handling. If I am not completely satisfied, I may return a shipment and cancel at any time. The free books and Mystery Gift remain mine to keep!

134 CIS KAVJ

FIRST NAME_____LAST NAME_____
(PLEASE PRINT)

ADDRESS_____APT._____

CITY_____

PROV./STATE_____POSTAL CODE/ZIP_____

PRINTED IN U.S.A.

Offer limited to one per household and not valid for present subscribers.
Prices subject to change."

"That's not enough! This isn't an office job. It's like being in combat. Your full concentration—your utmost devotion—must go to your unit! These five months—from the minute you were chosen until the last press conference and debriefing—belong to mission 61-J. *You* belong to Mark and to Paul and to me. And to the hundreds of people backing up our crew! You simply do not have time to romp about with Cupid until September! Do you understand?"

Instant fury ripped away her normal poise. "I understand that you're telling me to walk out on your friend!"

He shook his head. "We're not talking about friends here, Erin. We're talking about duty! If my relationship with a woman was getting in the way of this mission, I'd set her aside for the good of the crew. I don't ask any more of my men than I do of myself, and for the moment...you're like any other man who's ever been under my command." He paused to let his words sink in. "That's how you want to be treated, don't you?"

"Yes," she seethed, "but that doesn't give you the right to tell me what I can do with my free time."

"The point is that you don't *have* any free time. You're giving *our* time to Kyle. Put him on hold till September or forget him altogether, Erin, if you plan to carry your weight on this mission."

"Is that an order, Commander?" she asked in barely concealed rage.

He shook his head. He did not share her anger; he was just doing his job. "No. It's a suggestion from Jeb to Erin. If you try to satisfy *both* Kyle and this mission you'll end up torn right down the middle and be no good to any of us. I was hoping you'd realize that on your own, in time to do something about it, but since you haven't, I decided to stick my neck out a little bit and give you a second chance. I'm going to report exactly what I see, Erin, and if I see you making a major change in your priorities between now and the next time somebody asks me how you're doing, I'll cheerfully report your progress."

Erin straightened her spine, still angry but knowing that Jeb would do as he promised no matter who got hurt. "Nobody will have to clean up after me on this mission, Jeb. I'll be caught up with everything on Friday by the time I go home."

He nodded with a hint of respect. "Good. That's what I wanted to hear."

He turned to leave the room.

"Jeb?"

"Yes?"

"I won't give up Kyle for 61-J, and I have no intention of going under. I'm a damn fine swimmer."

Jeb shook his head and opened the door. "I hope there's a miracle headed your way, lady. I'd lend you one if I had one to spare."

BY THE TIME SHE GOT HOME, Erin was so tense she was ready to explode. She'd worked double-time all day, rushing from one spot to the next, reading through lunch, reading while she waited for people, simulators and jets. She'd mapped out a reading schedule for the week and figured that with five hours of sleep a night, she might have everything done by Friday.

When Kyle arrived at seven, Erin hurriedly kissed him hello, hauled him into the kitchen and pushed him into a chair.

"We need to talk." She rushed out the words. "We—"

Kyle stood up and laid one palm against her cheek,

nd the tension drained away by magic as he pulled her
p into his arms. "Turn off your motor, babe. What-
ver's wrong can wait a moment till I calm you
own."

Gratefully she leaned against him before she took
me for a more generous kiss. What had she ever done
 deserve such a patient, giving man? She wanted to
url up in his arms and forget the rest of the world. But
ne pulled away and forced herself into a chair at a
ober distance.

"What's wrong?" he asked her gently.

"I'm in trouble at NASA. I got called on the carpet
or not putting in enough time. They think I'm slowing
own the mission." She didn't want to tell him who
ad delivered this bad news, but he was too quick for
er.

"Who's 'they'?"

She looked away. "Jeb."

"Of course. What are friends for?"

"He honestly. . . said it like he was trying to help me
ut. Trying to give me a second chance to straighten
p before he had to report my. . . flakiness to the top."

"Erin, you don't have a flaky bone in your whole
ody," Kyle reassured her. "Did you tell him how
ard you're working already?"

"Yes. But he said it wasn't enough. He said that. . .
ntil September I didn't have any free time. I'm a cap-
ive of 61-J."

He grinned. "Then I guess I'll just have to ride up
n my white steed and set you free."

He leaned over to kiss her, but Erin stayed in her
eat. "This isn't funny, Kyle. He made me feel like I
vas actually in danger of losing my spot on this mis-
ion. He seemed to think that I. . . shouldn't see you at
ll until September."

This time gravity marked his face. No smiles, no sunshine, no morning warmth lurked in his eyes. "And is that what you've...decided to do?" It was obvious he was preparing himself for the worst.

"Of course not! I told him to stick it in his ear."

"You did?"

Erin tried to laugh. "Well, I told him what I did with you was my own business. But I also promised to have everything shipshape by Friday, and that does mean I shouldn't see you until then. I simply won't have a minute to spare."

For several minutes he met her eyes, then he stood up and looked away. He walked to the window and studied the garden as though it were for the last time. Then he walked back to Erin and bent to kiss her very tenderly, a lingering kiss that could almost have been goodbye.

"Good luck on your studying. I'll call you sometime."

He almost made it to the door before Erin stopped him, a strange fear rattling its way into her chest. "Kyle...it's only for a few days."

He turned around, his eyes unreadable. "Sure it is. A few days this week...a few days next week...a whole week the month after that. It'll get easier when you're out of the habit of waiting for me to call."

She stood up and walked to his side, holding his shoulders to keep him close. "You're scaring me, Kyle."

He touched her face, his eyes revealing hints of pain. "Rinny...I never wanted you to take this mission. I knew it would deplete your energy and your spirit, and I knew that sooner or later, it would force you to make a choice between me and your career." He released her and stood back. "I was just hoping we'd have a little more time before it happened. Enough time for me to...find a way to make you love me too much to let me go."

"Kyle, I have no intention of letting you go. I told Jeb—"

"Did you tell him that maybe he should find somebody else to replace Roger? Did you tell him that the mission was stealing *my* time with you? Did you tell him that if push came to shove and you had to make a choice, you'd choose Kyle Tatum over 61-J?"

She stared at him, knowing what he was asking... knowing she lacked the answer he craved. "I don't think it's come to that, Kyle."

"But it will. You're already showing signs of wear and tear, Rinny. And I'm getting restless."

"Restless?" The word frightened her. She had never imagined she'd have to worry about fidelity with Kyle!

"I'm tired of being pushed aside. I'm tired of coming in second place to the mission. And I sure as hell am tired of keeping our relationship a secret." He ran a hand through his hair. "Now it looks like it won't be much of a secret to keep."

She put her arms around him again, anxiety blocking her air. "That's not true. I just need this week to get caught up. Then I'll work out a schedule when I can see you and still—"

"*You'll* work out a schedule and *I'll* come running whenever her ladyship desires my touch?"

She dropped her hands and stood back, a flush of anger on her cheeks. "I don't think I like that, Kyle. You sound like all I want from you is sex."

"Is there something else you want? Time? Commitment? A wedding ring?"

Erin didn't know what to say.

"Have you ever noticed that you never use...endearments for me? You freely confess your hunger for me, Erin, but never your love. You always have time for me to spend the night, but nowadays you can't seem to find the energy to go anywhere I might want to go...or the interest to ask about the rest of my life. I don't think you know one damn thing about the Navy now that you didn't know before we met. You want to hear what I've learned about surgery and chimpanzees?''

Her hands were numb.

"I don't think you've ever noticed that two people are involved in this relationship. We do what you want to do. We go where you want to go. We keep secrets you want to keep! Why? Because of your career. Because of 61-J. I suppose you've forgotten by now that I also have a career. That I have a mission coming up I might like to talk about from time to time. People I might want you to meet. A future I might want to discuss with you. A future I might want you to be part of.''

By now Erin was watching the floor, shame branding her cheeks with bright color. Oh, he was overdoing it a bit in his anger, but he was too close to home for her to say he was dead wrong. Certainly they'd gotten together at a time when it was inevitable for her to be a bit selfish, but she had taken his good-hearted nature for granted. She had never really looked at anything from his point of view.

Slowly she met his eyes. *You'll be torn right down the middle and be no good to any of us,* Jeb had warned her. She felt herself starting to rip. "This...might be as good a time as any to discuss...your work and your future," Erin forced herself to say. "I'm not doing anything...more vital this evening." She tried to tack on an endearment, but she couldn't think of one that wouldn't stick on her tongue. She didn't come from a family where such words were freely bandied about; her parents had had quieter ways of showing their affection.

This time it was Kyle who looked contrite. "I'm sorry, Erin. I just feel. . . a little used sometimes."

She couldn't say he was wrong. "I have been a bit selfish, Kyle. The mission really is no excuse." She moved back to his side, waiting for him to touch her.

He didn't. "I know you've got a lot to do," he announced briskly. "So I'll call you in a few days and see how it's going."

He turned to leave, but Erin stopped him with a hand on his chest. He put an arm around her waist without really looking at her, then dropped a brief kiss on her cheek.

It wasn't nearly enough for Erin. She crawled into his arms, snuggling as close as she dared. Against his throat she whispered, "Please don't leave like this, Kyle. I won't get anything done."

The change in Kyle was instantaneous. He wrapped both arms around her and hugged her powerfully, kissing the top of her head. For several moments he rocked her without words, waiting for the hurt to subside. Only when they were both at peace did he lead her to the living-room couch and pull her onto his lap.

"We don't have to talk about this right now, Rinny," he suggested, his voice soothing her fears. "I know you've got a lot on your mind." He kissed her again for his own reassurance as well as hers.

"You. . . made it sound like I've been ignoring you, Kyle. I don't ever want to do that. If there's something important going on in your life that I'm missing, I really want to hear about it. You mentioned your mission—"

"I can't tell you very much about that. We've been trying to sand down a few rough edges—political more than technical, I guess—but...that's not really what's been on my mind."

She snuggled closer. "I'm listening."

He pulled her closer, his fingertips tender but chaste against her shoulder. "Rinny, the time's going to come... maybe not now, maybe not even on this mission... when you're going to have to make a decision about what really comes first in your life. I'm not always going to be here—" He stopped at the look of panic in her eyes. "I don't mean I won't be here for you, babe. But in four more years, my assignment to NASA will be over. I don't have any idea where my orders will take me, but it's a safe bet it won't be Houston. You might want to consider...I mean you just might want to think about whether it's worth killing yourself to break into a career that you might... choose to walk away from...not too much further down the line."

Erin watched him with a strange, still panic in her heart. The realization that he still planned to love her four years from now lifted her into clouds of joy. But the idea of leaving NASA...of jumping off the very summit of her lifelong dreams to follow him...terrified her. The tide tugged at the sand beneath her feet.

"All I'm saying is, before you make a decision that may...snuff me out of your life, I want you to know...for whatever it's worth...that my feelings for you are very permanent."

She knew she should have kissed him, pushed out the words, "I love you," and celebrated his confession of love. But she couldn't. She had to know just where she stood. She had to face her options squarely.

"What...exactly are you suggesting, Kyle?" she whispered.

He kissed her very lightly. "I'm asking you to con-
der spending the rest of your life with me. I don't
ink it's time just yet for me to...propose on one
nee, but I want you to know that...I'm moving in
at direction." He leaned down to kiss her again,
ith even more tenderness this time.

When he gently pulled away, Erin stared at him, un-
ble to speak. He covered her silence with tender
ords. "I know it frightens you when I mention mar-
age, but I'm still not sure why. I'm really pretty easy
o get along with. I'm financially responsible and un-
npeachably loyal. I'm handy around the house and I
ove children." He met her startled eyes before he
dded, "And I love you, Rinny. Very much."

Before she could marshall her thoughts he went on,
I never expected to have another career wife, but I'm
ot so antiquated that I can't see how miserable you'd
e as a full-time housemaker with all your surgical
alents. I can't say I like the idea of being married to a
octor, but I could probably find a way to live with
at if you could find a way to live with me. You
now—well, maybe you don't—that a Naval officer is
eassigned pretty often, and I know that might be hard
n your career, but at least doctors are needed every-
here."

Erin still could not speak. She couldn't even touch
im.

"I'm just asking you to think about it, Rinny. I just
ant you to...be aware of all your options."

Slowly she reached up and stroked his face. She felt
ke she'd been tossed into the sea without a life vest.
ut she had to say something! "Kyle...I think my
eelings for you are...pretty permanent, too. But
've...I've never really considered marriage before.
ust in general! And you're not really talking about

marriage just between the two of us. You're talking about...NASA and the Navy and Anthony Kyle Tatum the Fourth and the Fifth and the..." She broke off and buried her head against his throat. "I don't think you have any idea how much you're asking of me."

He sighed and touched her hair. His voice grew a little huskier. "I'm not asking for anything I'm not willing to give you back a hundredfold, Rinny. I want to live with you. I want to make a home with you...a family...a life together."

"You...you are...sort of living with me already, Kyle." She was stalling, struggling to offer him a comforting word. "You sleep here more often than you do at the base."

"Dammit, Erin!" he burst out, abruptly dumping her on the couch. "You just don't get it, do you? I'm not looking for a place to sleep. I'm looking for a home! For both of us!" He struggled for words to make his vision clear to her. "I'm talking about...a swing on the front porch in August. A crackling fire when it's snowing outside. Baseball bats and dolls in the living room! Teenagers asking for the keys to the car!" His eyes met hers with poignant regret. "Somebody who gives a damn if I can't get home for dinner."

He jammed his hands in his pockets and turned away from Erin. He'd been patient as long as he could; it wasn't easy for a man like Kyle to talk about marriage to a woman who didn't seem to be interested.

"Kyle, I'm sorry. I wasn't making light of—"

"I've lived all over the world, Rinny, in jungles and deserts and on ships at sea. The one thing I'm sure of is that home isn't *where* you go at night.... It's *who* you're going to...who you've got waiting for you even if you can't get to her for months at a time." His eyes were dark pools of loss; his voice grew soft and still. "When you've got to ask a lady's permission to come calling, Erin, you can be damn certain that no matter how welcome you may be in her bed—" he glared at her from a great height "—her house is *not* your home."

CHAPTER EIGHT

ERIN GOT PRECIOUS LITTLE SLEEP that night...and precious little studying done. Kyle's anger—so controlled and yet so terribly deep—reverberated in the house for hours after he was gone. He hadn't apologized for one single word, nor had he repeated his earlier promise to call. He had left her in a tailspin of fear and confusion.

She had always known that Kyle Tatum was the marrying kind, that somewhere down the road a vision of wife and family lured him to domestic bliss. She was deeply moved that he'd chosen her to fulfill his fantasy. But she didn't see how on earth she could approach space surgery like part-time volunteer work in between wiping tiny admirals' noses and packing for Kyle's new orders while he flew in and out of this year's war.

On the other hand, she could not imagine carrying on blithely in Houston four years from now, knowing that Kyle was coming home at night to...anyone but her. After just four days without the sound of his voice, even the walls of her little cottage seemed to miss him. The phone remained silent. The table where he so often ate dinner was unaccountably bare; the swimming pool looked huge without his tanned and muscular body doing laps. And the bed...Erin couldn't even bear to think about the bed. Each solitary night intensified her need for his touch...and for his morning smile.

She made good on her promise to Jeb, but still

walked into her house Friday night loaded with a new
pile of briefs. A weekend free to catch up on her work
held no allure for Erin when she felt so estranged from
Kyle. Every night she hoped he would call, and every
night she went to sleep fearing that *she* was the one
who would have to make the first move. But she
couldn't just call up and say she missed him; she knew
he'd demand a compromise, some substantial proof
that she shared the depth of his feelings and was willing to make some sacrifice to prove it. She also knew
that if she didn't make her move soon, it might well be
too late.

She was on her way to the phone when it issued its
own summons. Determined to veil her eagerness, she
let it ring three times before she reached for the
receiver.

"Good evening, Erin," Kyle greeted her in a neutral
tone. "I hope you've had a productive week."

"I've missed you," she confessed, melting the instant she heard him say her name. He couldn't have
sounded more normal! Her relief was immediate and
intense. All that anguish for nothing! It was only
eight-thirty; if he hurried they could have some healing
time together before she went to work. "I've had a terrible time concentrating on my work."

"Just following orders, ma'am. Staying out of your
way," he replied in what might have been a teasing
voice. "However, if it wouldn't be too presumptuous
of me, I wondered if you could spare some time to see
me tomorrow. There's an air show out here on the
base at noon. The Blue Angels are coming in. I always
go with some of the guys but I thought maybe you'd
like to come along."

Erin did some fast calculating. She'd heard of the
Blue Angels—the Navy's precision flying team that

gave demonstrations around the country. It was supposed to be a fantastic show for airplane buffs, but with her exhausting schedule she couldn't see spending the day in ninety percent humidity when she could get the jump on her newest pile of briefs and give Kyle her undivided attention tomorrow night.

"It's a nice thought, Kyle, but I don't think so. I've got so much to do that—"

"No problem," he replied indifferently. "Just thought I'd ask. I know you've got to go to work so I won't keep you."

"Kyle!" The word leaped out of her mouth before he could hang up.

"Did you say something, Erin?" His voice was perfectly calm.

"I . . . I . . . when am I going to see you?" She sounded about sixteen.

"Oh, I don't know. I'll give you a call in a week or two. Maybe we can take in a movie."

"A week or two?" she croaked, genuinely stunned. "A movie?" She breathed deeply and struggled for her voice. "Kyle, I . . . I really want to see you tonight."

"Tonight?" He sounded surprised. "If we made a date for tonight I sure don't remember it, Erin. I'm sorry. I've made other plans."

"Other plans?" She choked on the words. Surely he didn't have a date with some other woman! A week ago he'd wanted to marry her! *Dear God, what is happening here?* her heart asked, skittering back and forth across her chest. She couldn't think. She knew there should have been some suave and sophisticated answer, but she couldn't find one. "I . . . really want to see you, Kyle," she confessed. "This week has been endless, and I . . . I think we need to talk. Couldn't you come over for just a little while?"

"No, Erin, I can't. I'm sorry. I have to leave in about ten minutes." He paused to let his refusal sink in. "I was hoping to see you this weekend, too. But if you can't make the air show, I guess—"

"I'll make the damn air show," she ground out under her breath.

"Pardon?"

She sighed deeply. What was he doing to her? "I said I've changed my mind about the air show. I'd love to go."

"Hey, that's terrific!" he declared with what could have passed for genuine enthusiasm. "I really think you'll enjoy it."

"I hope so, Kyle."

"And I'm sure you'll have a lot in common with my friends. Several of the guys work at NASA."

This time there was no doubt about his intentions. He was boxing her in; forcing her to publicly acknowledge their relationship. Yet she didn't dare fight him. Something was terribly wrong, far more out of balance than she had feared. He had given up waiting for her to offer him a compromise; he'd come up with one of his own.

"That's...fine, Kyle." She forced out the words. 'I don't think we need to keep our...relationship a secret any longer. Since Roger and Jeb already know about us, everybody else will probably know soon enough anyway. I was going to tell you—"

"When, Erin? When your back was up against a wall and you knew if you didn't toss me a bone I'd walk?"

New panic slapped her in the face. She was losing him. In spite of this date—this dare—he was still angry. She had used up all of her chances.

"I said I'd go with you tomorrow, Kyle," she reminded him in a strained, hushed voice. "No more secrets. You can tell the whole world that I'm your lady...as long as I still am." She hadn't meant to add on that last confession of fear. But her heart was circling her ribs like a tiger in a cage. She was shaking. Never had she felt such uncertainty.

Several moments of silence passed. Too many moments. It was Kyle who finally spoke.

"I'm a logical man, Erin. I'm also a proud one. I've decided that it's ridiculous for me to put my personal life on hold for a woman who has not the slightest inclination toward any kind of public—or even private—commitment to me. If you want me full-time, you know you can have me, Rinny. But if you just want to see me whenever it suits your fancy, you can damn well bet that I'll see you whenever it suits *my* fancy. I've got a long list of appealing women who are eager to share their time with me." He paused to let his last line sink in. "You can't have your cake and eat it, too, lady."

Tiny firecrackers of fear went off in Erin's chest. When her words came they were not planned; they parachuted out of her heart in desperation. "I love you, Kyle," she whispered into the phone. "Please don't go out with anybody else."

His silence thundered against her ears for endless minutes. Then his low voice crossed the line to touch her, massaging her heart like she had once done for him. "I don't have a real date tonight, Erin. Commodore Everhardt's daughter has just graduated from Smith and he's giving her a coming-out party. Since I'm an eligible young officer with no...apparent... attachments, I have been 'invited' to attend. I have to go, babe, but I'm under no obligation to pursue the matter after that."

She tried to still her pounding heart. Silly jealous

words rushed out of her mouth. "Have you met her? Is she pretty?"

"Rinny!" he moaned in exasperation. "You're the only woman I want. You know that."

Erin felt relieved and ridiculous. She had to stop acting like an idiot. She had to tell him the truth.

"I. . .I've given a lot of thought to our. . .discussion Monday night, Kyle."

"Our discussion?" He sounded as though he had not the slightest idea what she meant.

"About. . .home and commitment. . .and marriage."

His voice was very cautious. "And what have you decided?"

She told him the only thing she was sure of. "I couldn't bear to lose you, Kyle."

This time his words were less than reassuring. "I'm not eager to give you up, either, sweetheart. But it's obvious that you're not ready to give me the kind of commitment I have in mind. You need more time—to work and to decide—and more freedom." Again he paused, letting his words sink in. "You can't expect me to just sit around like a lovesick schoolboy while I wait for you to change your mind."

Erin was near tears. "You make me sound so awful, Kyle. If you had any idea how much I've suffered this week. . .how terrible it's been without you. . .you wouldn't try to hurt me like this. I'm so frightened. Please don't go to that party. Please come over here and let us straighten everything out—"

"No." The single word was simply spoken. "It's a social obligation I couldn't get out of even if I wanted to. And I don't want to, Erin. I've got to carry on with my own life. If I had any sense, I wouldn't see you at all, and it may yet come to that. But—"

"No!" He'd said the word with calm assurance, but Erin uttered it as a desperate plea. She couldn't stop the tears now. She couldn't hide the trembling in her voice. "What do you want?" she burst out, knowing she'd say yes to anything but marriage. Marriage meant giving up NASA, and that was one thing she could not do. Even for Kyle. "What do you need from me to make everything all right between us?"

This time the silence was unbearable. Erin gripped the phone so hard that her fingers began to ache long before Kyle's voice came back to ask her, "I think the question is, what do *you* need to make everything all right between us?"

The answer to that was suddenly crystal clear. "I want you to move in here tonight. Completely. Permanently. Go to that party if you have to, Kyle, but remember who you're coming *home* to. And while you're there you can tell the whole damn Navy that you're no longer available as a single man!"

Once again Kyle's silence haunted her as he digested her words. Then he finally asked, "What would be the...terms of this...living arrangement, Rinny? Would we be planning a wedding or just...splitting the rent?"

Erin could hardly breathe. She was so frightened she was tempted to agree to anything. She knew what he wanted her to say, but twenty years of visions and a decade of blood, sweat and tears held her fast. "We would be making a public and private commitment to belong to each other, to make a home, to share our lives as long as...we're happy together. It would be a...trial period to...work out the wrinkles in our future, with every hope that somehow we can find a way to give each other our hearts without sacrificing our souls."

"What you're trying not to say is that you don't know how in hell you can ever marry me but you're willing to pretend there's a way if it'll keep me on the hook awhile longer?"

Erin leaned heavily against the wall, her love for him smothering all logic and restraint. "It's not...a pretense, Kyle. I don't know how I can give you what you want...children and...Navy wife and all...without becoming somebody who just isn't Erin Ness. But I—" she stopped and swallowed hard "—I do want to share my life with you, Kyle, and I don't think that's ever going to change. If there's any way—any way at all that I can figure out that I can marry you and still pursue my career...I'll do it."

Until the words left her mouth she didn't know they lurked in her heart. Her trembling intensified. A baseball of fear lodged in her throat. He couldn't leave her. He just couldn't walk out on—"

"You'll leave for work before I can get there," he declared in an odd, husky tone. "Wouldn't it be better if I came over in the morning?"

"There's a spare key under the potted palm," she gushed, suddenly desperate to find him in her bed when she came home at dawn. She was shaking all over with waves of unexpected relief. "You can keep it."

"Under the potted palm," he repeated, still a bit mesmerized by her declaration.

"Yes. Will you come? I'll serve you breakfast in bed. We can do whatever you want tomorrow—I'll lock my books in my desk. The whole day's yours." She had to take a gulp of air before she could carry on. "Will you be here when I get home?"

Wisps of silence fluttered through the wire as she waited for his reply. No words had ever mattered to her more.

"Yes, sweetheart," he promised with new sunlight in his voice. "I'll be there waiting when you get home."

IT WAS SEVEN-THIRTY in the morning when Erin returned. Kyle's red Saab was parked in the driveway, looking just like it belonged there. There was no sign of him in the living room or the kitchen, but as she entered the bedroom she saw him...asleep in her bed. His keys and wallet were on top of the dresser, and his uniforms and civilian clothes hung in the closet.

Her relief at the sight of him was even greater than her fear that she'd made a terrible mistake. She had made a commitment that might interfere with her work, but she'd also been completely honest and true to herself. She belonged to this man. It was senseless to fight it.

"You're late," Kyle declared from under the quilt, his eyes still closed. "I was promised breakfast in bed at seven A.M. when I checked into this hotel."

"I'm sorry," Erin mumbled, not quite sure if he was kidding. "I had to do an emergency cesarean at the last minute. The lady was forty-four and—"

"Hush." He pulled her down beside him. "You've been up all night. You're exhausted. Did you really think I expected breakfast in bed?"

Erin watched him tensely. His hair was tousled; he looked so sexy, so sleepy and warm. But she didn't dare touch him...didn't dare remind him that he'd once claimed she only wanted him to satisfy her body. "I guess I don't know what to expect right now, Kyle."

He pulled her very close and kissed her cheek. "You can expect me to be the most loving, considerate, patient roommate you've ever had. You can expect me to give you lots of room...lots of time to yourself. You can expect me to pick up after myself, pull the weeds and fix the hinges on that creaky front door. I promise not to get in your way."

Erin bowed her head against him. "I was so afraid," she whispered.

He rubbed the back of her neck. "I know. I'm sorry. I really didn't mean to scare you, Erin. I just couldn't stand coming in second place to that damn mission any more." He kissed the top of her head and stretched out on the bed with her against him. "I want to come first in your life, Rinny. I want you to come first in mine."

She snuggled up closer. "Let's try it for a while and see how it goes," she breathed into the thick black hair on his chest then moved away. "How do you want your breakfast served?"

"Erin...really..."

"Please let me do this for you, Kyle. Just this once."

Sensing that she needed to do this, he gave in. "Okay. I'd like breakfast served by the pool with my waitress dressed like she was the first night we made love."

Remembering that poignant night with sweet clarity, Erin asked, "Before or after we went swimming?"

He smiled devilishly. "Come to think of it... after."

Erin stared at him in some surprise. She'd never served breakfast in the nude before! Even though it was so private they might as well have been in the Garden of Eden.... "You're pulling my leg again, right?"

"No," he said with a twinkle in his eye. "I'll do that later."

By the time Erin served breakfast on the patio, the leg in question was adorned with a mock garter made of blue ribbon that matched the bow in her French braid and the extra eye shadow highlighting her eyes. She was wearing considerably more makeup than usual to make up for the lack of clothes. A silver chain around her neck and a heady dose of her finest perfume completed her ensemble.

"I hope this is what you wanted this morning, sir," she announced with a curtsy. Kyle examined the trayful of bacon, eggs, and biscuits with great care before he lifted his eyes to her face. With a slow, deliberate gaze he studied her breasts, her blue ribbon garter, and everything in between. Her nipples rose for him; the rest of her quivered.

"Yes, indeed, sweet thing," he murmured, brushing her skin with his eyes. "This is just what I had in mind." He grinned. "Better, in fact, than what I had in mind."

Erin set down the tray before him and studied his physique. He was wearing a ratty pair of denim cutoffs, as atypical a garb as she could imagine for Kyle Tatum. She was certain that the shorts were his silent way of saying that he really felt at home.

"May I sit down, sir?" she asked sweetly.

"Please do." He pulled her onto his lap, his left arm looping across her stomach. His hand took possession of her breast. "Are you hungry?"

In answer to his own question he stroked her rigid nipple, and suddenly Erin had no appetite for food. "No, sir, Commander Tatum," she answered smartly. "I'll just watch if you don't mind."

He kissed the back of her neck and released the pulsing center of her breast. He started eating with his right hand; idly his left caressed her hip. "This is excellent. I'll have to come here more often."

"Any time, sir. Everything is on the house."

"Everything?" His hand shifted to a more secure hold on her thigh.

"Everything. At least until tomorrow."

Kyle laughed. "If I can only expect this treatment for one day, I'd better make the most of it."

He finished the meal in silence. The morning sun warmed her back; Kyle's nearness warmed the rest of her.

"You know what?" he asked a few minutes later, leaning his face against her breasts.

"What?"

"I think what we need here—" he flicked the nearest nipple with his tongue "—is some sunscreen. I would not want my favorite waitress to burn."

At first Erin could not move. He was deliberately arousing her. And enjoying himself immensely. Was this punishment for the last week of separation?

"Go on," he urged her, his free hand contradicting his words as it slid up her thigh. "Go get the lotion. I'll put it on."

She did as he bid her. When she came back he was sitting on the chaise lounge, legs outspread. He gestured for her to sit between them, her back to his chest.

"Marvelous stuff, sunscreen. Without it girls like you could never serve breakfast without their clothes." He spread a good dollop over her back.

"And lechers like you would have to find more original methods of seduction."

Kyle laughed, slopping the cream over her shoulders toward her breasts. "Why Erin Elizabeth! Here I am doing my best to consider your welfare—" he saturated her areola "—and you accuse me of ungentlemanly schemes. I am appalled, Erin Elizabeth—" he moved to the other brown target "—simply appalled."

Erin was appalled at the way he'd circled her areola without ever touching her nipple, but she said nothing as he continued his sensual game. Kyle had never tried to seduce her quite so brazenly, and she wondered whether he was just trying out his new power or had some other plan in mind. It was obvious that he had no interest in relieving her torment soon.

He traced the base of her nipple a dozen more times, slowly, agonizingly, never once touching her aching peak. Finally his hand slid down over her stomach and covered everything he could reach from his angle behind her. His fingers stopped just short of her thighs.

"Better stand up so I can get your legs, Rinny," he suggested.

"I can do that." She knew she was running out of patience with his game. In another moment she would throw herself on him, proving all his accusations of her unseemly lust.

"So can I. It's my day. You promised me," he demanded like a playful child. She sighed in exasperation, but stood up and let him cover her legs with the creamy white lotion. He started at her toes and moved every so slowly upward, stopping at her knee on one leg before he started the other. Then he covered her thighs one at a time, front to back, deliberately stopping just short of the throbbing core of her womanhood.

Kyle, she moaned inside. *Dear God. Kyle....*

"Let's go swimming," he suggested brightly, tossing the sunscreen aside.

"What?"

"Let's go swimming. And don't tell me you're not in a suit. Neither am I."

He dived into the water in his cutoffs and harrassed

ier until she joined him. Almost immediately he swam
up behind her, looping his arms around her waist until
he seized a breast with each hand. He let her tow him
along, his fingers edging toward, but never quite reach-
ng, her now aching nipples. Finally she couldn't stand
it anymore. She pushed him away and climbed out of
the pool.

"Where are you going, waitress?" he called after
her gaily.

"To take a shower."

"Hot or cold?" he asked, knowing she'd taken one
about an hour ago.

"Solitary."

It was like waving a red flag to a bull. He bounced
out of the pool and followed her into the shower. He
undid her braid tress by tress and insisted on washing
her hair.

"How's that feel?" he asked from a place entirely
too near her neck.

"Surprisingly good," she confessed, trying to soap
her body before he tried to do that, too.

"And how's this feel?" he asked, his fingertips slipping down from her scalp in slow motion to massage
the nipples that had been waiting for him for half an
hour.

"Surprisingly good," she mumbled into the water
as she leaned back against him. He was naked now,
and she could vividly feel how much he wanted her.
Surely he was ready to relieve her torment! *God, how
I want you, Kyle. As much as I've wanted you
before, never, never, have I wanted you more than I
do now.*

"Let's go dry off, okay?" he whispered, punctuating the suggestion with a hot curl of tongue in her
ear. He twisted her nipples for another moment or

two, then tugged them like reins to lead her from the shower.

Erin closed her eyes and followed him blindly. She had never been more aroused in her life. Not even that first incredible night in the pool.

It took her a moment to realize that they were in the kitchen. She was sitting on his lap, and he was drying her very thoroughly with a towel. *Very* thoroughly. The towel was between her legs, and his fingers seemed to be on both sides of it. She leaned back against him, opening herself to his tender ministrations.

"Did that shower make you feel better, Rinny?" he asked, his tongue stroking her collarbone. "Is that what you wanted after a hard day's night?"

She put her arms around his neck and buried her mouth against his hair. "Yes," she whispered, one breast lifting toward his lips.

"Good," he declared matter of factly, plopping her on her feet. "Let me go hang up the towel and I'll be right back."

Erin was too stunned to respond. What game was he playing? She was nearly hysterical with desire. Surely he knew it! He was so damn cheerful. So relaxed! She had to calm down.

Irritably she marched out to the living room and settled down on the couch. She'd promised not to work today but he was cheating, so she could cheat, too. She picked up the nearest book and had just started to read it blindly when Kyle arrived, stretching out with his head in her lap before she could protest.

He was still naked, still smiling. His arousal was very evident, and her aching frustration gave way to new waves of desire. Two could play this game. Slowly she snaked one hand around his neck, down his chest, toward his—

He turned on his side, facing the couch, and propped himself up on one elbow. "Have you ever seen the Blue Angels before?" he asked conversationally, holding her hand on his hip. His lips grazed one nipple as he talked. She was powerless to answer.

"It's an incredible show." He settled back down on her lap, releasing her hand. His mouth moved lower as he spoke. "There are up to six Phantoms in the air, sometimes only three yards apart." His lips grazed her navel, the skin below...then skirted the uncharted hair that shielded her crying need. "Do you have any idea how far that is, Erin?" His mouth moved still lower as both hands met beneath her breasts. She leaned forward in unabashed desire, thrusting her nipples against his warm, brown skin. Instantly his fingertips honed in on the tiny summits of her desire, nails and skin combining in perfect balance to push her past sanity. "Sometimes something that seems so far away is only—" he dipped his head that last inch to reach the throbbing node of hunger he'd been stalking "—as close as—"

My God, Kyle, please! The words ripped out of her, a shriek of hunger, a naked cry of need. In less than a second Kyle rolled off the couch onto the carpet, pulling her with him, sliding her instantaneously over his waiting tower of glorious manhood. He clung to her nipples with his lips and hands as she rode him into oblivion, her need so potent, her relief so savagely intense that it dwarfed the most magical of moments she had ever spent in his arms before. It was worth every agonizing moment of the morning's slow torture, every start and stop of teasing foreplay, worth the waiting, the wondering, the merciless helplessness of yielding all control. She sobbed out her piercing celebration against his chest, gloried in the feel of his hands wildly galloping over every inch of her straining flesh. He thundered inside her at a pace designed for her pleasure, not for his, but when at last she finished this wild midnight ride of his contriving, she knew he, too, was sated and richly content.

Minutes passed before she could breathe normally. . . even longer before she could look at him. With the return of sanity came the unanswered question, *What was he trying to prove?* But one look at his face told her the answer. . . the sweetest declaration he could possibly have made.

He looked like a little boy who'd spent his last dime on a present for his grandmother, waiting desperately for assurance that he'd fulfilled her wildest dreams. There was not a trace of the cocky pilot in his eyes, despite the careful selection of his words.

"I. . . didn't want you to think the magic would wear off after I moved in, Rinny."

She shook her head, still unable to speak.

"You won't be sorry, babe. I'm going to make this work for us. I'm going to make you happy."

Erin collapsed against him in complete surrender. How could she ever have doubted this man? How could she have risked sending him away?

"I believe you," she whispered, brushing her fingers through his hair. "In fact, Kyle Tatum—" she paused to kiss one dimple "—I'm already ninety-nine percent convinced."

She felt his smile against her cheek. "I guess I'll have to keep working on that last percent, huh, Rinny?"

She tightened her legs around him. "I'm counting on it, Commander."

CLAD IN A PINK HALTER TOP and matching shorts, Erin was almost ready for the air show when Kyle walked into the bedroom and quietly asked if she'd mind putting on something a little less revealing. She was surprised. He'd never expressed concern about her clothing before. He generally preferred her half-dressed! "Well, I did promise you whatever you wanted today," she managed to say. "But in the future—"

"Rinny—" he stopped her, his hands touching her face "—this has nothing to do with my...sexual fantasies. We're not going to be alone in your pool. You're going to be introduced to other officers and their wives as Commander Tatum's lady. That means Navy etiquette must govern your comportment at all times."

The last line sounded like it came right out of Katie's Navy wife handbook, but Erin could tell that he was serious. With a pang of guilt she realized that she had not seen Katie since she'd been assigned to the mission, even though the young girl had called her several times since her husband had gone to sea.

"I understand the Navy's interest in your appearance on duty, Kyle. I'm not sure why it cares how I dress on my day off."

"It doesn't matter why. What matters is that the Navy is important to me, and therefore I'd like it to be important to you. Living together outside of marriage is still frowned upon by the older officers, Erin. Most of the people we'll be with today are our age, but still...I want you to make a good impression. Just dress modestly and act like a lady. I don't think that's asking too much for a woman of your cultural mien." He managed to make it sound like a compliment and Erin very much wanted to please him, so she changed into a modest blue sundress with lots of ruffles and sedate white lace.

The base was crowded when they got there, but the official sticker on Kyle's car got them a good parking place. He led Erin to a patch of lawn near the announcer's stand where they were able to hear interesting tidbits of information, which Kyle augmented and corrected throughout the afternoon. It really was an awesome performance; Erin watched with respect and more than a little fear for the pilots flying wingtip to wingtip in pairs and perfect formations, crisscrossing one another in the sky at staggering speeds. Sometimes they flew belly up or twirled sideways. One pair flew a hundred feet off the ground.

As the show went on, Kyle's officer friends and their wives began to drift toward the prearranged spot on the lawn. Many of them brought lawn chairs and blankets and babies, and all of them tried to make Erin feel welcome whether they knew her or not.

"We don't see Kyle at the O' Club much these days," Alan Clayburn, Kyle's mission commander, told her with a friendly grin. "Now we know why."

His wife, a loquacious young woman who reminded Erin of an older version of Katie, shook her finger at her husband in mock dismay. "Now don't have Kyle drag her to the Club until I tell her the ground rules, Alan," she insisted, pulling a blanket over the top of a stroller in an effort to shade her baby. "As soon as you walk in the door you're fair game until you make it clear that you're not available the instant your husband—or fiancé—is shipped out to sea. It doesn't matter how possessive he is. The bottom line is up to you."

Erin nodded uncomfortably, thinking of Vivian. "I...haven't had a lot of experience with bars, but I'd guess that a woman often gets pretty much what she asks for."

Leslie Clayburn shook her head. "It's worse in the Navy. Everybody knows when your husband is leaving

nd exactly how long he'll be gone. The simplest kind
f gesture can be misinterpreted by the wrong man.''

Deciding that this conversation was irrelevant, Erin
uickly changed the subject. ''That's a lovely dress,''
he told Leslie, making note of the demure striped
hirtwaist as a prototype for any future Naval events.
'ointing to a pair of tiny gold wings that were a per-
ect replica of the ones Kyle wore on his uniform, she
sked the other woman, ''Where did you get that dar-
ng pin?''

Leslie looked a little stunned. ''From Alan, of
ourse. Just before we were engaged.'' She smiled at
rin in some consternation. ''I...I got the impression
hat you and Kyle had been together for some time.
'm surprised that you don't have a pair of wings yet
ourself.''

''He brought me an air mattress the first time he
ame to dinner,'' Erin revealed, without batting an
yelash. ''It's given me a great deal of pleasure.''

Turning away before Leslie could determine the
ause of her suppressed laughter, Erin tuned in to the
nen's discussion. It was pilot talk, which did not sur-
rise her, but no one seemed to be giving patriotic
peeches or tossing around military terms or titles.
ven though most of the men from Kyle's crew and
1-J were there, nobody was talking about NASA.
hey spent a few minutes celebrating the news that an
ld flying buddy named Chip Denziger had received
ew orders and would be passing through in a few
veeks, but after that their focus was entirely on the
ets in the air. Erin noticed that it was Kyle who took
ime to explain the flight maneuvers to the younger
oys who clustered around their fathers.

''Howdy, Erin,'' Jeb greeted her during a break in
he action. ''I'm surprised to see you here today.''

"Why should that surprise you, Henson?" Kyle's voice suddenly cracked from behind her. One hand slid possessively around her waist as he faced his friend. "You got her all week. Today she's all mine." Their eyes met in challenge before Kyle added, "By the way, if you need to reach me, I'm no longer living on the base."

Jeb nodded as though it were no surprise, then turned courteously back to Erin before the tension between the two men became obvious to anyone else. "This should be an interesting spectacle for you, Erin. It'll give you some insight into what Kyle does when he's not playing astronaut."

Erin was a bit confused. She'd flown with the pilots in training of course, and felt the jets zip straight up and down in an effort to emulate zero gravity. But the Blue Angels were doing incredibly dangerous aerobatics, precision flying of consummate skill.

"You can fly like that? You *do* fly like that?" she asked Kyle in surprise.

Kyle shrugged.

"Don't be so damn modest, Tatum. Didn't you tell her you missed making the Angels by a hair?"

Erin's stomach turned over with more fear than pride.

"It's nothing to be proud of," Kyle muttered wistfully, unable to disguise his longing, even now, to join the pilots in the air. "Who remembers all the guys who *almost* made it?"

"Well I'm glad you didn't," Erin said without thinking. "That looks even more dangerous than space flight."

Leslie closed her eyes as though Erin had committed some unpardonable social offense. Jeb sighed in exasperation; even Kyle glared at her before he reminded her, "It's safer than flying in combat."

For several seconds she stared at him, knowing she'd missed the boat again. This was a professional pilot she had fallen in love with, a pilot who was doing time at NASA until the Navy sent him wherever it, in its patriotic bureaucratic wisdom, chose for him to go. *And what on earth will I do when it beckons its red, white and blue finger?* she asked herself. But she had no answer.

CHAPTER NINE

THE NEXT FEW WEEKS scurried together in a crush of work and preparation as the time for the launch kept sneaking closer. Erin spent a great deal of her time trying to bridge the gap between human and simian surgery. Her most disturbing discovery was that even though of all the great apes the chimpanzee was physiologically the closest to man, it also had the highest mortality rate in any kind of experimental surgery. Erin had located the world's foremost authority on chimps, a zoo vet from New York City, and was determined to meet with him at least once before the launch.

Not long after Kyle had moved in, she'd received a formal invitation to Admiral Tatum's retirement ceremony. A few days later she had also received a personal letter from Kyle's mother, who had generously welcomed Erin to her home for the weekend in question... and subtly welcomed her to the family as well. The tone of the letter both warmed and frightened Erin. While she was delighted that Kyle's parents apparently shared his enthusiasm for her, she was alarmed by how fast everyone seemed to be planning her future.

Roger was finally well enough to start discussing bits and pieces of his research with her, and Erin tried to schedule her regular visits early in the day before he got too tired. He seemed eager to help her, but there was a sorrow that overlay his words whenever he mentioned the actual surgery in space. He still had a lot of pain in his back, and neurological exams for his head injuries continued.

Just as Kyle had promised, he turned out to be a joy to live with. He cleaned up after himself but never complained about Erin's messiness. He kept her company with his tender smile but let her work without asking her to make impossible choices. The only time he seemed remotely upset was when Leslie Clayburn called to invite them to a dinner party and Erin forgot to tell him for five days.

She knew he was angry the minute he walked into the house. He didn't yell, or even glower particularly, but there was a tension in his beautiful body that the sleek white uniform could not hide.

"I just had a drink with Alan Clayburn," he stated baldly, as though this announcement should have had some particular meaning for Erin. "He's really looking forward to the dinner party he and Leslie are having this weekend for Chip Denziger."

He paused, reading the ill-concealed alarm in Erin's face as she remembered Leslie's long-since forgotten call. "I went to flight school with Chip. I haven't seen him in six or seven years and I've never even met his wife. They'll only be here for a few days."

He perched on the arm of the couch and studied Erin, who was, as usual, glued to her desk. Guilt flushed her features as he spoke.

"Since Alan would never mention a party he was throwing if I weren't invited, I had to ask myself how it was that I was not yet aware of the invitation. I figured that either his woman or mine probably made a mistake. Not knowing which, I kept my mouth shut." His voice was still controlled, still tight, still angry under the calm. "I guess the real question is, did it just slip your mind or were you hoping that if you didn't mention it maybe it would just go away?''

Finally she answered. "That's not fair, Kyle. She called just as I was leaving for the hospital Friday night. We had that four-car pile-up on Route—''

"This is Wednesday, Erin. Do you have an excuse for each of the past five days?''

She looked away. She really had no excuse—she'd just forgotten the call the minute she'd hung up the phone. "I'm sorry, Kyle. I really am," she told him with genuine regret. "But it wasn't deliberate. I just—''

"Maybe not consciously, Erin. But aside from the fact that it is absolutely imperative that you promptly relay any phone calls to me—whether you think they're important or not—if you had any particular interest in going you would surely have remembered it by now.'' He paled slightly as he added, "In fact, if you'd had any particular interest in the fact that *I* wanted to go, you would surely have remembered it by now.''

It was true. The last thing in the world Erin wanted to do with her nonexistent free time was spend it on the base with a bunch of strangers. Oh, she liked Leslie and Alan well enough, but—

"Look, Erin," he continued, his tone still quiet but tense, "the Clayburns are willing to go out of their way to treat you as. . .well, pretty much as my wife. In Navy circles a lot of people wouldn't be able to do that. Once our. . .living arrangement is generally accepted, I won't have to keep explaining it to people. We'll be invited everywhere as a couple—''

"Do you have to keep explaining it?''

He looked away. "More than I'd like.''

Erin straightened. "It's hardly an unusual occurrence, Kyle. People live together all the time.''

He sighed. "Not in the Navy, Erin. Not in officer

ountry. It's done, but it's not—'' he struggled to explain it ''—it's not top-of-the-line behavior. At NASA we're so mixed up with civilians it can slide by a bit better, but on a lot of bases... it would be considered pretty bad form.''

''Is it bad form for an officer to be married to a professional woman?'' she asked. ''One who doesn't have the time or inclination for bridge parties and ladies' teas?''

He scowled. ''It's awkward, Erin, but it could be done if the lady in question handled the situation with grace.'' His eyes grew darker. ''I have never at any time suggested that you should quit practicing medicine to marry me, Rinny. And that's a bigger sacrifice on my part than I think you realize.''

''And what about the sacrifice you're asking of me? You want me to give up space surgery for...for...''

Kyle stood up and moved away. ''If you don't know by now I guess it doesn't matter.''

He looked resigned rather than angry, but his stance filled Erin with shame...and more than a little bit of fear. ''I'm sorry, Kyle. I want to live with you. I just don't want to give up my dreams. I don't want to fall off the cliff halfway up the mountain. Can you understand that?''

''I want to marry you, Erin,'' he replied with fervor. ''Can you understand that?''

For a moment Erin was still. Then she suggested, ''Maybe there's...another avenue of compromise here we haven't considered.''

''Such as?''

''You told me once that it didn't matter where your home was as long as you knew someone was there waiting for you. Couldn't our home be...here...no matter where the Navy sent you? We could still get married, and I'd have something to do besides sit and wait and worry while you—''

"What about the children?" His tone was grim.

"The children?"

"Yes, the children! Where do you propose they would live in this fantasy scenario? Should we start a new fad—doing the weekend shuffle between mom and dad before the divorce instead of after?"

Erin looked away, defeated. "This isn't getting us anywhere."

"No, it's not," Kyle agreed in a tired voice. After a moment he crossed the room to stand beside her. Even though he was angry—perhaps *because* he was angry—Erin reached out to touch his hand. To her surprise the motion did not soothe him; he all but ignored her fingers.

Instead he announced abruptly, "I'm going to the Clayburns' party. I want you to come with me."

She was silent as she sought an answer. "Kyle, I'm barely keeping my head above water as it is. I hardly have time for you, let alone—"

"You *don't* have time for me! You never have. But when you asked me to move in here—begged me, as I recall—you promised to give our relationship, our future, your best shot. Part of that picture is the Navy, Erin...and the social benefits...and obligations... that are part of the service." Ignoring the plea in her fingertips that still grazed his hand, he stood up and crossed the room, stopping in the doorway to stare at her bleakly. "If I weren't living here, I'd at least be free to bring a date."

She didn't know how to cope with that. She didn't know how to cope with the zigzag of panic that slithered from her heart down to her knees and back up again as she tried to read his words. "What...what does that mean?"

He unbuttoned his shirt and met her eyes. A new look seemed to fill them. Not anger, not pain...defeat? "It means you can't have it both ways. Either you're my lady or you're not." He pulled off the shirt and draped it over his shoulder. "The writing's always been on the wall, Erin. Whether or not you decide to read it is up to you."

He strolled out of the room casually enough, but he'd made his point. She might be able to get out of this one evening—maybe—but she couldn't spend a lifetime with Kyle Tatum, boycotting everything that mattered to him.

Do I want to spend a lifetime with Kyle Tatum? she asked herself, not for the first time. She glanced up at the doorway he'd filled just moments before. He'd shared her life for just a few short months, yet already she knew that her house—her life—would be desolate without him. The man loved her. That much was visible to even the most jaundiced eye. It was Erin herself that stood in the way of their togetherness. She could give it another name—the mission, the Navy, fear of the finality of marriage—but it all boiled down to the same thing. Either Kyle came first or he didn't. And if he didn't, sooner or later he would leave her.

Quickly she tossed aside her NASA manual and trailed him into the bedroom. He lay on the quilt, reading a brief of his own. He did not look up when she entered the room.

"Do you think..." She swallowed hard. "Do you think it's too late to call Leslie?"

He glared at her. "It's been too late since Saturday. Sunday at the latest. By now she knows perfectly well that you don't want to come and didn't even have the courtesy to decline the invitation."

Erin held his gaze. "I meant too late to call her tonight. To tell her we're coming."

For a long moment he held her eyes, betraying nothing. Silence seemed to darken the room. Desire, hope, and a strange twisting pain seemed to carve its way across his features. Then he told her, "Better late than never."

She knew he was talking about a great deal more than the phone call to Leslie Clayburn.

KYLE SEEMED MORE RELAXED and friendly in the morning. Erin knew she hadn't done nearly enough to accept the Navy part of his life, and she'd resigned herself to the comparatively small sacrifice of the dinner party. Still, she was uneasy with the tone of his comments the previous night and felt the need to do a bit more giving. . . to offer a more visible sign of her desire to compromise and grow.

When Kyle got home that night the house was lit only by candles in the dining room. A lace tablecloth with matching napkins graced the scene. The menu included a full turkey dinner complete with peas, potatoes, gravy and cranberry sauce, followed by angel food cake topped with cherries and cream for dessert.

Erin herself was clad in a floor length emerald-green gown with a slit up to her knee. One side of her strawberry blond hair was swept up past her ear and crowned with a fresh gardenia from the backyard. The rest of her tresses cascaded down her neck in waterfall curls. Subtle green eye shadow and dangling emerald earrings complimented the display of female art.

She smiled almost tentatively at the look of shock on Kyle's face as he sauntered through the door, dressed in casual blue slacks and a short-sleeved white cotton shirt.

"Rinny?" he asked, as though he didn't quite recognize her at first. "Did I. . . forget something?"

Her grin widened. "Not that I know of, Commander."

He took a moment to look her over, his appreciation
blatant and most reassuring. "What..." He seemed to
have trouble speaking. "What are we celebrating?"

She moved a little closer, tucking herself easily into
his arms. "Us. Our love. Our future."

He lifted his hands to her cheeks and studied her eyes.
Secret jubilation creased the dimples by his mouth.
"How long do we have... to celebrate this... event?"

This time the smile was unforced. "Till dawn, Commander Tatum. I've arranged to take the entire night
off." To herself she added, *Even though I'll probably
be paying for it for a week.*

But the look in his eyes assured her it would be worth
it.

DINNER WAS SPECTACULAR. Afterward they decided to
go to a movie Kyle had been eager to see; they even
stopped off at the O' Club for a drink on the way home
and spent over an hour chatting with two of his friends.
Erin learned more about his background as a flier in
that hour than she had in all the time they'd been
together. Once or twice he even talked about his time in
Vietnam.

She didn't count the hours away from studying as she
perched proudly by his side. She didn't even think
about how tired she'd be in the morning. Tonight belonged to Kyle. Tonight *she* belonged to Kyle.

Every time he looked at her, new warmth radiated
from her spine. Every time he touched her she wanted to
drag him off to some private place! But she was calm
and friendly and snuggled as close as he would let her
until he decided it was time to go home.

"There are just a few things I want to tell you about

the Clayburns' dinner party," he announced in the car on the way home. Erin leaned against him and lay one hand on his knee. "It will be casual, as far as Navy functions go, but don't be surprised if we're seated by rank."

"By rank?" Erin asked. "I don't have any rank."

He chuckled, not unkindly, then dropped a kiss on her hair. "You will always have my rank, whatever it is. The wives have a hierarchy that is every bit as rigid as the officers'. The only guy likely to be invited who outranks me is Tom Rallings." He glanced at Erin in the car. "He's a captain. Fortunately, his wife doesn't abuse his rank like some women do."

Erin nodded, trying to decipher his last cryptic comment. Katie had told her more than once that as a junior officer's wife she was at the mercy of most of the women on the base. Some were very good to her, and some were not. Erin didn't have time to ferret out the fine points. "Do I call these guys by their rank?"

Kyle shook his head. "Not at a party. Just be respectful. Everybody here will be my friends, so there's not really any danger. But sometimes we'll *have* to go to events where there are lots of cracks to fall through. I'll try to warn you when we're mingling with anybody who could influence my career."

"Okay." She didn't really know what else to say. She just wanted to let him know she would try to please him.

"It's trickier when you're the hostess, babe, but if you watch Leslie you'll learn a lot. We'll need to return the Clayburns' hospitality within a week or two."

That was a twist Erin hadn't counted on. She couldn't imagine staging any kind of Naval social affair before the launch no matter whom she had to ad-

'ise her. But she forced herself to say, "I'll do my best, Kyle."

He stopped the car when they reached Erin's house. Tenderly he gathered her hair back from her face, his eyes foreshadowing a night of passionate reunion she would not soon forget. "I know that, babe. And that's going to be more than good enough for me."

THE NIGHT THEY WENT TO THE CLAYBURNS', Erin dressed the part of a Navy wife. Taking her cue from Leslie, she wore a sophisticated but modest apricot polycotton knit with dolman sleeves and a wide matching belt. She made the ultimate sacrifice and put on nylons and heels, desperately hoping that the base provided decent air conditioning for its residents. Kyle wore a dark blue suit—not quite Navy issue, but the similarities were obvious. He smiled at her with devastating charm as he escorted her up the Clayburns' front walk.

"I love you, Rinny Ness," he whispered just before he rang the bell. He put one arm around her and kissed her on the cheek, a tender gesture that she had not expected on the eve of this formal event. Was he going to be warm and fun this evening? She'd anticipated spending the evening with formal Commander Tatum, not her playful lover Kyle.

"Kyle! Erin!" Alan greeted them enthusiastically at the door. He was also dressed in a suit—dark brown with a suitably staid matching tie. "Glad you could come. Chip and Sarah are already here. Leslie's in the kitchen."

The house was modest and unassuming, but it was spotless and graced here and there with photographs and knickknacks that reminded Erin of her own home. The smell of a roast cooking wafted out to the living room and hinted at Leslie's culinary skills.

In the lving room Erin found two men and one woman. The latter was stiff and serious and more than a little uncomfortable with the robust greeting Kyle gave her husband, a huge man with dark, bushy eyebrows.

"Denziger!" he shouted, thudding the other man's back with one fist as they shook hands with alacrity. "How've you been? I heard you were stationed in Guam for a while."

"Guam and sixteen other places," he agreed with a wide smile that seemed to convert his rather awesome appearance into that of a teddy bear. "But look what I picked up before I left the States!" Proudly he gestured toward the rigid woman on the other side of the room. She wore a simple white dress that made her look very pale. She tried to smile at Kyle but failed.

"This is Sarah," the giant man announced with love in his voice. "Looked for her all over the world and finally found her in my own backyard."

Sarah glanced up at her husband with warmth in her eyes that Erin had not expected, sending him a secret message that she could not read. She offered Kyle her hand and visibly glowed just a tad as he told her, "I'm honored to meet you, Sarah. Chip's letters—rare though they are—give you nothing but rave reviews."

She almost smiled. "He is rather fond of me."

Kyle laughed and released her hand. "I'm rather fond of my lady, too." He turned back to Erin and favored her with a smile that left not the slightest doubt in the minds of anyone in the room that she was his sunrise and his sunset. He put his arm around her in a tender, protective caress as he announced almost reverently, "This is Erin."

"Hello," she said to the others, feeling almost shy in the face of his praise. "It's nice to meet you all."

She glanced at the other man whom Kyle had ignored up till now and ventured, "I didn't catch your name."

"Tom Rallings. Chip was in my squadron in San Diego." He smiled pleasantly, causing Erin to wonder why she'd expected him to look smug just because he was a captain. "My wife Joan is in the kitchen helping Leslie."

Taking the cue, Erin announced, "I think that might be a good place for me, too. If you'll all excuse me..."

She had the strangest feeling that Sarah Denziger was sorry to see her go.

ALL IN ALL the dinner went pretty well. Chip, being the guest of honor, sat at Leslie's right and Sarah sat next to Alan. The rest of the guests sat informally, for which Erin was very grateful. After the party she would ask Kyle everybody's rank and try to memorize it if he thought it was important.

Another couple, Don and Carol Harrison, had arrived shortly before dinner. Afterward, the women had gravitated into the den while the men—all of them pilots or astronauts whom Erin might have had something in common with—congregated in the living room. She could see them through the doorway, vibrantly discussing the sorts of things that made men laugh out loud. Now and again she noticed that their voices dropped, a sure sign that they were discussing some aspect of Navy business. Once or twice she thought she caught the word "Russian."

They weren't so quiet when they recounted their stupendous flying feats. Chip and Kyle compared notes on who was really the most frightened the first time he "hit the boat," an aviator's term for landing a fighter jet on the tiny deck of an aircraft carrier. Katie had told her that the Navy had counseled each wife in Billy's flight-school class to be prepared for a dramatic change in her husband right after the first time he "hit the boat." Euphoria, hysteria, exultant pride, feelings of godlike power were all to be expected after such a difficult, heroic feat. With time, a strong man got used to it.

"So did you leave your things in storage or send them on ahead, Sarah?" Leslie asked as she settled into an overstuffed chair. "When we moved to Heron Bay it took me six months to find everything."

"And that's almost long enough to get new orders," said Joan Rallings.

Everyone laughed except for Sarah and Erin.

"Actually, I'm hoping it won't be too bad this time," Chip's wife admitted cautiously. "On the move to Guam I lost a lot of things."

They all clucked sympathetically, then Leslie asked, "So what's Chip going to be doing in California? I can't get anything out of Alan."

Again the other woman shifted uncomfortably. "I don't know very much. He'll still be flying, and supervising something new."

"What kind of a something?" Carol Harrison asked. "A plane, a project?"

Sarah flushed. "I really don't know."

"Back off, ladies," Joan announced perceptively. "Looks like Sarah's got her orders, too."

Erin was starting to feel sorry for Sarah. Here she was in a brand new place, meeting her husband's friends for the first time and trying to make a good impression. But clearly her loyalty to her husband—and his loyalty to the Navy—had to take precedence. There were things, Kyle had once told her, that a Navy wife simply could not say. The nature of Chip's assignment was clearly one of them.

"Where are you from originally, Sarah?" she asked in a deliberate effort to refocus the conversation.

The other woman took the lifeline and hung on with both hands. "Arizona. My father was with the government and worked on a Navajo reservation."

"Really!" Erin replied with genuine interest. "That's where I'm from, too. I have a friend on base from Tucson—married to a pilot. Katie Matthews. You two ought to get together."

Sarah looked almost happy. "It's really nice to meet folks from back home, isn't it?"

Before Erin could answer, a piercing infant wail greeted them from the back of the house. Erin was surprised. She'd almost forgotten that the Clayburns had a baby.

"Oh, no!" Leslie groaned. "I gave Kristie distinct orders to sleep through the night."

"Would you like me to get her?" Joan offered. "You've worked hard enough already."

Leslie hesitated, then admitted, "If you wouldn't mind, Joan. I get to do this every night!"

Joan laughed, then said to Erin and Sarah, "Mine are in their teens, so this baby stuff seems fun again."

"You've just forgotten what it's like," Carol teased her.

"I'll be a grandma soon enough. I've got to stay in practice."

Erin said nothing. She didn't want to spend the evening discussing babies and why she didn't have any. Sarah, she noticed, made no effort to contribute to this part of the conversation, either.

"Sarah," she tried again, "Kyle told me that he was in flight school with Chip. He was really looking forward to meeting you."

Sarah smiled. "Chip was excited about seeing all

these guys. Sometimes you're stationed with a dozen old friends, and sometimes you don't know a soul. And sometimes you don't stay anywhere long enough to find out *who* you're stationed with.'' Sarah offered her a cautious smile. ''Chip was Alan's wingman in Vietnam. Don served under him in his first command. I guess you heard Tom say they were together in San Diego.''

Erin had heard a lot more than that. She had heard the depth of feeling these men had for each other once they'd shared the same load, no matter how long it was between joint squadron assignments or casual visits. She'd heard the way their wives honored those friendships and framed them with womanly support systems of their own. In a way, it was all starting to make sense to her.

The idea that Navy life was logical and reassuring was a new one for Erin. Before she could ask herself if her new perception was the result of her recent experiences or her ever growing love for Kyle, Joan returned, alone.

''You got her back to sleep already?'' Leslie asked in disbelief.

Joan shook her head. ''No. I was going to bring her out here but I got intercepted in the living room by a paternal volunteer.''

Leslie looked shocked. ''Alan? *Alan* volunteered to hold her when she's fussing?''

Looking more than a little confused, Joan answered, ''No. Believe it or not, it was Kyle.''

They all turned to stare at Erin as Joan continued, ''That man is a natural-born baby-rocker. I've never seen anything like it.''

As Erin turned to look at Kyle and the baby, a tailwind of feelings pulled her off guard. The little girl was probably eight or nine months old and dressed in a lacy pink nightie with matching knitted booties. Her tiny knees were tucked under Kyle's elbow as he held her close. She gurgled with delight as he swooped her back and forth, crooning airplane sounds to fit his actions. His face was lit by a beatific smile that Erin had never seen before.

"Is there something you're not telling us, Erin?" Carol asked, her voice full of maternal glee.

"Of course not!" Leslie intercepted. "They're not even mar—" She stopped herself just in time.

Erin turned to glance at her sharply. Hadn't she told her friends the truth? Were she and Kyle supposed to pretend they were married here? But Leslie's face told her another story. She was casting no judgments, but didn't want to reveal any secrets, either. She was just uncomfortable. She honestly didn't know how to handle this situation tactfully.

"The simple truth is, Kyle and I both have missions coming up in the next few months," Erin offered in an attempt to spare her hostess. "We just aren't in any position to think about babies right now."

Leslie stood up quickly. "Anybody for dessert?"

"I am," Carol declared. "But let me help you, Leslie."

"Me, too," Joan added, again choosing to help out despite the fact that her husband's rank could have allowed her to be as lazy as she liked.

Suddenly Sarah and Erin were alone in the den. Leslie didn't need all five women in the kitchen! Erin tried to think of something else to ask Sarah about Arizona, but before she could speak, the other woman declared, "You're an astronaut." The strange look on her face could have been envy or disapproval.

"Yes," Erin declared evenly.

"And proud of it, I'll bet," Sarah finished for her.

"*Yes.*" Her tone was cautious, now. "It's not something I need to apologize for." *Even though somebody in this Navy wife setting might think I should.*

Her words razored Sarah's cool demeanor. "Erin!" she exclaimed, her face flushing a deep red. "I didn't mean anything..." She looked desperate for understanding. "I thought you, at least, understood how I was feeling. Please, don't be angry." Now the words gushed out. "I'm such a shy person. In new places I just...clam up and people think I'm so cold. By the time they get to know me Chip gets new orders and..." She stopped as her husband's name came to her lips. "Not that I'm complaining. I wouldn't change one single moment of my life with Chip, and this is what he wants. He's a pilot—you know what that means. He wouldn't be the same man outside of the Navy. But sometimes...sometimes—"

She stopped, clearly embarrassed. She would never know how her sudden stammering apology had won Erin's instant affection.

"Oh, Sarah, I know exactly how you feel. I don't have any idea what to do with the Navy, either, but I'm trying...not as hard as I should be, but at least I'm trying...because Kyle is the same way. Sometimes I wish there was some way to get him out of the Navy, but—"

"But you'd never get the Navy out of *him.*" Sarah finished the sentence for her. "He wouldn't be the same man you fell in love with."

Erin nodded, strangely at peace in the knowledge that somebody, anybody, understood how she felt. "This is only the second time I've ever been to any Navy gathering. I'm just not used to worrying about rank and orders and promotions."

Sarah laughed, knowing she'd found a friend. "I can handle that. It's the constant woman-talk about babies that's hard for me."

"I know what you mean. You'd think the whole world revolved around babies! Why can't people understand that some of us are perfectly happy without children? Maybe even happier, in fact? I've just got so much to do—" She stopped, longing to pull her foot out of her mouth, as she read the disavowal in Sarah's eyes. She had, apparently, completely misunderstood Sarah's words.

"How long have you been married, Sarah?" she asked quietly.

Sarah's eyes darkened. "Three years."

Erin was about to put on her doctor's hat and do a little infertility counseling when Kyle strolled into the room. He was carrying the baby who now lay in blissful slumber. A tiny smile graced her mouth even in sleep. Kyle wore a matching grin on his face.

"Could you help me out a minute here, babe?" he asked Erin, depositing the sleeping baby in her lap. "There's some lemon meringue pie out there that looks like it might almost rival yours and I think I deserve a reward. Getting a baby to sleep is the hard part, isn't it? I'm giving you the easy job."

Erin met his eyes as she took the delicate sleeping bundle and tucked it gently against her chest. Instinctively an ancient lullaby began to whisper in her heart.

She heard Sarah sigh as Kyle left the room, but she didn't dare look at her. She didn't dare look at the baby, either.

Kyle was wrong. Holding a sleeping baby dressed in pink ruffles and lace wasn't an easy job at all.

CHAPTER TEN

"YOU'RE EXHAUSTED, ERIN," Roger said one morning after he had repeated himself at least six times. "I'm beginning to think you're in worse shape than I am."

A month ago she would have given him a pale grin. Now she didn't bother—partly because she knew Roger too well to play games and partly because he was right. She was too exhausted to think. Her days were jam packed with simulated surgery in weightlessness; her nights were still a juggling act between research and Kyle. His patience was remarkable, but the sweeter he was the more she ached to be with him. . . and the more she resented the demands of 61-J.

Roger was having his own problems with the mission. Even though he'd been grounded, he desperately wanted to be part of the event. While several senior astronauts, including Kyle, would serve as CAPCOMs for different parts of Erin's flight, Roger had been denied this post because nobody at NASA thought he would be well enough by the launch date to take the strain. The CAPCOM was in charge of all formal communication between the shuttle and the ground. . .the voice that people around the world heard on television as they watched the flight crew in orbit. The top brass had consented to allow Roger in Mission Control as a consultant during Erin's surgery on the chimp, but everyone, including Roger, knew that it was just an honorary appointment. By the time

51-J left the ground, Erin really wouldn't need him anymore.

"I know they think I may have brain damage," Roger declared as he hobbled toward the window to peer down at the street. "But I don't."

For several weeks now he'd been able to dress himself and move around, but ongoing tests still kept him at the hospital. His frustration was beginning to alter his disposition. "I wasn't sure at first because I was so foggy. But now I'm off the medication and I know." Even though Erin had heard this speech more than once, she tried to listen attentively. "I still know more about this mission than you do, Erin. Doesn't that mean something?"

"Of course it does. But you don't have to convince me, Roger. I've always been your head cheerleader." On a whim she stood up and threw out her arms in boisterous demonstration. "Give me an R, give me an O, give me a G, E, R!"

He turned back from the window and gave her one of those sunbeam smiles that had been melting women since Roger Shaw's fifteenth birthday. "Thank you, Erin. It really helps a lot knowing that you and Kyle are behind me." He lowered himself onto the bed, being careful not to strain his back. "Do you know that Kyle hasn't missed one single day here since I was first injured? With all he's got on his plate, he's always managed to fit me in."

"What do you mean 'with all he's got on his plate'? He's living with me and scheduled for a mission that's his heart's desire! What more could he possibly ask for?"

The warmth in Roger's brown eyes faded just a little. "You...uh...think that Kyle is happy as a clam and has absolutely nothing to worry about."

Erin closed her notepad and focused on her friend. Was he kidding or trying to tell her something she needed to know? "We've been living together for six weeks, Roger, without a noteworthy disagreement since the day he moved in." She thrust from her mind her clumsy handling of Leslie Clayburn's call. "All the snags we had before just seem to have disappeared. We're still in paradise, if you'll permit such a mushy phrase."

Roger did not respond to her good humor. His eyes were grave.

"What...what are you trying to tell me, Roger?" Erin asked uncertainly.

"I don't want to be the one to burst your bubble, Erin, and I want to make it very clear that Kyle has *never* complained about living with you. But...I know him. He's wound up like a rattler. He won't talk about his mission and he won't talk about yours. There's a sadness in his eyes that doesn't match the picture you just painted of conjugal harmony and bliss."

He paused, then declared very softly, "Erin, I've been married and I've been divorced...because of 61-J. And I know that the only way any two people can live together full-time without an occasional spat is if one of them is bending over backward to make sure that all is sweetness and light." He stood up and stared her right in the eye. "Are you feeling any weight on your spine?"

"I'M WORRIED ABOUT ROGER," Kyle announced a few hours later. He'd spent longer than usual at the hospital and hadn't said much to Erin since he got home. Now, as she nestled in the crook of his arm during a ten-minute break from her studies, his words echoed

er own thoughts. "He's getting more depressed every
ay, Rinny. We've got to do something."

Erin snuggled closer, wishing that she had a solution.
Kyle was worried about Roger, and Roger was worried
bout Kyle. She wasn't sure she was helping either one
f them very much. "There's a chimp specialist—a zoo
et from New York—who's going to be coming to
Houston at the end of July to meet with me. Roger
ould meet him instead."

Kyle kissed the top of her head. "A noble thought,
abe, but he'd see through it in a minute. I was think-
ng...I know you're already on overload, but...is
here any chance you could handle a welcome home
arty for Roger? It looks like they'll be releasing him
airly soon." He rushed on before she could object.
Just a small group...a few close friends...people
who'd love him the same if he were a ditch digger."

Erin didn't answer at first. She couldn't imagine
paring another evening even to *go* to a party, let alone
lan one that included Kyle's hierarchy of Navy
riends. Sidestepping that issue, she voiced another gen-
ine concern. "It's a nice idea, Kyle, but I'm not sure
oger will be up to it. When a patient first leaves the
ospital he's very tired and—"

"He's depressed as hell, Erin! Right now I think
hat's his biggest medical problem. His whole world has
ropped out from under him. He needs to know that
1-J isn't the beginning and end of his life. It's the peo-
le who love you that make all the difference."

Erin knew that his speech could have been intended
or her as well as for Roger, but she made no comment.
Kyle was watching her carefully.

"I'll do all the work, Rinny. I just want a cake—I'll
rder it—and drinks and munchies. We'll keep it casual.
All you have to do is smile and give him a big hug."

Erin rubbed her forehead and gave up. After all, how could one lighthearted evening leave her any more exhausted than she was right now?

"Okay." She tried to conceal her apprehension. "Will you take care of the invitations?"

He smiled, elated with her capitulation. "Yes ma'am. I promise not to let this be a burden to you, Rinny." He looked so happy she was sure she'd made the right decision. "Speaking of invitations, have you written to my mother yet?"

Erin closed her eyes. *Not again. Why do I forget everything that matters to him?* "I'm sorry, Kyle. I haven't gotten around to it."

He looked surprised. "Sweetheart, it's been over three weeks since she wrote to you. I've arranged everything by phone myself, of course, but I thought I made it clear that my parents are accustomed to very traditional expressions of courtesy. I'd really like you to make a good impression."

"I was hardly planning to embarrass you at your dad's retirement party," she snapped, resenting his minilecture—and the fact that she deserved it.

The arm around her shoulders stiffened. "It's not a party, Erin. It's a very formal shipboard ceremony. Full dress uniform. The admiral of the fleet will be there and everybody else in CAR DIV—"

"I know. You've told me all that. It's just easier to call it a party than to remember all the Navy terminology."

He glanced at the pile of briefs on her desk and frowned. "Certainly a woman of your education could master a simple phrase like 'change of command.'"

"Maybe you should give me a list of phrases to study, Kyle. Along with the etiquette of rank and how to pull my foot out of my mouth." Her brief flare of

nger died as she watched his somber eyes just inches
om her own. He didn't deserve this! She was ex-
austed and uncomfortable with his parents' expecta-
ons of her, but that was no reason to take it out on
yle.

"I'm sorry, Kyle," she told him, slipping her free
and across his chest. "I guess I'm afraid I'll feel out
f my depth at your dad's part—change-of-command
eremony."

He pulled her a little closer, trying to understand. "I
ought you were feeling a little more comfortable
ith Navy social life these days."

She nodded. "I am. I almost managed to relax at
e Clayburns', and I really liked Sarah—I told
ou that. But your dad's ceremony sounds so formal,
 terribly important.... Like a wedding, I guess, or
—"

This time he stood up, leaving her alone on the
ouch. "That's the problem, isn't it? You don't want
e to take you home to meet my parents. You're feel-
g pressured."

When he phrased it like that she had to admit he was
ght. She had not the slightest doubt that Kyle and his
arents viewed her trip to Washington as a chance to
ass final inspection on his choice of a bride. But she
asn't ready to be a bride. At the moment she wasn't
eady to be anything but the mission specialist assigned
 61-J.

"I'm just a little nervous, Kyle. That's all." She
ached for his hand as he stood beside the couch.
I'm sure it will work out all right."

He nodded slowly, not quite convinced. Gingerly he
queezed her fingers. "You will...write to her soon,
on't you, sweetheart?"

Erin nodded. "Tomorrow. I promise."

A WEEK OF TOMORROWS passed before Erin remembered her promise again. By then it was the night of Roger's party, and she had sixteen thousand things to worry about before Kyle got home.

The whole day had been crazy. She'd spent the morning taping a television interview and the afternoon practicing simian surgery in the underwater neutral buoyancy simulator. Nothing seemed to go right with the operation, but she wasn't sure whether weightlessness or fatigue was to blame. She had so little control of her hands that she felt like she was drunk or terribly ill.

By five o'clock Erin was utterly exhausted. She wanted a nap, a bath, and a chance to talk to Roger about zero gravity, in that order. With any luck at all she could corner him for a while during the party.

"Well? Are we ready?" Kyle asked playfully when he got home a few moments behind her, carrying a chocolate cake iced with Roger's name.

Erin stared at him from the depths of fatigue. "I am ready to drop," she told him bluntly. "I just want to go to bed."

In the early days of their relationship, Kyle would have responded with a sensuous pun, then joined her under the blankets to cajole her into a better mood. Tonight he sobered instantly, asking what he could do to help. He finished all the decorations in silence while Erin tried to rest.

He didn't complain, but she still felt guilty napping while Kyle worked so energetically on the house. She knew how important this evening was to him. It wasn't just an affair to honor Roger; it was also the first time they'd opened their home to his Navy friends. He'd always wanted to return Alan's and Leslie's hospitality and welcome his O' Club crowd. Even Jeb was invited,

espite the current uneasiness between the two men.
yle had informed her that Jeb still remembered the
arties at Point Mugu that Vivian had managed to spoil
ith her last-minute excuses and deliberate breaches of
avy etiquette. Erin was determined not to follow suit.

"I have to go to the store," she declared just minutes
efore she'd planned to start her bath. "I forgot to get
our cream for the dip."

"I'll go get it," Kyle volunteered. "There's no need
or you to rush."

Erin shook her head. "I can't remember what brand
as the recipe I need. It'll only take a minute."

"At least let me drive you, babe. You look worn to
e bone."

Erin did not argue. She could not remember a time in
er life when she'd felt this tired, not even in residency
hen she'd often worked around the clock. Somehow
e had to stage this party that she'd never wanted to
ve in the first place and still go to NASA in the morn-
g. Thank God she didn't have to sandwich in surgery,
o!

Her resentment was intense by the time they reached
e store.

"Do you want me to go in with you?" Kyle asked.

"No," she snapped. "Just let me get this over with."

He looked away, his face dark and grim. "I told you
e didn't have to do this, Erin. I explicitly said—"

"You have made it very clear that entertaining is part
nd parcel of an officer's life in the Navy. But you knew
wanted to wait until the mission is over—"

"Roger can't wait. He needs some support *now*. If he
eeded surgery you wouldn't ask him to wait for your
onvenience. What makes you think that his feelings
re any less important?"

She sighed. He was so damn right it killed her. "I

want to do my best for Roger. And for you. But I'm just hanging by a thread as it is, Kyle. I sure didn't need the pressure of a party—even with people I don't have to prove anything to, let alone a bunch of strangers with wings and anchors tatooed all over their hearts.''

Kyle clenched the steering wheel and glared at the people walking by. He didn't say a word.

Erin shrunk in her seat. He was so good to her. He deserved better than this! ''I'm sorry, Kyle. I don't know what I'm saying. I'm just so damn tired—''

''Get the sour cream, Erin. Let's go home and get the party over with so you can rest.''

She left the car without another word. Kyle tapped out an irritated beat on the steering wheel while he waited for her. He knew she was exhausted. He knew the party was the last thing she needed. But she wasn't the only person involved, dammit! *He* needed the party. He needed the fun, the relaxation with friends, the knowledge that her house was his home and he was free to do as he liked there. And Roger needed the party even more—the gathering of people who loved him and believed in him.

When the undulating wail first saluted his consciousness, Kyle wasn't sure whether it was a fire engine or something else. But when the ambulance sirened into the parking lot, he bolted for the store in tandem with the paramedics, feverishly searching for Erin amidst the crowd that blocked the glass doors.

She told me she was ready to drop. I've never seen her look so weary. I shouldn't let her push herself so much. I should have—

He found her near the checkout stand, hunched over on the floor with her back to him. The two white-coated men ran to her instantly, deflecting Kyle from his goal. A strangled cry died on his lips as he realized that Erin was not the one in trouble. Her hands were pumping a man's chest. Her mouth was giving him air . . . giving him life.

The paramedics scooped up the balding, overweight man on the floor, making no move to dislodge the beautiful strawberry blonde who was still attached to his chest. She was calling out crisp technical orders that were meaningless to Kyle. Her eyes fluttered past him as she bulldozed her way to the ambulance, but if she saw the man she'd promised to love and cherish until the Navy changed his orders, she gave no sign.

"So where's the star of 61-J?" Roger asked cheerfully when he arrived an hour later, his eyes casting an appreciative glance at the flowers, balloons and streamers that adorned Erin's friendly old house. "I'm not used to seeing you with an apron on, Kyle."

"Neither am I," Kyle growled, then forced himself to stay calm for Roger. The party had perked him up a bit; he wasn't going to undo whatever good the evening might do his friend. "But I'm afraid Erin had to put on her doctor hat tonight."

"What's that mean? They're short on staff?"

"No. It means she went to the store to pick up some sour cream—sour cream, for Pete's sake—and ended up in the back of an ambulance with a heart attack victim. I haven't the slightest idea when she'll be home." He could not conceal his frustration.

"It's not the end of the world, Kyle," Roger assured him. "The party's for me, after all, and *I* understand. Don't you?"

Kyle studied Roger with a keen eye. "Understanding it and being happy about it are two different things."

"You think she should have let him die?"

Kyle tossed up his hands. "Of course not! But couldn't she let somebody else take over once she got him to the hospital?"

Roger shook his head. "That's very hard for a surgeon of Erin's caliber to do. When somebody's life is in your hands, you can't just hand it over to somebody else like a...load of dirty dishes." Roger stared at him for a moment. "Hell, Tatum, it could have been your father! It could have been *me*."

"I know that! She's a doctor. She has to do what a doctor has to do! But dammit, Roger, the simple truth is that I'd be a lot happier living with an average cook than a superior surgeon. Fame and fatigue aren't traits I particularly treasure in a woman."

"Then you sure as hell don't treasure Erin, Kyle, because no two words could describe her better." His words were tart.

"I'm hoping that's only a temporary condition. I keep telling myself—"

"Try telling yourself the truth for a change. Erin Ness is never, I repeat *never* going to be the kind of sweet, humble housewife you created in your dreams. Frankly, I don't think she should have to be, but that's not the point."

"What exactly is your point?"

"My point is that Erin will always be a very talented, very successful, very ambitious lady who will cast her long shadow on your own achievements from time to time. Even if she married you, had babies, and never worked outside the home again—a medical tragedy as far as I'm concerned—she'd still find something terrific to do. If she ran the Ladies' Aid Society at the local church, it would be the best damn Ladies' Aid Society that Houston has ever seen. If she joined the Garden Club she'd—"

"All right! She's marvelous. She's terrific. But dammit, Roger, she's not *here*!" He slammed the dip down on the table. "She's never here. Not really. She just drops in to sleep and change and study whenever she can get away from NASA and the hospital. I thought I'd see her more if I was underfoot, but all it's done is made it easier for her to ignore me. One night last week I left here for over an hour and she never even knew I was gone!

"She never sets aside any time just for me. An hour a day—hell, an hour a week—that's all I'm asking for. Just a moment when I'm all that matters... really matters to her." His voice dropped off. "I'm not sure I can take this too much longer, Roge."

Roger sat down, slouching in a way his back wouldn't have tolerated a few weeks before. "I'm not sure Erin can, either. She doesn't show it, but she's ready to snap. She has so much pressure on her—"

"Pressure? Roger, I'm bending over backward to make life easier for her!"

"She knows that. Don't you think she's worried about how much she's neglecting you?"

"Not particularly. I think she's so damn sure of me that she doesn't waste much time thinking about me at all."

Roger was silent for several minutes before he stated simply, "You've always loved her, Kyle. Just hold on till the mission's done. Then see what she can give you." When Kyle didn't answer, he went on, "Erin's smile is worth the laughter of a dozen other women. If you can't see that, I'm sure there's plenty of men who could."

Kyle's head snapped up angrily. "Including you?"

Roger let the words sink in, then looked his friend squarely in the eye. "I try to forgive my friends under trying circumstances."

Kyle held up both hands in mute surrender. "I'm sorry."

"You should be," Roger retorted unmercifully.

Kyle smiled, glad that their friendship could survive such blunders. "She talks about you all the time, Roge. Hell, she spends more time with you than she does with me! I feel like an extra in a musical production as it is, waiting in the wings for a glimpse of the leading lady's smile. I'm jealous of everybody. Even that stupid chimp. The last time she went to see him she spent half an hour telling me everything he did. I don't think she's ever thought about me for a half an hour straight except—" He was going to say "in bed," but even in his anger he refused to dishonor the woman he treasured.

When the doorbell rang, Roger went to get it, subtly filling in for Erin as cohost. About half of the guests were Navy with the rest from the hospital, and they all seemed to take Erin's unscheduled absence in their stride.

Overall the party went pretty well. But after Roger had been toasted and roasted and warmly welcomed back, Jeb asked Kyle if the group could watch the TV interview Erin had taped that morning. Everybody was excited about the brief news segment except for Kyle.

As he stood in the kitchen doorway and watched his absent lady on the screen, he began to ask himself what he was doing in this house. He was the host this evening, yet he felt like a guest, an intruder who'd borrowed a friend's bachelor pad to throw a secret party. This was Erin's home...Erin's show...Erin's world.

During the interview she held her own and repeatedly praised Roger's work, insisting that he was still a vital part of the 61-J team. The reporter didn't seem too interested in Erin's colleague; he was determined

make her the celebrity. He also made a great fuss
over Quinto.

"Quite an unusual crew we have now, huh, Jeb?"
Roger declared quietly when Kyle snapped off the set.
"Three men, a woman, a chimp and a chump." He
thrust one thumb toward his own chest on the last
word.

Everybody laughed at the joke except Kyle. It hurt
him to see Roger waiting crippled on the sidelines,
even if it *was* Erin winning the race. He knew what it
was like to stand behind Erin Ness while she took the
bows.

So much for the homecoming celebration.

CHAPTER ELEVEN

IT WAS FOUR O'CLOCK in the morning when Erin got home. One light burned on the front porch, another in the hall. Not one scrap of party crumbs or decorations remained. The door to the bedroom was closed.

Wearily she staggered into the living room, stubbing her toe on the empty quilting frame. Like a sleep-walker she crossed the floor to her quilting bag, taking out the tiny green pieces that belonged to Katie's baby. She sat down on the couch, her eyes half-closed, and began to sew.

Less than five minutes had passed before the door behind her opened. She could feel Kyle's anger clear across the room.

"What the hell are you doing?" he growled at her. "It's the middle of the night, you left here ready to drop and you've got to go to work in three hours, so you've decided to sew. Have you lost your mind?"

Erin did not answer. She could have explained that sewing worked on her like a sedative, and she badly needed some help to get to sleep. She could have explained that she was past tension, past fatigue, past rational thought of any kind. She could have explained that the last few hours had been the hardest in her life.

Instead she asked dutifully, "How was the party?"

"The party? Oh, it was just terrific, Erin. Jeb walked in with déjà vu written all over his face, and the applause I'd planned for Roger turned out to be the sound

f one hand clapping. But—'' Abruptly he stopped as
e saw her face, numb and cold and without expression.
Rinny?'' he whispered, his tone now hushed and ten-
er. ''Are you all right?''

Slowly her eyes lifted to his, the knowledge that he
ill loved her suddenly vital. ''I lost him, Kyle. He died
n hour ago.''

Kyle moved closer, kneeling beside her. One hand
ipped her face. ''I'm sorry, babe. You can't save them
ll no matter how hard you try.'' His anger seemed to
ave vanished. ''I'm sure you did the best you could.''

She shook her head. Rising hysteria began to fill her
iroat. ''No. I didn't do the best I could. A med student
ould have done a better job!'' she forced out shrilly. ''I
ouldn't focus. . . I couldn't concentrate. I was thinking
bout you and the party and Roger. . . and sometimes I
ist couldn't think at all!'' She began to sob explosive-
'. Her words were incoherent. ''I'm so scrambled. I'm
illing apart. I'm just. . . just—''

The rest of her words were lost in the warm skin of
yle's bare chest as he crushed her tightly against him.
ie didn't tell her not to cry; he just whispered com-
ortingly against her hair as she poured out her anguish,
owing from her like a waterfall with no final destina-
on. ''I'm not doing anything right,'' she gasped when
ie got her second wind. ''I'm only half there at NASA,
alf there at Our Lady, and I'm not giving you even a
raction of what you deserve. I love you, Kyle. I don't
now what I'd do without you!'' Her eyes met his in
enuine regret. ''I'm so sorry about tonight.''

He pulled her closer but did not speak, knowing that
hug was the only answer she needed. She wept until
ie had no more tears, no more words. At last she fell
sleep against him.

After a while he carried her to bed and lay down beside her. "It's okay, Rinny," he whispered into the dark. "I'm going to take care of you. That's a promise."

An hour later he was still awake. Erin was still nestled in his arms.

WHEN SHE WOKE UP it was late afternoon. Sometime during the night Kyle had undressed her and wrapped her in a silky yellow robe. Vaguely she realized she had missed work, but she was certain that Kyle had called Jeb to explain her absence. Unfortunately, she still had evening duty at the hospital. She dragged herself out to the kitchen and found Kyle there fixing dinner.

"Hello," she greeted him meekly, still a bit dazed from last night. "I'm sorry I . . . went berserk."

He crossed to her side and cuddled her in his arms. "Don't be silly. You helped me get my values in perspective. I've spent the whole day figuring out a solution to your problem."

She raised her eyebrows. "You didn't go to work either?"

"No, ma'am." He looked very serious. "I wasn't sure whether or not you'd need me."

She buried her head in his shoulder, remembering that just last night he'd pointed out that Roger's feelings were every bit as vital as his medical condition. ". . . really don't deserve you," she confessed.

He kissed the top of her head and pulled her closer. "That's probably true, but as luck would have it you're stuck with me anyway. You want to hear how I've solved your problem?"

"Okay."

He sat down on the nearest chair and pulled her onto his lap. "Actually I've considered several alternatives.

he first is to quit the mission altogether, which I
new you would discard.''

She nodded.

"The second is to go on the way you've been going
ntil you die of exhaustion. That one *I'm* going to dis-
ard.''

She had to agree, but she couldn't stifle her growing
pprehension.

"So, something has to go. Starting with Friday
ights at the hospital.''

"No! I'm a surgeon first of all—''

"No, ma'am. You are an astronaut first of all if you
ecide to stay on the mission...if you spend your life
a Houston. That's a value decision you've got to
ake sooner or later, as last night should surely have
aught you. Now, for the time being, that extra stress
n't helping you or the patients, and it's not necessary
or your work at NASA. You're not going to forget
ow to do an appendectomy in two months. You're in
ar greater risk of botching surgery on the chimp
arough fatigue and hysteria than lack of experience.''

She hated to agree with him, but it did make sense.
You're probably right, Kyle. But surgery really isn't
ae biggest drain on my time.''

"No. I am.'' The words came out so starkly that
rin instinctively huddled closer. "That's why I'm go-
ag to move back to the base.''

"No!" The word was ripped from her throat. "I
eed you here. You're my...you're my life. Kyle—''

He kissed her in an effort to calm her down, but she
ulled away. "Please don't give up on me, Kyle.
lease wait till the mission's over—''

"Sweetheart, listen to me. I'm *not* giving up on you.
will see you just as much as you can fit me in. I'm
lso going to arrange for a housekeeper so you don't

have any domestic responsibilities at all. Then you can
work around the clock with just time out to eat and
sleep. That's the only way you're going to live through
this thing.''

"I don't want to live through it without you. Don't
leave me, Kyle!''

Frustrated, he pulled her closer. "Rinny, I'm trying
to do what's best for you. It's hard enough for me to
sacrifice what little time I've got with you. Don't make
it impossible.''

"It is impossible. If we were married would you offer to move out every time I had a hard week at
work?''

He scowled, but he did not answer.

"What if you...just arranged to be gone a little
more? Spent more time with your friends...or what
ever. I need to know that everything's all right between
us or I won't get anything done.''

She watched his face tensely as he weighed her
words. She knew she'd said them before; knew she'd
given him the impression that she just wanted him
close—on standby—so she wouldn't have to worry
about anything but the mission.

"That didn't come out quite the way I meant it,
Kyle. We made a decision—a commitment—when you
moved in here that we would be a—'' she struggled for
the word "family" but just couldn't say it "—a couple. A unit. Now just because I'm going through a
rough patch with my job doesn't change that. It
doesn't affect my love for you in the least.'' He'd
stopped looking at her; he seemed to be studying the
stove in the kitchen. "Please don't move back to the
base, Kyle. No matter what your motives are, I'd feel
like you were walking out on me. Nothing would be
the same.''

She wondered, fleetingly, if his motives for moving back to the base had nothing to do with her immediate crisis. So far nothing about their arrangement had turned out the way he'd envisioned it, and if Erin didn't make a sharp turn somewhere down the road, their future wouldn't turn out the way he wanted it, either.

For a long time Kyle said nothing, then without looking at her he capitulated. "Okay, babe," he breathed in defeat. "I'll stay here awhile longer and see how it goes. But I'll do my damnedest not to make any demands on our time. Except..." He hesitated, but Erin urged him to go on.

"What? Tell me."

"Could you...still manage to come to Washington with me? We could just go for the ceremony and come back—twenty-four hours—you wouldn't have to lose a whole weekend of study." His eyes were earnest. "I hate to ask you, Rinny, but my folks are counting on it and I think they'd be terribly disappointed if you didn't come."

By the look in his eyes it was obvious that he'd be terribly disappointed, too. How many times had she already disappointed this man! How many times had he forgiven her shortcomings, her busyness, her exhaustion! He'd been talking about this trip since that first glorious day on the beach. There was no way she could turn him down.

"Of course I'll still go. No matter what happens, I'll find time to meet your parents." *And I'll find time to write to your mother before you ask me about it again.*

He smiled, then kissed her very gently. "I love you, Erin. I'm going to do whatever I can to get you through the next two months."

His words touched her deeply. Her need to merge with him in every way was suddenly overwhelming.

"Starting right now?" she asked him.

He nodded. "Starting right now."

She pulled the sash on her robe just enough for her lovely breasts to greet his eyes. "I think I need some relaxation."

"Relaxation," he repeated, his eyes, then his hands, brushing the soft skin below her neck. "What...exactly...does the doctor prescribe?"

Slowly his fingertips swept down toward the rising rosy peaks that seemed to lift in invitation, testimony to his sensual skill. Erin's breath caught in her throat. She framed his virile face with her hands and guided his mouth toward her right breast. His tongue reached out to tease the darker center, carving slow, erotic circles around the circumference of her desire.

Instinctively Erin turned on his lap until she was astride him, feeling his hunger rise against her. She opened the robe completely so his hands could sweep down her back to massage her hips. She was already braced against his thighs, but he pulled her harder yet against him, a low growl of need escaping from his throat.

"The doctor," she whispered into his hair, "thinks she needs to spend the night in bed. Do you think we should get a second opinion?"

He stood up, pressing her intimately against him as he let her slide ever so slowly to the floor. He kissed her throat with fire hot enough to brand her, then met her mouth as his fingertips hiked back up her midriff toward her fully awakened nipples. He closed a thumb and forefinger around each confession of desire before he murmured, "The pilot seconds the motion. Does that make it unanimous?"

Without waiting for an answer, he picked her up like Rhett Butler might have carried Scarlett to bed in a fade-out scene from *Gone with the Wind*. There were no stairs to climb, but the trip to the bedroom still consumed the whole panoramic screen. By morning Erin was certain that it was the finest movie she had ever seen.

EVERYTHING LOOKED BRIGHTER after a few days' rest. Erin spent the weekend reading, sleeping and swimming. Kyle spent most of Saturday and Sunday with Roger, but when he was home his silent presence boosted her spirits and gave her hope that she would somehow survive the duration. Each time he passed her he'd drop a kiss on her forehead or squeeze her shoulder, silently reiterating his support.

On Monday Erin arrived at work feeling almost refreshed. She suspected she should have taken a day off weeks ago. She also should have given up her surgical duties when she'd first received her mission assignment.

"Erin?" Jeb greeted her with some concern the instant she reached her office. "Are you feeling better?"

She nodded, still not certain just where she stood with this man. "Yes. Sorry I had to miss a day, but I was up all night at the hospital and I don't think I would have been much of an asset to the team." She was afraid he would tell her she wasn't much of an asset anyway, but Jeb quickly relieved her fears.

"Erin. . . I'm well aware that you're working around the clock to pull this mission together, and I wish I could tell you to take it easy. But I can't. All I can tell you is that you're doing a good job now and I think it will all be worth it in the end."

She smiled. "We're in agreement there."

He grinned for just an instant, reminding her of the charm she knew Jeb Henson could show to a woman who wasn't on his crew. "I know that. . . I haven't always seemed. . . grateful for your efforts, Erin. I suspect you think that I haven't always been fair to you. But I've never worked professionally with a woman before and there are times when I'm. . . really not sure what I should do with you. If you. . . if you were just Kyle's wife and not a member of my crew. . . or if you were just a member of my crew and not involved with such a close friend. . . I don't think it would be so hard for me. But as it is, sometimes I'm torn between what's good for Kyle and what's good for 61-J. Can you understand that?"

She could understand it. She just wished he'd told her that on the first day instead of giving her his Navy commander's speech. "I do understand, Jeb. I don't always like it, but—I know you'll always make a decision that will be for the good of the crew. There may come a time when I'll have to thank you for it." She pointed to the sky with one finger, indicating the uncertainties of space. "Kyle once told me he'd be a lot more worried about sending me into orbit if you weren't in command of the mission."

"He did?" Jeb was clearly flattered.

"Yes. He said there's nobody he'd rather have as his wing man in a pinch. And he was rather upset with you at the time, as I recall, so it was hardly idle flattery."

Jeb managed a smile. "We're all going to get through this thing, Erin. And we're all going to be damn proud. Even Kyle."

Erin wanted to say that Kyle should get part of the credit just for putting up with the pair of them, but she held her tongue.

"I'll meet you downstairs, okay? This is the lucky day you get to wrestle with that chimp."

Erin had almost forgotten about Quinto. After all

he time they'd spent in the simulator, today they were
going to bring the chimp on board just to get a hands-
on idea of how he fit into the picture.

The whole crew seemed to be feeling cheerful, if not
downright silly, by the time Erin reached the mock
Odyssey. Mark was imitating Quinto, who looked
pretty spry in spite of the mild sedative he'd received,
and even Paul seemed to be in the mood for jokes.

The chimp greeted Erin with a slobbery hug, and
Mark tried to do likewise.

"All right, already! Only one ape allowed on each
mission," she told him with a laugh. "NASA regula-
tions."

"Then it better be me," Mark told her. "I've always
had simian tendencies. Besides, Quinto can't fly the
shuttle."

"He'd probably do a better job," Jeb teased him.

Mark responded with mock fury, instantly assuming
a boxer's stance. This time it was quiet Paul Stevenson
who laughed. He, like Erin, had been around the pilots
long enough to understand their fliers' pride. "They're
going to take their gloves off, Erin. You and I better
stay out of the way."

"All right you guys," Seth, the flight trainer,
ordered as he entered the room. "We're going to have
to get the chimp hooked up. Let's just take this slow
and easy and see how long it takes."

It took longer than anyone could have imagined. A
"fully instrumented chimpanzee," as Erin's books
described poor Quinto, was strapped, wrapped and
wired in so many different ways that he might as well
have been chained to the cabin. Each connection
monitored some vital sign and would give medical
science some valuable piece of data, but Erin had to
admit the chimp looked positively miserable. She knew

she should have viewed him solely as a lab subject, bu
ever since she'd learned that Roger treated him like a
pet, she'd been inclined in the same direction.

"Erin," Mark said after they'd been working in the
simulator for an hour, "I think his medication is wear
ing off."

"Sure, Mark," she chuckled, thinking he must be
teasing her. Actually, the sedative was very important
and one of the many things they had to determine
precisely. Too much could kill Quinto, especially in
the uncertain atmosphere of space. Too little would
leave them with a weightless monkey bouncing all over
the sensitive instrumentation of the cabin. Fortunate
ly, at Quinto's age he was still pretty mild and tracta
ble. Full-grown chimps were often as big as a short
man and could be quite nasty when provoked.

Suddenly Quinto went haywire, as Mark's predic
tion came true. Before anyone could reach him he
started unplugging each of his connectors, punctuating
each achievement with a wild simian shriek o
triumph.

"Ayeeeee!" he bellowed in delight, ripping loose the
last of his fetters. "Ayeeeee!" He did several turns
around the cabin before he landed in Erin's lap, sud
denly in need of a hug.

By this time the whole crew was laughing hysterical
ly, and even Seth was forced to smile.

"Me, too!" Mark babbled, imitating Quinto as he
tried to push the chimp off her lap. "I need a hug or
kiss or—"

"A psychiatrist!" Jeb finished for him.

Erin carried the squirming patient-to-be over to
Paul and dropped him in his lap. "I simply canno
abide this sort of disorganization in my operating
room," she declared with mock solemnity. "This i

your responsibility, Dr. Stevenson. What kind of an anesthesiologist are you, anyway?''

The chimp wrapped his arms around Paul, who groaned and threatened to put Quinto out for good next time. The rest of the crew crawled out of the simulator, chuckling in unison, and gave up work for the rest of the day.

WITH KYLE'S STEADFAST SUPPORT, the pressure seemed to ease over the next few weeks. Miraculously a housekeeper appeared even though Erin never recalled interviewing one. The dishes were done, the house was clean, and a warm supper awaited her every evening. Kyle arrived in time to eat with her, rub her shoulders, and tell her jokes to lighten her day, then disappeared for several hours while she studied. He always came back to lull her joyously into sleep. He went flying every Saturday and spent Sunday afternoons with Roger.

The tenderness between them grew almost daily until the Monday evening in late July when he came home with an envelope in his hand.

"I picked up your ticket, babe," he greeted her cheerfully, flopping down on the couch for a comfortable kiss. "I just found out I'm going to have to fly out ahead along with Alan to take care of some NASA business, so you're on your own until I meet you at the airport. Is there anything in particular you need to know before I go? I have to leave in the morning."

Erin looked up from her reading—a comparative analysis of the cardiovascular system of the chimpanzee and *Homo sapiens*—and stared at him blankly. "At this point I'd be grateful for a vacation with you almost anywhere, Kyle, but would you give me a hint what we're talking about here?"

"Washington, sweetheart," he reminded her with a

patient smile. "Friday is the change-of-command ceremony, remember?"

He waited, his face clearly expecting her to say, "Of course! The change-of-command ceremony." But she couldn't. Friday was the day she was scheduled to see the New York City zoo vet who specialized in chimpanzees. She hadn't thought of his father's retirement in almost three weeks.

"Uh. . . Friday, you say. What time?"

"What does it matter what time? Eight or nine in the morning, I imagine. But my folks are expecting you Thursday night and me whenever I can wind things up at the Pentagon. When did you tell mom you were coming? When you answered her letter?"

This time she couldn't cover up her faux pas. One look at her face told him everything.

"You never wrote to her at all?" His voice held barely concealed anger. "Erin. . . I know you're carrying a heavy load, but I can't believe you let that slide again. Under the circumstances it's more than thoughtless. It's just plain rude. My mother—" He stopped, his eyes suddenly growing from reproachful to incredulous. "You. . . are still planning to go with me, aren't you, Erin?"

The living room grew deathly still. Erin could not look at him. "I have a vital appointment scheduled Friday morning. I didn't pick the time, Kyle. It—"

"What the hell is the appointment? Unless you're dying of cancer or something—"

"It's for the mission, Kyle."

"Of course! The mission! The mission that surrounds your heart like chain-link fencing! The mission I've been running a length behind since the first moment I bulldozed my way into your life!"

"Kyle. . ." She started awkwardly, ashamed of her

blunder and frightened by the look on his face. "You know how much I love you. I'm doing my best to juggle you with everything—"

"Juggle is a good word for it. Three things in two hands...and one of them always ends up getting dropped." He gestured sharply toward the hardwood floor. "Hear that thud? It was me, Erin. I've got bruises to prove it."

Erin swallowed hard and tried to keep from quivering. His voice was so stiff she could hardly hear a trace of his love for her. "Kyle, I know what you've been doing for me these past few weeks and I am...overwhelmingly grateful."

"And what have you been doing for me, Erin? What have you ever done for me since the weekend Roger got hurt? Have you once, even *once*, noticed that I'm preparing for a mission that's got six dozen problems for every one you've got on 61-J? Have you made the slightest effort to find a way to accommodate your plans—even your long-term plans—to my life in the Navy? Have you even given a moment's thought to how much I want to raise a family with you?"

Erin could not answer.

"I've done every damn thing I could to help you through this rough patch, Erin, even though I never wanted you to take this mission in the first place. I knew the strain would level you, and I was afraid it would destroy our love before it even had a chance to put down roots." His voice grew quieter. "There are nights when I've been just as tired as you were, but I've gone out to let you study just the same. I've pretended that I felt at home here just to give you that security, but for the last month, I've really missed living on the base. I honestly felt more at home there. At least I didn't have to ask permission to show up at my own quarters!''

He walked away from her, his hands in his pockets as he continued grimly. ''I've lost all count of the number of times I've wanted to come home at night to somebody who'd smile at me and say, 'How was your day, darling?' and offer me a back rub and a smile. But have I asked you for that? No. Have I added to your stress? No. I've only asked for one simple thing: twenty-four hours of your time for the most important event of my father's life.'' He shook his head and turned back to face her. ''You couldn't even give me that, Erin. Hell, you couldn't even *remember* that!''

She was trembling now. He was calm, too calm. He should have been yelling, carving her up with insults he'd have to beg her to forgive him for later. She struggled for magical words of apology that would somehow make everything all right. ''Kyle, I know I'm in the wrong here. I made a mistake. I'm really sorry that I forgot about the letter—''

''Erin,'' he stated baldly, ''you didn't forget about the damn letter. You forgot about *me*.'' He stared at her with a terrifying mixture of anguish and despair, then crossed the room to pick up the air-line ticket on his way out the door. ''And I think the time has finally come for me to. . . forget about you.''

For the next five minutes, Erin stood perfectly still as the sickness washed over her. *My God, what have I done? What have I done? What have I done?*

The words echoed in her brain like a horse in full canter. She began to shiver so violently that she had to wrap herself in a quilt, despite the stifling Houston heat before sundown. She was beyond all thought, beyond all hope. Her world had come to an end when her man had walked out the front door.

And then, very slowly, another voice began to whisper in her ear. *What can I do to get him back? What can I do? What can I do?*

She didn't have the answer, but she knew someone who might. Pausing only to pull on jeans and a T-shirt over her bikini, she bolted outside and headed straight for Roger.

"Erin?" he asked the minute she slunk into his apartment, her fractured composure evident to anyone who cared for her at all. "What the—"

"He left me, Roger," she whispered like a dying person. "I can't breathe."

Without another word Roger took her in his arms, banishing her fears that he would tell her she'd gotten her just deserts. He rocked her like a small child while she sobbed against his chest, the pain exploding from a volcano somewhere deep within her.

Almost twenty minutes passed before he let her go, easing her into a comfortable armchair. He didn't ask her for any explanations; he just brought her some coffee and gently stroked her hair.

"I'm so miserable, Roger," she whispered, spilling out the whole tattered tale in bits and pieces over the next hour. "You warned me. I didn't hear you. I was so damn sure he loved me."

"He does love you, Erin." Roger's voice was very low. "That's not the problem. It's never been the problem."

She peered at him through sodden eyes that still hurt from the salty tears. "He was so cold when he left, Roger. So quiet. It was...like he just made his decision, put me behind him, and trotted right off to a new life without a backward glance. Just like the Navy had shipped him out and there was nothing I could do but wave goodbye from the shore."

Roger patted her on the knee and settled down on the couch across the room, then tried to warm her with a smile. "I want you to spend the night here, Erin. I don't think you should be alone right now."

Erin's relief at his words was overwhelming. If Roger would just stay near her, she might make it through the next few days. She might be able to think of a way to get Kyle back. "Oh, Roger! You're so good to me. I—" She stopped, suddenly awash with a different set of feelings. Kyle's feelings. Feelings she had always either laughed at or ignored.

"I don't think I can stay here, Roger," she told him slowly, still not fully certain of the reasons herself.

"Of course you can. I've got a perfectly good guest room going to waste. It would be a privilege to repay some of the care I've been getting all these months."

"From Kyle or from me?"

He pondered the question for a minute. "Both."

But Erin knew that Kyle's devotion to Roger had greatly outstripped her own. She also knew that Kyle could never accept her explanation of why she spent the night with Roger. "Don't you see, Roger? Kyle won't understand. As much as he trusts you, he's always pointing out that I spend more time with you than with him. He'll think I just went from him to you."

"Well, maybe it's time he woke up. The whole world does not operate on his antiquated standards. As long as you and I know exactly what our intentions are, why does it matter what Kyle might think if and when he finds out? I'll square it with him later. Your feelings are the ones I'm worried about right now."

Erin brushed her hair out of her face. Why was it only now that she had lost Kyle that she was beginning to understand him? "It doesn't matter, Roger. I've

ailed him in so many ways. Even though he doesn't
want me anymore, it'll kill him if he thinks we're having
an affair. I won't do that to him. I won't hurt him any
more than I already have.''

Suddenly she covered her face with her hands, new
pain lancing her soul. "Oh, God, Roger! What am I going to do? How could I possibly have driven him
away?''

For several moments Roger was silent. Then he
asked, "What would you change if you could get him
back? What would you do differently?''

"Everything! I'd call him darling and give him back
rubs every night! I'd honor the Navy. . . I'd go see his
parents. . . I'd stuff half of your wonderful briefs in the
trash. But I don't have the slightest idea how to get him
back. Even if I begged him on my hands and knees—''

She stopped as the words came out of her mouth.
Roger studied her for a long minute, then nodded sage-
ly. "It's worth a shot.''

"Worth a shot! Roger, you didn't see his face when
he said goodbye! I don't think he ever wants to see me
again. If you think it will do any good for me to beg him
to come back home, you are out of your mind!''

He stood up slowly. "Think about it, Erin. He didn't
walk out on you just because you forgot his father's
ceremony. That was just the straw that broke the
camel's back.''

She knew he was right. The plain, naked truth was
that she was lucky Kyle hadn't walked out on her a long
time ago.

"I know Kyle,'' Roger said. "I know what Vivian did
to his pride and self-respect. I know what *you* did to his
pride and self-respect. But he probably could have
made it until after your mission if you hadn't insulted
his family.''

Roger walked back to her side, his eyes reflective. "He loves you terribly, Erin. He'll never be happy without you. But if you want him back, you're going to have to convince him that you're ready to put him first in your life. That means you're going to have to play Navy in Washington and wait on him hand and foot for a while to make up for all the time you've so blithely ignored him."

"I'm willing to do that, Roger. I'm willing to do anything at all—"

"Are you willing to give up the mission?"

She grew so still that even her tears stopped flowing. "Is that what it would take, Roger?"

He lifted his hands. "It's your best chance."

"You said begging was my best chance."

"You're going to have to beg just to get a private hearing. You still need something to bargain with once you've got his attention."

Erin shook her head. "I can't bargain with the mission, Roger! I'm not even sure I can bargain with my pride. I've never begged a man for anything. I'm not at all sure that I can do it now."

Roger leaned back on the couch. "Then forget him. Give him up right here and now. Because there's no other way you'll ever get Kyle Tatum back."

WITH KATIE'S HELP Erin got on the base and reached the Heron Bay Officers' Club at precisely eight o'clock. The dinner hour was over, and most of the men had straggled off to their evening plans. Those who lingered turned their heads interestedly as Erin walked in. Their instincts were uncanny; no one here had ever approached her when she had belonged to Kyle.

She found him near the dance floor at a table large

ough to accommodate six or seven of his friends...
vo of whom were women. One wore tiny gold wings
n her blouse...proof that she belonged to a pilot.
he other seemed to be sitting with Kyle.

His face was pale instead of bronze, and the expres-
on in his eyes was dull.

"Hello," she greeted him simply. The word got lost
omewhere in her throat.

His eyes read the swollen lids and red blotches only
artly hidden by the artful use of her finest makeup.
Ie ignored her lovely rose silk dress. Nothing in his
ace gave her the slightest reason to hope.

He asked curtly, "Do you need something?"

Erin looked down at her hands. Her mouth was too
ry to form words. "May I...speak to you for a sec-
nd?"

"Sure. Speak." He said it the way he'd command a
og.

"Alone, please, if you'd be so kind."

For several moments he stared at her pink waistline,
eighing his options. He knew he had her in the palm
f his hand; he knew he could humiliate her in front of
is friends. He'd sounded almost neutral when he'd
ft the house, but now he looked less forgiving. The
niform helped make him look totally intimidating!

Putting all her eggs in one basket, Erin forced her-
elf to wait. Finally his eyes met hers. His blue eyes,
ardened against her, seemed determined to stay
ardened against her no matter what the cost. In a
oice that was low but still audible to his companions
he admitted, "If you want me to beg you, Kyle, I
vill."

They were the hardest words Erin had ever spoken,
nd she knew that nothing else could hurt much more.
f he laughed at her now she would never forgive him.

Maybe that's what Roger had in mind. A quick and sure way to cauterize the open wound.

But Kyle's eyes changed in the face of her plea, and for just a second she caught a glimpse of his love for her. Abruptly he looked away, but he stood and faced his friends. "Excuse me just a moment, will you?"

They all nodded absently as Kyle led Erin to a semi-private table in the back of the room and gestured for her to sit down. But when he joined her there, his eyes were hard again. His first words took her utterly by surprise.

"Are you pregnant?"

"Am I *what*?"

"Pregnant. With child. You've heard of the concept. I can't imagine what else could force you to grovel." Before she could answer he marched on, "Forgive my moment of irrational thought. If you were carrying my child you'd just get rid of it, wouldn't you, Erin? You wouldn't let some other human being stand in the way of your career, now, would you?"

She stared at him, too wounded to speak. She didn't want a baby. She didn't have time for a baby. But if she ever got pregnant by accident, she knew that aborting Kyle's child would be impossible for her...as impossible as giving up Kyle himself.

"I came," she forced out, then started over, "I came to see—"

"There's no point in this, Erin," he interrupted her tonelessly. "We had a good time in the beginning. But it's not fun anymore. As busy as you are you won't miss me more than a few days anyway, and by then you'll be congratulating yourself on all the work you've caught up on without me there to pester you—"

"Kyle, please! I have to tell you—"

"Erin, when you told me you didn't have time to come to meet my parents—when you told me you didn't even have time to *remember* you were supposed to meet my parents—you told me everything I ever need to hear." He rose abruptly. Without thinking, Erin reached out and grabbed his hand with both of hers. Instinctively his fingers closed around hers, giving her new hope.

"Please, Kyle. Please listen to me—"

"Rinny," he said almost tenderly, clearly touched by her desperation, "I'm really sorry you're hurting. I mean that. I'm not feeling terrific about this myself. But it's just not going to work, sweetheart. Can't you see that? You were right all along. It's time to admit that and say goodbye while we can still part as friends."

"You wanted to marry me!" she pleaded. "Could you walk out like this if I were your wife?"

Abruptly he pulled free of her hands. "You're not my wife, Erin. That's the whole point. You wanted a relationship free of commitments. You fought every move I ever made to plan a future for us. The way I see it, you're getting exactly what you asked for . . . which, coincidentally, is just what you deserve."

He didn't get an inch from the table before Erin was on her feet. "You owe me the chance to apologize, Kyle. At least hear me out."

He turned around, surprised and a little hostile. "I don't owe you a damn thing. If you ask me the deck is stacked the other way around."

"The night you came to me . . . the first night we really got together . . . I didn't want to listen to you. You'd said absolutely unforgivable things to me, Kyle. But I loved you enough to hear you out. I listened.

Just do that much for me. I'm begging you." Tears filled her still-red eyes, then slid down her face. "I love you so much, Kyle. Just because I don't know how to show it doesn't mean it isn't there. I'm dying inside." She covered her face, suddenly out of control. "I'm just dying, Kyle."

He didn't say a word, but he sat back down at the table. She had never seen him look so grim. "What do you want to tell me? People are waiting for me. I've got an important flight in the morning."

She swallowed her desperation and returned to her chair, suddenly realizing that she didn't have the slightest idea what she wanted to say. "I never...I never for a moment thought you could leave me, Kyle. Maybe I did take you for granted, but I also...I really thought...that we were past that stage. Maybe we didn't talk about commitments anymore, but we...we were committed. We were...so very together. I wish I'd paid attention to you sooner...I wish I hadn't been so caught up in myself that I didn't see this coming, but I can't change that now. All I can do is tell you I'll *crawl* all the way to Washington if I have to. Please give me another chance. I'll find a way to make things right with your parents. Don't take somebody else in my place." It wasn't really what she wanted to say to him, but the words splashed out anyhow.

Slowly Kyle shook his head, his eyes refuting every word she'd spoken. In silence he let her absorb the finality of his rejection before he spoke. "I'll come get my things after I get back from Washington, and I'll leave a check for the housekeeper to cover the time from now till the launch. I promised you that."

"You promised me more than that," she heard herself whisper, the words punctured with futile new tears. "You promised me—"

"You're the only woman I want, Erin," he hushed her, refusing to meet her eyes. "You know that. But the time has come for me to accept the fact that I can't have you. Not as my special full-time lady. Certainly not as my wife. A trip to D.C. isn't going to change that."

"No, it's not," she replied urgently. "*I'm* going to change our relationship, Kyle. I'm going to listen to you, really listen to what you need from me, and do whatever I have to, to put you first in my schedule." His impassive eyes told her he didn't believe a single word. "I love you, Kyle," she pleaded in desperation. "I don't know how you managed to wedge yourself into my life so permanently, but I don't think I can put one foot in front of the other without you anymore." Despite his grim mask she reached across the table to take both his hands in hers. "Please, please come home. Don't destroy what we have. Not when we still have so much love for each other."

He watched her from a long distance, across the miles of table, his hands flat before him as he ignored her desperate grip. "Are you done? May I go now?"

Erin leaned forward in new panic. "Just like that? Aren't you going to say anything?"

"I've already said everything I have to say."

She closed her eyes. *It's not working, Roger. I've humbled myself for nothing.* Yet she had to try one more time. "Is there...anything...*anything* at all I can do at this point...to get you to come home?"

His eyes swept over her face, her ivory skin, her flowing strawberry blond hair. He read the anguish in her soft gray eyes, her genuine determination to do whatever she had to do to reclaim his love. For a funeral procession of endless moments he studied her, studied her question. Then at last, very slowly, he nodded.

"Yes, as a matter of fact. There is something you could do."

She sat up straight, new hope thudding in her heart. "Anything. Name it."

"Will you quit the program and marry me? Tomorrow?"

She tried to read his face, but it was completely blank, the Navy officer's mask under stress. Defeat flushed her cheeks. Why had he deliberately asked her the one thing she simply could not do? "I...I was serious, Kyle."

He stood up and tucked his cap under his arm. "So was I, Erin. So was I."

CHAPTER TWELVE

AT PRECISELY FIVE O'CLOCK the next morning, the phone began to ring. Erin was already awake... or, more accurately, still awake. *He waited till morning to call me,* her heart pounded in jubilant, desperate hope. *He didn't want to disturb my sleep. Oh, Kyle! I love you. I love you. I love you....*

"Hello?" she whispered hoarsely into the phone.

"Good morning, ma'am," a stranger's voice greeted her. It was cool and precise and unquestionably formal. "I'm sorry to disturb you at this hour but it is imperative that Admiral McDermott speak to Commander Tatum before he leaves for Washington."

Instantly Erin was alert. What could she say? *Yes, Kyle Tatum lives here. No, I don't know where he is.* How she fielded the awkward question could help or hurt this man she loved, this man who had so coolly tossed her out of his life the night before. But it made not the slightest bit of difference that Kyle had ceased to think of her as his partner. She still belonged to him, one hundred fifty percent, and if the man on the other end of the line ordered her to swim the English Channel in her flight suit to help Kyle, she would have done it without a moment's hesitation.

But she honestly had not the slightest idea where Kyle was. He'd said he was flying in the morning; he might already have left for Washington. Her ignorance, not to mention the circumstances that had produced it, was hardly going to weigh in Kyle's favor. Carefully, Erin announced, "I'm sorry, sir, but Commander Tatum has already left the house. I can give you the number of Air Operations at the base in the event he hasn't taken off yet. I also have the home phone number of his mission commander, Alan Clayburn, who could possibly relay a message. The two of them are flying together."

It seemed to be the right thing to say. The aide took both numbers and thanked Erin formally for her assistance. She didn't like the idea of Leslie Clayburn knowing that Kyle had moved out. . . and she didn't like the idea that Leslie probably knew more than she did about where Kyle would spend the next few days.

Quietly she asked herself why it was that now, *after* she'd lost Kyle, she was beginning to take his military concerns to heart. He'd never received a call like that before, and the grave, almost urgent, tone of the officer continued to haunt her. *Has it ever once occurred to you that I'm preparing for a mission that's got six dozen problems for every one on 61-J?* he'd asked her in his fury. What were the problems? He had sidestepped the few questions she'd asked him, but that didn't mean he wasn't worried. Was it more than concern about his parents that had caused him to respond so potently to her mistake? Was he just so weighed down with mission problems that he couldn't cope with an unsupportive wife?

It struck Erin that she had gradually come to think of herself as his wife, and his defection now was no less than a step toward divorce. She still didn't know how it had happened. He loved her—she knew he did! So how could he possibly walk out on her now?

All the answers to that question were humiliating and didn't change a thing. Kyle was a proud man who

ad been pushed as far as he could go. Ultimately he
ad abandoned a woman who had sealed her own des-
ny, then raged at fate for giving her precisely what
e deserved.

IT SEEMED TO ERIN that the next forty-eight hours
sted for seven and a half years. She stumbled
rough work in a somnambulent state. It didn't help
at Jeb told her gently that the breakup was probably
ll for the best and refused to share anything he might
ave known about Kyle's trip to D.C. It didn't help
at Mark tried to cheer her up by telling silly jokes
hile they worked in the simulator; it didn't help that
aul came right out and said he was sorry to hear
bout Kyle. But the absolute nadir of the week was the
all from the chimp expert in New York postponing his
ip to Houston for personal reasons. He hoped Erin
ouldn't be inconvenienced by his change in plans.

"Of course not!" Erin wanted to scream at him.
This appointment, which you've cancelled so non-
halantly, has just cost me the only man I've ever
anted to share my life with...." She had remained
ifficiently calm on the phone, but she'd taken an ear-
lunch and spent most of the hour in the privacy of
er car, weeping in fury and despair. With twenty-
wenty hindsight, she realized that she could have
voided this entire catastrophe if she had just asked
oger to fill in for her. Under the circumstances, he
ould hardly have considered it a featherbed assign-
ient.

The only flicker of light in the black cave of her pain
as Katie's invitation to dinner on Wednesday night.
Vhen Katie had discovered that Erin's mission to the
' Club had been a dismal failure, she had insisted on
ying to cheer her up.

Of course cheer was not possible in the numb state Erin was in, but the agony did ease just a bit in Katie's ebullient company. She seemed to have adjusted to Billy's seafaring absence remarkably well, having made several new friends among the close network of Navy wives. One or two had even promised to help out when the baby came, but Katie still asked Erin to stay with her at the hospital during her labor—not as a doctor, but as a friend. Erin readily agreed.

After a splendid dinner with all of Erin's favorite delicacies, Katie towed her guest into the nursery for a preview display. Erin was not at all sure she was in the mood to summon up the necessary oohs and ahs.

But the small room was a wonderland of tiny fixtures, each one so entrancing that even Erin felt a wispy ache of yearning. The jungle animals had won the decorating battle, and Erin had to admit that the giraffe curtains really were adorable.

"I haven't bought many blankets for the crib since you're making a quilt," Katie told her earnestly. "How is it coming along?"

Erin's expression was bleak. She was too depressed to prevaricate with an old friend. "When's your *next* baby due?"

Katie sighed. "Maybe you'll have more time when the mission's over," she suggested hopefully.

"I'm sure I will. No one will be making any demands on my time."

Katie touched her shoulder, then tried to move on to a cheerier topic. "Look what mother sent me, Rinny," she declared, holding up a fuzzy gray bunny that looked like it had just hopped out of a Beatrix Potter book. "Isn't it adorable?"

In spite of herself, Erin had to agree. One huge floppy ear covered most of the bunny's face, and a

air of blue patchwork pajamas made it look almost
uman.

"These are the kimonos," Katie went on, opening
rawers stuffed with miniature bits of clothing. "My
aby book says I'll need six to ten, but we can only af-
ord four to start with. And these little booties will
iatch. Over here—"

Erin couldn't focus on Katie's voice after that.
he'd gotten lost in the hand-crocheted pair of blue
ooties Katie had thrust in her hand. They were so
mall they would have fit on Kyle's thumbs. What
mall person would wear such tiny things! A newborn
aby about the size of the floppy bunny that Katie's
iother had sent. Without thinking, Erin picked up the
unny and slipped the booties on his feet.

"I did the same thing the first day he came!" Katie
ozed, watching Erin in delight.

But there was no delight in Erin's face. It was way
oo late to be feeling sentimental about babies. Even if
iis weren't just a momentary aberration caused by
yle's cruel accusations and her own ongoing pain,
ie had no more time for babies now than she ever
ad.

How could you accuse me of aborting your child?
ie asked Kyle from a wounded place inside her heart.
he pressed the bunny against her shoulder and fought
ew tears. *Oh, God, Kyle, how can I possibly carry on
ithout you?*

"Rinny," Katie finally whispered, "why don't you
ist marry him? Right now while you've still got the
hance?"

Erin sighed. *Damned if I know,* her heart replied.
ut aloud she repeated her unconvincing logic. "Be-
ause he wants babies. He doesn't understand why I
ave to stay in Houston. He wants me to give up a

thousand years of hard work to follow him around the world."

"Are you sure he wouldn't be willing to compromise if you. . . gave in on just a few of those points?"

"Katie, he gave me an ultimatum! Give up the mission and marry him tomorrow. Does that sound like a compromise to you?"

"Well. . . no," Katie had to acknowledge. "But Rinny, it seems to me that he's done all the compromising so far. Maybe it's just your turn to make the. . . grand gesture."

"I did that! I went to him on my knees! I bled for him in front of his friends! What else can I possibly do?"

"Give up the mission and marry him, Rinny! You can still be a doctor anywhere the Navy goes, and that's really what you want to be. All this. . . space stuff has more to do with your pride than your career. I've listened to you when you talk about your patients. I've listened to you talk about the mission. One's your life blood. The other is just a victory! A chance to prove that by God, Rinny Ness really did it!" Indignantly, she jammed her fists on her hips. "Do you really think one week in space is worth spending the rest of your life without Kyle? Do you?"

Erin had not yet found an answer to that question when she walked into her empty house an hour later, armed with an impromptu gift from her hostess—a book called *Navy Wife: Service Etiquette and Household Management for the New Bride*. Katie insisted that if Erin would just make an effort to accommodate the Navy, the Navy would make an effort to accommodate her.

Erin tossed the book on top of her bookshelf, thinking she should throw it into the trash bin. Once, she could have read it for a good laugh; right now she

anted to forget the Navy—even the sight of a uni-
orm could make her cry. She decided that the day's
nk mail would make better reading.

She read three advertising brochures cover to cover
efore she opened the envelope from United Air Lines,
xpecting to find a summer schedule or a discount
oupon for the Bahamas. But when she recognized the
olored carbon copies that all bore her name, the pulse
 her neck began to pound like a ticking bomb set to
xplode.

It was a round-trip ticket for Washington, D.C.

HE TATUMS LIVED off the base in a comfortable
rownstone with dozens of potted plants on the front
orch. Two children played catch in the street. They
ood aside to let Admiral Tatum drive up to his
ouse, calling out a cheerful greeting, which he quickly
turned.

Erin, sitting primly beside him in the Chevrolet, felt
ke the trip from the airport to the house had taken
vice as long as the flight from Texas, largely because
e'd had to struggle so hard to make conversation.
lthough Kyle's silver-haired father had been gra-
ous, assuring Erin that it was an honor to be en-
usted with his son's "most treasured possession"
hile Kyle was held up at the Pentagon, Erin had real-
ed in their first few minutes together that Kyle had
ld him very little about her. He didn't know she was
 doctor; he didn't know she was an astronaut; he cer-
inly didn't know that she and Kyle had been living
ogether for most of the summer. Not knowing what
yle expected her to say—not even knowing what
avy business could possibly be more important to
im than greeting her at the airport after this hellish
eek of separation—she had remained silent for most

of the ride. Kyle's father probably thought she wasn'
bright enough to have much to say.

She hadn't heard a word from Kyle since she'd re
ceived the ticket, her only link to their uncertain future
In desperation she'd spent last night poring over Katie'
Navy wife handbook in hopes of gleaning enough to ge
her through the weekend without devastating thi:
miracle. . . this one last chance. She had taken time of
work to go shopping and had bankrupted her clothing
budget in an effort to dress the part—modest, feminine
formal. She'd even spent money on white gloves and a
hat, although she suspected—and certainly hoped—
that the handbook might be a little out of date in thi
respect.

Stopping to shag a fly ball on his way to Erin's side o
the car, the admiral reminded Erin of Kyle playing with
the kids on the beach. As he opened her door he reache
down for the evening newspaper in the driveway jus
like any normal man coming home from work. Erin
wasn't sure why his actions surprised her; admirals, sh
decided, were people, too.

"It's been a long time since Kyle and I played ball
and I still don't have a grandson to teach," he told Erin
with a smile. "But it shouldn't be too much longer, I'
wager. I imagine you've noticed that Kyle's crazy abou
kids."

Erin swallowed hard. How long could she keep field
ing his well-meaning questions? Why hadn't Kyle pre
pared her for this? Why wasn't he here to meet her?

"Yes, I've noticed," she said as warmly as she could
"I think his eagerness for a family must stem from hi
own childhood memories. I've never heard a man ex
press more joy and pride in his parents." Not only wa
it the right thing to say, it was true.

Admiral Tatum could not conceal his smile. "We'r

mighty proud of him, too, Miss Ness. Even if the Navy *didn't* think he was a hero, his mother and I still would.''

He picked up her bags and gestured for her to precede him toward the house. She had just enough sense not to offer to help him. To fill the silence and assuage her curiosity she asked instead, ''Why does the Navy think Kyle's a hero? Because he'll be flying the shuttle?''

Kyle's father laughed as though he'd just heard a good joke. Then his eyes caught the baffled look on Erin's face and he stopped in his tracks. He set down both suitcases. ''You're not pulling my leg?'' he asked, clearly stunned.

''No.'' She felt like shrinking into the grass. ''He's a hero to me, of course, but—''

''You've never seen him in uniform? Never asked him about his record? Never heard about his tours of duty in Vietnam?''

''I...I've seen him in uniform,'' she stalled, uncertain how to explain that the only time she'd ever examined his record she'd just been looking for proof that he was divorced. ''I've noticed the ribbons, of course, but I...can't say that I know what they mean.''

And you've never asked? his eyes reproached her. But like his son, he was all Navy, and he remained chivalrously silent.

''Kyle's mother will have dinner waiting, Miss Ness.'' He opened the front door and ushered her inside. ''Please make yourself at home.''

Erin couldn't have felt less at home as she stood in the hallway, eyeing the silver candy dish that Katie's book said was for leaving one's ''card'' while making formal calls in the Navy. She was still stinging from Admiral Tatum's courteously unspoken rebuke.

Her relief was enormous when Betty Tatum swept

into the room, her eyes full of warmth and welcome. She
was wearing a lovely salmon dress with matching scrim-
shaw earrings, a perfect compliment to her soft, aging
skin and natural salt and pepper hair. Without a word
she took both of Erin's hands in hers and squeezed a
heartfelt greeting. Erin wanted to hug her right there
and then. No wonder Kyle loved this woman!

"Betty, this is Erin Ness," Kyle's father introduced
them formally.

Erin's response was enthusiastic and unforced. "I'm
so glad to meet you! Kyle's talked about you so much I
feel like we're already the best of friends."

"So we are, Erin." She smiled in a way that only
another woman would understand. "Why don't you
follow me upstairs and get settled in before dinner? I
planned a meal that we can have right now if you're
hungry or ignore till eight. Maybe you'd rather have a
little time to unwind and clean up. It's up to you."

What a considerate person! Erin thought. No wonder
Kyle was so easy to get along with. "Frankly, I would
sell my soul for a shower and a half hour nap, Mrs.
Tatum, if that could be arranged."

"Consider it done, dear. And please call me Betty."

"Betty," she started again as they climbed up the
stairs. "When exactly are you expecting Kyle?"

"I really don't know, Erin." It was obvious that she
was accustomed to her menfolk coming and going on
unpredictable Navy schedules. "He said not to hold
dinner for him."

They reached the landing and turned into a lovely
blue room full of lace and ruffles and feminine frills. In
the corner stood a sewing table adorned with a lovely
floral voile dress with pins in the hem. Above it hung a
picture gallery of Kyle Tatum—a collage of his life from
infancy to the uniform she now saw him wear.

Suddenly there was no one else in the room but Kyle. His photos filled Erin's heart so completely that she could almost feel the warmth of his hands on her face, the aching relief that a moment in his arms would bring her after so many days of anguish. She had realized that Kyle would not be sleeping with her in his parents' house...but that didn't lessen her desire to be with him. If they were married, of course, everything would be different. *If we were married, he would never have left me. He would have known how much I love him.*

Her grief remained in her heart while her eyes remained on the wall. She could hardly bear to be mesmerized by so many faces of Kyle and be denied the real thing! Slowly she moved toward the collection, her eyes caressing the ten-year-old playing ball with his dad, the sixteen-year-old with his first prom date, the midshipman graduating from the Naval Academy. How innocent he looked! How unfettered by memories of Vivian and Vietnam!

At the center of the frame was a redfaced newborn baby, wispy hair black as coal, eyes blue and bright as he held his arms out to the woman who cradled him in the picture. A warm and beautiful Betty Tatum almost three decades younger. Erin's age.

As she studied the picture, Erin noticed a miniature pair of gold wings on Betty's white blouse. Once she'd laughed at these women's "wings of gold," but now the sight of them creased a tiny fold in her heart. If this was the way a Navy pilot honored his lady, why hadn't Kyle ever once mentioned such a gift to her? Katie's book said that many men gave their wives a pair when they earned their own pilot's wings at Pensacola...in tribute to the women's loyalty and support during the marathon training. Whenever the gift was given, it was always an honor, a public demonstration of respect and affection. Some pilots didn't feel right about giving wings to their wives or girlfriends and never did. *What about me?* Erin asked herself. *Do I have to earn the right to be a Navy pilot's wife?*

"Erin," Betty's voice behind her interrupted very gently. "I'll just move this dress out of here if you'd like to be alone now. Anthony brought up your bags."

Erin turned around quickly, a dazed look on her face. She hadn't even heard him enter the room! "I'm. . . sorry. I was just. . . admiring your pictures of Kyle. I don't. . . have any. He's been gone since Tuesday."

She sounded ridiculous, even to herself. But Kyle's mother seemed to understand. "The waiting gets easier with time, Erin," she sympathized. "And it has its own blessings. A Navy marriage always stays fresh and young."

Erin couldn't explain the real cause of her anguish, so she accepted the other woman's comfort the way it was intended. "This is the longest we've ever been apart. I can't imagine ever getting used to it."

Betty smiled and gestured across the room to a very large portrait of Kyle that hung on the wall above the bed. "This is a more recent picture," she explained. "It was taken just before he went to Houston."

Eagerly Erin approached the dramatic color image of the man she ached for. He looked even more glorious than he did in person! He was wearing his beautiful summer dress whites with his cap and gold braid. But instead of the bars of ribbons she'd so often seen him wear above his left pocket, there were rows of medals about the size of silver dollars, each one hanging from a few inches of ribbon. As usual, his burnished-gold pilot's wings proudly crowned the collection of honors.

But then another medal caught her eye, one she was certain she'd never seen before. It was no bigger than the others in the picture, but the gold star topped with tiny anchors hung from a pale blue ribbon around his neck. Kyle's father's words skated across her mind. *Even if the Navy* didn't *think he was a hero*... She'd never paid attention to Kyle's military honors before, but suddenly the need to know about this one was overwhelming.

But she decided not to ask his mother. It was time to find out from Kyle.

THE EVENING PASSED comfortably enough, with Kyle's charming father responding well to his wife's obvious enthusiasm for Erin. After dinner Erin sat with Betty while she hemmed her dress, and they chatted about quilting and Kyle's mission and life in the Navy. It was obvious that Betty loved the service every bit as much as her husband did and considered it an honor and a privilege to be an admiral's wife. She was worried about his health, though, and had urged him to retire because his father had died of a heart attack at an early age, and she wanted him to slow down before it was too late.

By bedtime Erin was reasonably sure that she'd done nothing cataclysmic with Kyle's parents, in spite of her early faux pas with his dad. But still she could not sleep. Insomnia had been her regular bed partner since Kyle had moved out, so she was still reading in her new pink peignoir set when the knock came on her door.

"Erin? May I come in?"

Despite the low tone, the voice was so familiar that Erin's stomach did a jackknife dive. "Yes, Kyle!" she called back without thinking. She was on her feet and heading for the door even before he nudged it open.

But she stopped cold when she saw his face. He

looked deathly pale, even worse than he had the last time she'd seen him, and not for the first time it occurred to her that his business in Washington must be terribly serious.

His eyes took in her silky robe in a brief glance, then settled on her face. He studied her as hungrily as she had fed upon his pictures just hours ago, yet he kept his distance, standing almost stiffly by the door. "My mother seemed to think you might still be up."

She nodded, paralyzed by the awkward space between them. "Yes. I was waiting for you."

Another layer of emotion swept across his face, but still he kept his distance. "I'm sorry I couldn't meet you at the airport, Rinny. I didn't want you to feel... uncertain of your welcome here." His tone was hushed. "But I've been trapped in a meeting since four o'clock. I had to make waves just to get out long enough to call my dad to ask him to meet you."

"Oh, Kyle," she whispered, aching for both of them. "You must be exhausted. Are you hungry?"

His eyes swept over her body again, then settled on the soft curves of her throat. "Yes," he answered hoarsely.

Suddenly she couldn't stand it anymore. This was no time for cowardice! She swept across the room, pressing her cheek against him as she slipped her arms around his neck. His answering grip was intense; his relief naked as he kissed her throat, then her cheek, then her lips again and again and again.

"I need you, Rinny," he breathed into her hair. "I need you with me tonight."

She clutched him tighter, meeting his brief, hard kisses with a desperate kind of longing. "I'm here, Kyle. Whatever you want... whatever you—"

"Oh, sweetheart! How I wish we could go some

where else! Anywhere that we could be alone!'' He pulled away from her face, then pressed his lips against her hair. His regret was vibrant as he murmured, ''I've already been up here too long.''

She knew he was uncomfortable with his parents being downstairs. She also knew that something in his life was out of kilter...something that had more to do with his mission and the Navy than his relationship with her. Thrusting aside her own needs, she whispered, ''Can you just take a minute to tell me what happened at the Pentagon? Just to get it off your chest?''

She felt him shake his head before he hugged her closer. ''I can't, Rinny, but thanks for asking. I'll talk to my dad after mom goes to bed.''

She tried not to stiffen; in fact she spread her fingers tenderly across his back as she tried to conceal her hurt. But Kyle read it anyway. He pulled back until their eyes met, then gently brushed her cheek with the back of one dark hand. ''I'm not pushing you away, sweetheart. It's not that he's my dad. He's a fellow officer. It's not that I don't want to tell you—it's that I can't.'' Carefully he kissed her again. ''Do you understand?''

''Of course,'' she said, even though she didn't.

He pulled her closer. ''Erin...aren't there times when you...as a doctor...are told things in confidence that you wouldn't feel right about telling me? Not that you don't trust me, not that I'd tell anybody, but...it would violate a professional confidence. Isn't there some kind of doctor-patient ethic there?''

This time she did understand, and felt a lot better. ''Of course, Kyle. There are secrets a person with integrity just has to keep.''

They both tried to smile, and both failed. And then, quite suddenly, Erin began to cry.

''I love you so much, Kyle!'' All the week's stored-up

tears stormed down her face as she pressed against him. "I didn't know anything could hurt like this. I didn't know—"

"Hush, sweetheart," he whispered, his arms pulling her tightly to his chest. "I didn't want to hurt you. You know I never wanted to leave. You just gave me no other choice."

"I know," she sobbed, burying her reddened face against his shoulder. "I know it was my fault. I've had plenty of time to think it over—all of it—and I know why you had to leave me." Abruptly she met his eyes. "But it's going to be different now. I swear it. I'm going to make you so happy that wild horses couldn't pull you away!"

This time he did smile, but too sadly to reassure her. Tenderly he bent to kiss her lips. It was a bittersweet kiss, a kiss of acceptance and forgiveness and. . . goodbye?

"Kyle?" she breathed with new panic in her heart. "When you sent for me I was sure you were going to give me another chance!"

His massive hands embraced her face again, and his sad eyes met hers with love he could not hide. "I am. I'm giving you another chance."

She shook her head, clutching him so tightly he could not escape. "Then why are you looking at me like that? Why do I still feel so afraid?"

Once more he kissed her, as though he could not help himself. Then he cuddled her head against his chin and linked his fingers in her hair. "Rinny, sweetheart, you know that there's nothing I want more in this world than to spend the rest of my life with you. But you—" he seemed to swallow a hard lump "—you still have a lot to learn about loving a Navy pilot."

"I know that, Kyle," she breathed against his chest.

'But I'm ready...I'm *eager* to learn now. I want to understand you. I want to understand what the Navy means to you.'' She wanted to tell him she'd spent hours with Katie's Navy wife handbook, but somehow it seemed too trite. ''I'm ready to give you everything you want. Doesn't that count for something?''

He could have asked her if ''everything'' included marriage and a lifetime spent around the world. But he didn't. Instead he agreed in a husky tone, ''Sure it does, babe. I hope that...we both can learn whatever it takes to make a life together.''

He kissed her again, quickly, fiercely, hinting at the crushing passion he was straining to suppress in his father's house. Then his voice grew hoarse as he tried to pull away. ''But we've got to be honest with each other, Rinny. We've got to face reality.'' He brushed her hair back from her face and met her glistening eyes. ''I sent you that ticket because I couldn't bear to see you in such pain, babe. Because I love you too much to give you up without one hell of a good fight.'' He swallowed hard. ''Not because I think there's a chance in hell that anything's really going to change between us.''

KYLE GREETED HER at breakfast looking just like the picture over her bed—complete with the distant look in his eyes and blue-ribboned medal around his neck. Erin hoped that his new sobriety reflected only the gravity of the occasion. He was courteous but distracted; nothing in his demeanor revealed his feelings for her.

It was not until they approached the dock, chauffeured in a car behind his parents, that Erin gingerly touched the gold star and whispered, ''I've never seen you wear this one before.''

He did not look at her; he seemed to pull away from the curious touch. "The Medal of Honor is only worn for special occasions. There's no miniature to wear over the pocket."

Erin gaped at him. His father had been telling her the truth! "The Medal of Honor? You mean the Congressional Medal of Honor?"

He looked down at her from what seemed like a great height. "That's a civilian misnomer. All Navy awards are originally established by Congress, not just this one. We just call it the Medal of Honor."

She breathed deeply. Ignorant of military tradition as she was, even Erin knew how few noble men had been bestowed with a Medal of Honor! How incredible that he'd never even mentioned it! How lightly she'd taken his career, his devotion to the service! "How...how did you come to earn it, Kyle?" she asked cautiously, not at all certain he would tell her.

"I helped out some folks who were in a bad way."

He threw out the words, defying her to catch them, daring her to ask him more. Before she could, he went on, "As thorough as you are, I imagine you scrutinized my biography in the early days. Didn't you even notice my service record?"

There was no answer to that but the obvious one. Trying not to lose any more ground than necessary, she told him simply, "There are a lot of things I care about now that I didn't really notice in the beginning."

Slowly he turned his eyes back to hers, reading her uncertainty for a long, hurtful time. She knew he still had little hope for their future, and when he looked like that, it was hard for her to be hopeful, either. Somehow she'd have to convince him that she really had changed.

When the car stopped Kyle broke the look, helping her out with quiet chivalry.

Erin had been on a dock before, but never one lined with Navy ships. The gray haze of metal was everywhere, an interior decorator's most boring nightmare. As her eyes swept the saltwater waves before her, Kyle asked, "Did my mother tell you what to expect? Or didn't you care enough to ask?"

Erin could have told him that his mother, bless her heart, had assumed that Kyle had told her everything. Instead she muttered, "I did my own research."

He looked puzzled; he knew she wasn't close to many Navy people. "Leslie?"

"No."

"Jeb?"

When Erin shook her head, Kyle gave up the guessing game. "So what are you expecting? What are you prepared for?"

She felt like a child being drilled before church on Sunday morning. "I know I'll follow you when you're piped aboard, then I'll sit with the other guests "decorously" during the opening remarks and fanfare. Your dad and the officer relieving him will read their orders. After that we'll go below for a reception where I should say nothing, smile a lot, and refrain from any exhibition that could possibly embarrass you or your father. I should be as charming and colorless as possible."

His eyes hardened for just a moment at her last line, but he still looked impressed that she'd done her homework. "You still haven't told me how you came by this sketchy information."

"Do I have to?" she asked, suddenly afraid he really would make her confess that she'd read Katie's book.

"Yes," he said with a tinge of suspicion. "I don't know why you should be afraid to tell me."

"Because I'm embarrassed, that's why!" she burst out, still careful to keep her voice low. "Katie gave me her. . .Navy wife handbook." She closed her eyes and shuddered. "How do you think I knew what to wear? I've never owned a pair of white gloves in my whole life!"

Kyle laughed. Right there on the dock in front of his father's aides and the gathering dignitaries, he laughed out loud. At first she was furious, but then, in the midst of the red blooming on her face, she caught his eye and realized that he was utterly delighted. His dimples punctuated his exultation. Before Erin could imagine what she ought to say next, he suddenly sobered. His eyes swept appreciatively over her subtle mauve summer dress and matching hat. It was obvious that he liked what he saw.

"You did it, Rinny. You've beguiled my folks and you look absolutely perfect for a change-of-command ceremony in the end of July. You really did come through for me."

Erin swallowed hard. New tears were finding their way to her eyes. "I did my best."

He reached out and fingered the hat ribbon that floated in the wind. "You did a super job. I know you'll make me proud today."

Erin's heart was bursting in the face of his praise. It occurred to her that he had never praised her before in quite this fashion. He'd thanked her for spectacular meals and sizzling nights in bed, but he'd never said, "You really came through for me." Probably because this was the first time she ever had. *If I'd known it would feel this good to please you, I would have trotted at heel beside you to every Navy event from here to Hawaii.*

"I love you, Kyle," she whispered.

He nodded just once, then let the hand on the ribbon ide down to her face. "It's going to be all right, Rin-, " he declared with more hope than confidence. Just keep your promises this time, and we can make it ork."

Ignoring the implied threat in his words, Erin nodded gerly. "Count on it, Commander."

He stroked her cheek one more time, then turned hen his father called him from farther down the dock. Time for us to go on board, babe. Follow me."

She did follow him...with the grace of a beached al. It would have been fun climbing down into a otorboat dressed in a swimsuit on a sunny day. But in r current apparel, it was almost impossible to main- in a sense of balance, let alone dignity.

There was a healthy breeze on the ocean—just ough to whip the ribbons of her hat in her face as they pproached the great gray monolith where the cere- ony would take place. Several flags flapped in greet- g from the mast, but Erin only recognized the red, hite and blue. Belatedly she realized that she'd failed study the different kinds of ships in a Navy fleet. rely Navy wives were conversant with all of these ips and their purposes! Kyle most likely spent his time aircraft carriers, the sea-based landing strips for jets. ut Erin wasn't even sure what a carrier looked like— ey could be boarding one for all she knew!

Even from a distance she could tell that dramatic eparations were already in effect. Lines of white- iformed men were clearly visible from the dock. A oup of riflemen waited on one side of the deck while a ilitary band played on the other, filling the air with rains of John Philip Sousa. Erin followed Kyle onto e deck accompanied by the shrill piping sound of the boatswain's whistle, her heels threatening to fall between the wooden slats on the gangplank. Even Kyle's steadying hand on her arm didn't seem to help.

There was a moment of stillness while he exchanged salutes with several men. She couldn't tell whether they stood in awe of his rank or the prestigious Medal of Honor around his neck, but it was obvious that they greeted him with high respect. A new kind of feeling touched Erin's heart...an almost possessive kind of pride. *This* was her man. He had chosen her above all others. Her chin rose just a little as she took her place by his side.

After that she felt as though she was wandering through a maze. Chairs seemed to fill up every spare nook and cranny of the deck that was not already claimed by an elephantine gun or a vent spewing hot air from a below-deck kitchen. A trail of purple velvet ropes on brass poles did little to help steer them to their seats, and after wobbling beside Kyle on this moving obstacle course, Erin was more than happy to lower herself into a stationary object.

Beside her, Kyle sat tall and looked straight ahead.

"This is my place, Rinny," he announced in a voice so low she had to strain to hear him. "I'm only on loan to NASA."

Erin studied the ships in the harbor and the wharf that seemed so very far away. She did not know what to say.

"It's not always like this at sea," he continued, his eyes focused on the parade of flags before him. "Sun in the sky and sunbeams in everybody's heart. Sometimes it's night in a storm. Sometimes the ocean goes berserk and you can't find the deck. You can't bring the jet down. Sometimes you can't even bring the plane back if you've been shot down. Over land. Over sea."

She wanted to stop him, but she knew he needed to
ll her about life at war, and possibly her life, too...a
ality they'd both tried to run away from for far too
ng.

"And all the time, your wife is waiting. For days,
r weeks...for months sometimes. She can be state-
de or stuck in some unappetizing little hole on the
earest base. She can be pregnant or sick or just lonely
hell, and it won't make any difference. You have to
where your orders send you. You don't whimper,
ou don't fight back. You save your fury for the
nemy. If there's no enemy, you stay ready. If the
avy's not ready, this country's in trouble. Your wife,
ur children, your parents, your president...
veryone you know, everyone you care about, is
ulnerable. Every civilian in the country is depending
n you, whether he has enough sense to know it or
ot." His voice faded away, but his eyes remained
ained on the mast. "That's why you ask your wife to
llow you. That's why you ask her to sit and wait.
hat's why you ask her to understand that the Navy
as to come first."

Erin's first instinct was to dive overboard and swim
l the way to Houston in her hat and gloves. She knew
e needed to test her, needed to make her accept this
art of his life, but did he have to hit so hard? *You
ade a decision, Erin,* she told herself sternly. *You
romised to love him. You promised to understand.*

Hoping it was not a breach of shipboard etiquette to
uch one's beloved, she slid her gloved hand over
yle's fingers, squeezing them just once in silent af-
rmation. Then she straightened her hat with dignity
d looked straight ahead as the ceremony began.

CHAPTER THIRTEEN

THE NEXT WEEK was very hard on Erin. She desperately wanted to be with Kyle, but he'd had to stay on in Washington after she left. Despite the quiet healing that had begun to take place over the weekend, he had kissed her goodbye at the airport and nonchalantly promised to call her for a date when he got back to Houston. So much for her vibrant hope that he was ready to move back home!

He didn't call until Thursday night, his voice a mask of indifference—or perhaps exhaustion—as he asked her out as formally as though it would be their first date. It was, in fact, the third time in two years that he'd invited her to spend a Friday evening on board the *Obsession*. This time she said yes.

It occurred to Erin that if Kyle hadn't convinced her to give up doctoring for the time being, her duty schedule would have precluded the cruise. She really missed the hospital—the miracle of surgery and the camaraderie of the staff—yet she knew that Kyle had perceived her situation quite well. NASA had chosen her because she was a surgeon, yet as long as she was an astronaut, surgery would have to take a back seat.

So would Kyle. That was the problem; that was why they were going on a formal date tonight instead of making love in her pool after he came home from work. Determined to recapture his passion, Erin spent over an hour getting ready for the evening.

She started with a pale blue camisole and half slip
vered by a lilac floral skirt-and-blouse set that
orted tiny pearl buttons from her cleavage to her
ees. It was simply too hot to wear a bra, let alone
lons, but Erin hoped the sheer fabric conveyed a
nse of casual elegance. Tucking a yellow rose bud in
r hair, she wore a little more makeup than usual just
make sure Kyle would know she'd dressed up for
m.

He arrived precisely at seven, as she had expected,
aring gray cotton trousers and a royal-blue shirt,
ich exactly matched his eyes. He looked so beautiful
e could hardly resist touching him, but so sad and
stant that she forced her hands against her sides. A
onth ago she would have attributed his reticence to
nsion or fatigue, but now she couldn't be sure.

"Hi," she said simply, facing him on the front
rch. She wanted to add "darling" but the word
uldn't come. "You want to come in for a drink
fore we go?"

He shook his head. "We don't have time."

Unable to restrain herself, she asked more gently,
Do we have time for a hello kiss? It's been a week."

This time his eyes met hers, anticipation lurking
hind the courteous restraint. "We'll catch up on our
ssing later, Erin. Let's get out to the boat."

He didn't say much as they drove to the shore.
sually they talked about NASA, a subject which
emed to be off limits at the moment, even though
in's mission was only ten days away and Kyle's was
st a few months later. She wondered what else they
uld safely discuss.

"Did you get to spend much more time with your
rents, Kyle?"

"A little. I went fishing with my dad."

"That's nice," she murmured, wondering why she'd never heard him mention fishing before. "I . . . I really enjoyed your parents, Kyle."

He nodded. "I think they enjoyed you, too. My mother got the book you sent her. She was cutting up little blue squares and triangles when I left."

"She's making a quilt for the guest room?" Erin was delighted.

"Yep. Said to tell you it was the pattern you suggested. Rocky Road to somewhere."

"Kansas? Oklahoma?"

"Take your pick. I know it wasn't Texas." Very slowly he smiled. It was the most beautiful smile she'd ever seen. Her own answering grin expressed her delight. Without warning he pulled over to the edge of the road.

"What's wrong?"

"I forgot something."

"What?"

Leaving the engine running, he turned in the seat, put his hands on her shoulders, and pulled her as close as their positions allowed. "I forgot to tell you how much I missed you, Rinny."

Before she could answer he had claimed her lips, searing her with sweet promise that filled her with instant hunger and renewed hope. It was not a gentle kiss, the hello kiss she'd so casually asked for. It was a bedroom kiss, a meet-me-later kiss, that started outside her mouth and ended deep within it, branding the warm recesses of her sweetness with his perennial fire. She slid her hands around his waist, then instinctively pressed lower until she cupped his round bottom with her right hand.

"Sure you don't want to go back home?" she asked provocatively.

He shook his head, slid back to his seat, and eased the Saab back into traffic. "Later, Rinny. I've planned this evening with great care. We are not going to spend it making love at your house."

She didn't like the way he referred to "her house" but she was so delighted with the warmth of his kiss that she refused to be offended. He reached for her hand as soon as he was safely on the highway, and she snuggled as close to him as she dared.

The mood remained unbroken as they reached the boat. The evening breeze was delightfully refreshing; the fresh lobster and prawns absolutely scrumptious. After dinner they strolled to the edge of the deck and watched the sun go down as the boat rocked in the gentle waves.

"I guess you're always stationed near the ocean, aren't you, Kyle?"

"Yes, ma'am," he answered, using the formal courtesy she hadn't heard much in their recent private months. "And I'm glad. No matter how I feel, the sea always soothes me."

Erin nodded. "That's how I feel about my pool."

As if the memory of the pool triggered something deep within him, Kyle rested his hand against the small of her back and nuzzled her hair. Without speaking, he let his thumb trace and retrace the last three vertebrae before his palm moved slowly up her back. The effect was paralytic, electrifying. Erin felt like a year had passed since the last time he'd touched her. She wanted to press herself against him, to beg for a kiss in spite of the presence of the others on board. But Kyle's touch remained casual. If he knew what he was doing to her he gave no sign.

But as they neared the shore thirty minutes later, Kyle breathed into her hair, "Unless you're in a hurry to get home, I have a private spot in mind where we could enjoy a little champagne and music.''

Champagne and music sounded nice, but home alone with Kyle sounded nicer. Remembering his earlier resistance to her house, Erin forced herself to answer, ''That sounds lovely, Kyle. I don't care where we go as long as we're together.''

He kissed her temple. ''I want you to practice that line a dozen times a day until it spills out by accident the next time I ask you to marry me.'' As if to emphasize his point, he swept her hair aside and kissed the nape of her neck. She shivered and huddled closer, craving his touch, desperately hoping that he wouldn't ask her to marry him at a moment when she'd be willing to say anything at all to please him. She was still walking along the top of a fence, looking down at Kyle on one side and NASA on the other. She could fall to either side and she would be leaving half of her loyalty behind.

By the time they reached the shore it was nearly dark and starting to cool. They drove for several minutes before Erin realized that they were heading away from the nearest commercial area. ''Kyle,'' she finally asked him, ''where are we going?''

''We are going,'' he announced with quiet pride, ''to the loveliest private beach house in all of Heron Bay. Which, coincidentally, I have taken the liberty of renting for the entire weekend, assuming you have no objections.''

It was a shame the night was too dark for him to see her euphoric smile. ''I have no objections, Commander.''

''Good. Then I won't have to move to plan two.''

''Which is?''

''Rope and hog-tie you and throw you over my shoulder.''

"Come now! Have I ever been that hard to persuade?"

"Depends on the issue," he answered quietly.

Damn. I wish he'd stop doing that, she thought. *One minute he's my old Kyle, then he's some distant stranger.* Determined to make this weekend work out for the two of them, she asked quietly, "How did you manage to arrange this all the way from Washington?"

"Roger did it for me."

"Roger knew and he didn't tell me?" She was amazed. "I've seen him almost every day this week!" She didn't add that she'd noticed that Roger had been getting more and more depressed the closer it came for 1-J to launch.

"Think of it as a Christmas present, Erin. It was a secret he kept for your own good."

Kyle's mood seemed to change as they reached the beach house. Erin couldn't really put her finger on it, but it was as if it were their first date and he was trying to impress her. Proudly he led her through the modern kitchen, the cathedral-ceilinged living room, the sun deck, which practically sat on the water, and last of all, the ultramodern bedroom, complete with a water bed and a furry bedspread of geometric stripes. In lieu of a headboard, an enormous photomural of a single red rose occupied one wall.

It couldn't have looked any less like Erin's own old-fashioned cottage, yet she liked it. The color scheme was black and white with red accents, chic and striking. Huge vases of fresh-cut flowers adorned every room in the house—unmistakably the touch of Kyle Tatum. He plucked out the wilted rose bud from her hair and replaced it with a fresh cornflower about the shade of her dress. His eyes were warm, playful, promising, but still he did not kiss her.

"What do you think?" he asked with a smug smile as he poured her champagne.

"Stunning. Really. The view of the ocean is spectacular."

"My sentiments exactly. If it's cool enough for you out there now, could we go sit on the sun deck?"

"Sure. I'd like to feel the breeze."

She followed him outside, sipping her champagne very slowly. Kyle settled down on a cushioned redwood chaise lounge and motioned for her to take the one next to him. The sea breeze lifted her hair and seemed the perfect foil to the soft strains of Tommy Dorsey on the stereo. It took her a moment to place the music; then she remembered the first night they'd danced on the pier. He caught her eye, then stood up and held out his hand.

Wordlessly she joined him as they danced outside. There was not a soul for a thousand miles, or so it seemed to Erin. Cautiously she laid her head on his shoulder. He pulled her closer.

"Do you remember the first time we ever danced together, Erin?"

"Perfectly."

"We weren't alone."

"No."

"It drove you crazy."

"Yes."

He pressed her against his chest as his lips nibbled at her hair. "You wanted me to touch your breasts," he whispered, leaving her hand against his shoulder as he caressed her throat. "Would you like me to do that now?"

White heat seared her. "Yes." Her voice was hoarse.

Erin's nipples rose in anticipation, but Kyle made

er wait. Ever so slowly he fondled the ivory skin above
er neckline, edging lower at a pace she could hardly
ear. When his fingertips creased the fabric she pressed
er mouth against his shirt; when they circled her breast
he crushed in closer; when they finally closed over the
rst nipple she cried out in need. With his other hand he
ently massaged the other side, then captured both
enters between his thumbs and palms, and she pressed
o close against him that the dancing stopped.

"Do you know," he whispered against her throat,
what I wanted to do that night while we danced?"

She shook her head...beyond speech, beyond
hought.

"I wanted to slide my fingers up your hips...under
hat white gauze skirt...and hold your perfect bottom
the palms of my hands."

The effect of his words was electric; she could almost
eel his hands against her naked skin.

"Would you like me to do that now?"

She put both arms around his neck, nodding fever-
hly as his hands abandoned her breasts, tucking under
er back waistband to plunge under her panties and lay
ege to her bare skin. At the same time his mouth took
ers fiercely, declaring in indelible terms that whatever
ad passed between them in these past hurtful days,
onight she would be his lady again. She clung to him
indly, incredulous that she had survived more than a
eek without his touch.

His mouth left hers, then found her throat. His hands
id forward, still beneath her clothes, teasing her waist
ad the softness below as he undid the top button of her
kirt. "These pearly buttons are beautiful to look at,"
e breathed against the bare upper curve of her breasts,
but I think they're getting in the way."

Impatiently she waited while he undid the buttons

and deliberately caressed the portion of her anatomy that lay beneath them. When her skirt was open to her thighs, he let it fall on the redwood deck. Abruptly he slid his hands back down her hips, ostensibly to pull her away from the floored skirt but actually to press her hungry body intimately against his pelvis. His powerful male strength enticed her, and her arms slid down his back to press him even closer.

"I think these buttons are in the way, too," he whispered, kissing the space between her breasts. A little more quickly he unbuttoned her blouse, the heels of his hands rubbing her breasts as his fingers freed each tiny button from its hole.

"I wanted to do this when we were dancing," he confessed against her ear, then followed his words with a lazy circle of tongue. "I wanted to take everything off. . . right then and there."

As if to make sure she understood, he swept off her half slip and panties, dropping to his knees to slip them off her feet. He was so close she could feel his hair between her thighs, then his hands as he retraced his path up to her waist. Without comment he slid his fingers under her camisole, bracing each throbbing breast. She swayed against him, naked except for the lingerie top, aching for completion.

"Kyle," she moaned against him. "Kyle, I—"

"Undress me, Erin." His voice was quiet but firm. He knew it was an order she would eagerly carry out. Quickly she battled with his own buttons, her fingers unbelievably clumsy with the simple task. His continuing tactile onslaught on her breasts didn't help. When he lifted the camisole to capture one nipple in his mouth, she cried out sharply, too deeply aroused to continue undressing him.

"If you're going to stop, so will I," he warned her.

Desperately she reached for his belt, struggling to ⊃en his trousers and slide them off. She pushed him ⊾ck on the chaise lounge, and instantly his hands slid ⊃wn the front of her body. One came to rest between ⊱r legs, slowly searching out new secrets.

"Oh, Kyle," she moaned again, tugging off his ⊾oes. His hands still fondled her as she reached for his ⁻iefs, but as soon as he was free of clothing he stood ⊃ abruptly, then helped her to her feet. He pulled her ⦙ close as he could without entering her body, then ⁻ted the camisole until she pressed naked against him. ⥾e waited while his hands slid up to her face, tender-⊱ss underneath the searing hunger. He bent to kiss ⦙r, then whispered against her mouth, "I love you, ⥾nny Ness. That's never going to change."

She kissed him back, too moved to speak. For an in-⊾ant he stood there, watching her, his hands still on ⊱r face. Then he kissed her again, with fiery new ⥾nger, and she gave up the last vestiges of restraint. ⥾ mutual consent they lowered themselves to the ⦙arest cushion as one unit. He entered her before she ⥾en had time to stretch out flat, and even that was too ⥾g a wait for Erin. She wrapped her legs around his ⦙d slipped her hands down over his buttocks, knead-⥾g them with wild hunger and urgent command. She ⦙led out his name as he thundered inside her, lifting ⊱r with him to love's highest peak.

⥾ TUESDAY MORNING the glow in Erin's heart had not ⊱t started to subside. Not even the hurricane warnings ⥾at had canceled her day of zero-gravity jet training ⦙uld diminish her celestial energy. The weekend with ⥾le had been everything she could possibly have ⦙ped for...except for one thing. He had made love ⦙ her, charmed her and pampered her for two glori-

ous days, but on Sunday he had picked up the suitcas
of his clothes Erin had packed at his request, then gon
back to the base to spend the night. She had bee
shocked at the gentle disclaimers between his kisses a
the door. Despite his tenderness and immutable lov
for her, he would not set foot inside her house.

She was in conference with Paul and Mark the nex
time she saw him. He knocked on her door and stuc
his head in, then stopped cold when he realized she wa
not alone.

"Sorry to disturb you, Erin. I'll get back to yo
later."

"No problem, Kyle," she gushed, unable to mas
the thousand-watt smile just the sight of him induced
Glancing at the two men who were waiting, she decid
ed that a moment with Kyle was worth their possibl
disapproval. "Excuse me just a moment, guys."

They nodded patiently while Erin slipped out of th
room behind him. He was wearing his dress whites to
day—something he seemed to be doing a lot more o
lately—and he looked as perfect as she'd ever see
him. Somehow knowing that the gold-and-blue ribbo
bar was the Air Medal and the red-and-white one wa
the Silver Star made the uniform seem much more spe
cial to her; she'd memorized half of his medals alread
and was working on the rest. Over the weekend he'
even told her the story of how he'd gotten each one.

But the smile on Kyle's face was the most specia
sight of all. It seemed to spell her name.

"Rinny," he whispered. His eyes brushed back he
hair, kissed her beneath the ear, slid across the modes
neckline of her Oxford blouse.

"Me, too," she answered simply, the magic betwee
them too forceful for mere words.

He grinned at her eagerness. "I was going to ca

ou about Saturday," he admitted. "I'd like to take
ou to see an outdoor production of *A Midsummer
ight's Dream* in Hermann Park if the hurricane has
me and gone by then. But I guess I couldn't pass up
chance to see you sooner, no matter how transparent
is."

"Yes," she whispered from a place deep in her
roat.

He chuckled so that only she could hear. "Yes to
hich question? The show or the excuse?"

"Both," she admitted, "and also to the one you
n't ask me here in the hallway."

A force of primal desire swept between them as they
ood two feet apart in public view. "Don't do this to
e, Rinny," he breathed. "I've got a conference in
lf an hour that won't give me any second chances."

"Then come see me when you're done." In a gesture
o subtle for anyone watching to understand, she un-
d the top button of her modest pink blouse. Al-
ough the action revealed almost nothing, the tension
Kyle seemed to soar.

"I'll be busy all day, babe." He seemed to be short
breath.

"Then come over tonight. I'll be home." Too late
e remembered his adamancy about her house, the
x where he seemed to be storing all his bad mem-
ies. Hurriedly she tacked on, "Or I can meet you
mewhere else. On the base...a hotel... anywhere,
st..." She stopped, embarrassed, knowing she was
ead of him again. He wanted her, but he wanted her
his own terms.

She looked at the floor, straining for control. In
w motion Kyle took one step toward her; the back
his hand brushed her temple in a gesture of tender-
ss that called tears to her eyes.

"When I break loose here I'll give you a call, sweet
heart. Maybe we can meet somewhere if it's not too
late."

Her eyes met his swiftly. "I don't care how late
it is. I miss you so much, Kyle. I know you don'
want to come home yet but if there's any other way
we can be together—any way at all—just tell me. I'
do it."

He took a step back and watched her face, gauging
the depth of her words. She hadn't meant to say "any
way at all." He might misunderstand. But at the mo
ment she didn't care. She longed for his touch, hi
smile, his morning beard tickling her stomach. What
ever point he was trying to prove surely he'd already
made! Two weeks had passed since he'd moved out o
her house. It already seemed like two years.

"Are you still hurting, Rinny?" he asked unex
pectedly. "Are you still afraid?"

There weren't too many answers to a question like
that, and none of them were safe. Short on options
Erin told him the truth. "Of course I'm still afraid
Until last weekend I couldn't even think straight.
know I'm still on trial and you still think I'm going t
let you down. How can I possibly not be afraid?"

His eyes grew very dark, as they did whenever hi
thoughts were grave. Now he studied her with infinit
care. Suddenly she saw sorrow in his face that was no
just a reflection of her own; suddenly she knew tha
Kyle was hurting, too, despite the proud distance he'
kept between them.

"Rinny, I've had an awful lot on my mind the las
few weeks. It ought to all come to a head today. May
be then it will be easier for me to...swallow a bit o
my pilot's pride with you."

Erin ached so much she could hardly speak. "B

roud if you want to. Be angry. Be anything you want,
Kyle, just don't push me away.''

His eyes swept over the tiny bit of skin she'd exposed
or him, new fire latent in his glance. ''Do I look like a
man who's trying to escape?''

She shook her head. He looked like a man who was
bout to forget his values, his priorities. . . and his con-
erence. Abruptly Erin remembered the last time a hall-
ay rendezvous between them had interfered with one
f Kyle's military meetings at NASA. Stiffly she forced
erself to remember what was best for him.

''You're due upstairs, Commander. I'll see you
aturday for sure—storm or no storm—and whenever
ou can fit me in before that.'' On some other day she
ould have laughed at her own words. It had always
een Kyle who'd had to wait until she could fit him in.

But Kyle wasn't laughing. His eyes were on her face in
different kind of way. ''Rinny, if this meeting—'' He
topped, studying her with new restraint. ''If I seem. . . a
ttle distant with you tonight, don't. . . don't think I'm
ushing you away, all right? Because no matter what
appens this morning. . .'' He sighed with a grave uncer-
ainty that was new to him. ''Frankly, babe, I don't think
've ever needed you more than I do right now.''

A thousand questions washed into her mind, and
Erin suddenly realized she should have asked them a
ong time ago. In her own selfish worries she had missed
omething crucial. He hadn't come to ask her for a
ate! He'd come to say goodbye before he marched into
attle! But where was the war? What was the problem?
he studied his beautiful face, full of well-concealed
orry and ill-concealed desire, and said goodbye the
nly way she could.

''My arms will be open,'' she promised him. ''No
atter what. No matter when. I'll be waiting.''

BY MIDAFTERNOON the black clouds hovering over the
Gulf of Mexico matched the sense of dread in Erin's
heart. A voice deep within her, in the part of her heart
where only Kyle lived, kept whispering hints that
something was terribly wrong.

At exactly 3:14 P.M. Jeb Henson confirmed it.

"Whatever you're doing can wait," he announced
gruffly to the technician beside her as he marched into
the equipment area where she was having a final check
on her flight clothes. "I need to see Dr. Ness alone."

He hadn't called her Dr. Ness in months, even with
the cold shoulder he'd given her in her first few weeks
on the job. They'd been getting along so much better
lately—even after Kyle had moved out—that she
couldn't believe Jeb's barely restrained anger was di-
rected at her. A spike of panic that had nothing to do
with the mission pierced her chest as he led her into the
nearest private room and shut the door.

"Jeb—"

"Erin, you've given me the impression that Kyle
means a great deal to you. Do you have any idea what
you mean to him?"

Erin stared at him blankly. "I . . . I think I'm important to him, Jeb, but—"

"There's his family, the Navy and there's you, lady,
and I don't think he even knows what order they come
in any more. But I think I can guess where he'll be
heading tonight. Straight to you. And if you blow it
this time, Erin . . . well, you already know I think that
to do so might be all for the best. But right now I've
got a buddy in trouble, and because of you he's not going to come to me, or to any of us who might understand. When he lands in this storm—"

"He's flying? With a hurricane coming in?" Terror
snaked down her back. Disbelief shook her heart.

"Of course he's flying! That's what pilots do, especially when they're so damned angry they can't think straight. And right now—"

"Jeb, for God's sake tell me what's going on! We parted very well this morning. He was uneasy about a meeting but *I* didn't upset him! I swear to you—"

"Don't be a fool!" His anger was fully unleashed now. "Do you think you're the only problem he's got in his life? He's going to fall facedown on your doorstep tonight, Erin, and if you're not going to be there for him I'll wring your neck."

Breathless, Erin stared at Jeb, objective mission commander, Kyle's loyal friend. Nothing ever seemed to shake his calm, but he was furious now, incensed, and Erin still had no idea why. With enormous self-control and surface calm she told him, "I'd do anything in the world for Kyle, Jeb. Just tell me what's wrong."

Jeb slumped down on a wooden chair and faced her squarely, his anger reshaped as genuine concern for his friend. "Erin—I can't reveal all the details. But the bottom line is that the Russians and the White House have been tangling over a new arms agreement for months. Somehow Kyle's mission got tossed in as a bargaining chip. The Russians flatly refuse to continue negotiations as long as we're experimenting with an antiballistic satellite system." He shook his head, disbelief and grief for Kyle still naked on his face. "The bald truth, Erin, is that Kyle's mission has just been scrubbed."

Scrubbed. The word clattered in her brain all evening. It was a word that could also mean things got cleaner, yet today it meant that everything in her life and Kyle's would be muddied up. It would be hard for anybody to withstand a scrubbed mission at this late date. Look at poor Roger! But with Kyle it was so much more complicated, because of the way he felt about serving the Navy, because of the way he felt about making his father proud and...because of the way he felt about her.

"Maybe I'll be able to swallow a bit more of my pilot's pride," he'd suggested just that morning. Had he known this was coming? Feared it...guessed it, certainly. But he hadn't shared it with her, even when she'd made an attempt at his parents' house to find out what was going on. Was it really too classified to share? Or did he just feel that she'd offered him too little...too late?

Jeb thought Kyle would come to her house tonight, but Erin wasn't at all sure. With such a broadside hit to his pride, and his previous refusal to enter her house, it seemed as though almost anywhere might be preferable as a place to lick his wounds.

Hours and hours passed without a word. Before the meeting, Kyle had implied he might be late, yet they had never really discussed what "late" might be. He'd wanted to meet her somewhere...but he was too courteous to ask her to go out in the middle of the night.

By midnight Erin had cleaned and shined the house to perfection, baked two batches of cookies and a pie. She'd dipped in the pool half a dozen times to calm down, but stayed tense listening for the phone. She was too anxious to sleep and too exhausted from the day's stress not to lie down.

Is this what he meant when he gave me that lecture on the ship? she asked herself, staring at the black storm outside her window, yearning to know if Kyle was still in the air or safely on the ground. *Is this wha*

*'s like for a Navy wife like Katie or Sarah? To wait
while her husband is in combat—at night in a storm—
never knowing when he'll come home,* if he'll come
home, how he'll feel when he gets there. . . .

"I can't spend a lifetime like this," she moaned
against her hands. "I'll be lucky to survive just this
one night. And the war is only going on inside him."

Swiftly it occurred to Erin that she was being selfish.
What the scrubbed mission did to their relationship—
to *her* feelings—was simply not important at the moment. This wasn't the time to worry about a future
that waited some four years down the road! Kyle—just
Kyle—must fill her heart and her concern tonight.
Home isn't where you go, he'd told her once. *It's who
you've got waiting. . . .*

With sudden pristine clarity Erin knew that she was
still "home" to Kyle Tatum. She must assume that he
would come to her; she must be ready when he did.

CHAPTER FOURTEEN

IT WAS AFTER MIDNIGHT when Kyle pulled up to the house in his Saab, but there was a light on in every room. A message of welcome? Maybe. But just as likely a sign that Erin was working late. Kyle sighed. What a redundant notion. Erin wasn't Erin if she wasn't working late.

Did she know what had happened to his life today? Did she care? This morning she'd been eager to see him, the magic between them as potent as ever. He'd tried to pretend it could be enough. But this evening he could not pretend. He needed a friend, his best friend, the other half of his own heart. He could not tell her what he needed. Not tonight. She either understood him at last or she never would.

He took his key out as he crunched over the gravel toward the front door. *Just this once, Rinny,* he prayed silently. *Don't let me down.*

The door opened smoothly, as though it had been waiting for him. He stared at the empty living room, remarkably clean and bare of Erin's books and papers. The night he'd walked out on her he'd promised himself that he would not return to this magical, hurtful place until Erin had changed or her mission had ended. Tonight he wasn't at all sure that he'd kept his promise. He just knew that he couldn't bear to hurt her any more, and he needed her so badly that the only thing that could keep him from her love was if Erin herself turned him away.

Without hesitation he made his way to the bedroom. The door was open and a tiny night-light cast a warm glow on the bed.

She was not reading. Her eyes were on him, waiting, as he entered the room. She looked even more beautiful than he remembered; her eyes were full of love and leftover fear. A single sheet covered her to the waist; her upper half was barely clad with some sort of blue feminine lacy thing. As he watched her nipples through the wispy fabric, he was swept by a sudden urge to bury his face in the lace, to hold her and weep, to make love to her without a word. Would she understand? Just this once, would she understand what was tearing him apart? She did not speak as he stood at the doorway, struggling for a way to reach her.

"How would you feel about. . .having me spend the night here?" he asked almost awkwardly.

She tried to smile. "That would be nice."

He swallowed, aching to touch her breasts. "How about tomorrow night, too?"

"That would be even nicer." She worked harder for the smile this time, but she still couldn't hide her apprehension. The wind slapped the window, reminding them both of the hurricane he'd just piloted through. She swept a lock of hair out of her face, and he longed to kiss the patch of throat the move left bare.

"How about. . ." He battled for speech, his eyes begging her to understand. "How about the night after that?"

Suddenly she tossed aside the sheet, the high-cut teddy revealing her beautiful legs as she literally ran to embrace him. She buried her face against his neck as they clutched each other, her own grip even mightier than his. He took her face in his hands and kissed her, hard, his frustration still unchecked after hours in the air. She did not flinch. She met him kiss for kiss, absorbed his anger, clinging to him as he pulled her close.

Abruptly the anger died. He slumped against the door frame, holding her against his heart. His hands kneaded the back of her head; she strapped herself to his chest so tightly that he felt as though they were one person. Her body seemed to drain away his anguish. The relief was intense.

They stood that way for several minutes before she whispered, "Do you know what I'd like to do, Kyle?"

He didn't answer. Whatever it was, he was sure he didn't want to do it. He didn't want to go swimming, or be assuaged with food, or listen to another lecture on how lucky he was to serve in the Navy and know that none of this was his fault and he would get another mission in two or three years if he didn't get new orders that would take him away from Houston. He didn't want to be reassured that he hadn't really let down his father and his grandfather and the son he'd never have if he persisted in the folly of loving Erin Ness. He just wanted her to hold him, to ease the pain, to smother him with adulation.

"I'd like to give you a back rub, darling," she whispered, the tender word alone a panacea for his ills. "Would you trust yourself in my hands?"

He hugged her so tightly he thought he might crush her, but she didn't demur. *It's going to work, Erin.* His heart started to hope. *Maybe, just maybe, we can pull this off after all.*

"I have always had the greatest of faith in your hands, Dr. Ness," he whispered, kissing the tiny hollow below her ear.

"Then follow me."

She led him to the bed and undressed him in a loving but almost platonic fashion. She could not have looked

exier in the lacy lingerie she was wearing, yet he knew
e was not yet ready to touch her. Too much had hap-
ened that had to be repaired.

"Roll over. Trust me. Relax."

She straddled his back with her weight on her knees,
olling his shoulders in great circles. Then she clenched
er knuckles into tiny marbles of delight. She stretched
ut his arms and rubbed the knotted muscles; she freed
he tension in his neck. She did not worry him with
enseless chatter. Ever so slowly she moved down his
pine, easing the lumps and bumps of this horrible day
nd the last two agonizing weeks. Then without hesita-
ion she moved on below the base of his spine, spread-
ng out over his buttocks and down to his thighs.

The change in mood was subtle, artful, and it felt
ery good. A grin found its way to his face. . .his first
mile since he'd seen her that morning. "I thought you
romised to relax me, Doctor," he teased her. "In
which case you're doing a lousy job."

Erin chuckled from somewhere near the base of his
pine. "I promised to make you feel good. That's not
lways the same thing."

"Touché."

She laughed and made a play on his words. "Turn
ver and I will."

He laughed with her and did as she commanded. She
erched on his chest this time, the lace leaving most of
er thighs exposed as she rubbed the front of his shoul-
ers. She leaned down to kiss him very gently. It was
ot a kiss that begged for satisfaction, or a perfunc-
ory goodbye-dear-I'll-see-you-later kiss. It was a kiss
hat ached to ease his hurting, a kiss that lingered be-
ween them for a long moment of silent union.

Erin retraced her trail down the front of his body,
ut this time she made no pretense of massage. By the

time she reached his proud statement of desire, his body was fully aroused and his heart more fully at peace than he would have believed possible just moments ago. He reached out for her face in a tender, grateful touch, then let his knuckles slide down the front of her lace. Slipping his hand inside the sheer blue fabric, he lightly netted one of her breasts with his fingertips. As he watched her face change from the giver to the receiver, she rubbed him even more forcefully.

"You're cheating," she whispered, her smile one of pure Texas sunshine. "I'm trying to do this without any distractions."

"Are you implying—" he flicked her nipple "—that these little tiny strokes—" he tugged it gently toward his mouth "—could even hope to attract your notice when you're working so hard?"

He waited for the satisfying sound of her moan as he teased her gently to new arousal. He pulled her flat on his chest, pushing the fabric aside as his tongue lapped the tip of her breast repeatedly. He slid his hands down to her hips—over the fabric and then beneath it—and pressed her hard against him. When she began to move in his rhythm, he knew the time had come.

"Give me a hint, babe," he breathed deeply into the rich curves of her breasts. "How does this thing come off?"

She laughed, guiding his hands to the snaps between her legs. "It's called a teddy. I bought it just for you. It's supposed to be the height of glamour."

"It's glamorous, sweetheart, and I've enjoyed the show. But right now I'd rather have my teddy bare."

They laughed together at his pun, Erin's eager hands helping his to free her of the lace and satin. When she was naked he rolled on his side to tuck her beneath him, his eyes never leaving her lovely face.

There was joy there, but also a trace of pain that
ould take a long time to erase. He knew she'd been
ven more frightened by the thought of losing him to
ne storm than she'd been at losing him through her
wn folly. He'd never forget the anguish he'd put her
nrough the last few weeks; the tears in her eyes when
ne'd crawled for him in front of his friends, the fear
n her voice when he'd first seen her at his parents'
ouse. Even now she wasn't sure why he had come or
ow long he would stay. But she had put every one of
er feelings on hold for him tonight, given herself ut-
erly to meeting his needs.

Erin reached up to trace the firm bones of his face as
to reclaim what had once been hers. She lifted her
ace for a kiss, and he gave her one that merged his
ain with her fears, forging a bond of greater love than
ney had ever shared before. Home at last, he joined
er body with his own, pouring out his lingering
nguish into the deepest wells of her love for him.

Kyle did not release her before he fell asleep, and he
new she would cradle him all night long.

RIN WOKE UP very late the next morning, sweetly
angled in Kyle's loving arms. Deep peace filled her.
ler man had come home; she was certain he would
ever leave her again.

Almost half an hour passed before Kyle began to
ir, but Erin never moved, determined to be right
eside him when he remembered that he'd lost his bid
) pilot into space. When he opened his eyes long
nough to see where he was, he gave her a warm,
eepy smile that promised a lifetime of mornings just
ke this one.

"Better?" she asked gently, knowing the loss would
ill hurt despite the comfort he'd received.

He nodded as she rubbed his shoulders. "A little. I
helps to know it's not my fault." He read her eyes and
then admitted slowly, "It also helps to know I'm no
alone."

She pulled him as close as their bodies would allow
"I belong to you, Kyle Tatum. And you belong to
me."

He gave her a long, promising kiss before he pulled
back to whisper in her hair, "You earned your wing
last night, lady."

She met his eyes with surprise and a quick dash of
pride. "Does that mean you're finally going to give me
a pair?"

"You want a pair of wings?" he asked in surprise
"I was only...speaking metaphorically."

Erin was a little embarrassed. "I wouldn't care i
you weren't a pilot, Kyle. But since flying means so
much to you, I can't help but wonder why you've...
sidestepped that particular Navy custom."

He had to think about it for a minute. "Well, babe
in my mind it's more than a custom. It's an honor for
a pilot's lady. The ultimate statement of his persona
respect. She's got to earn the right and once it's been
awarded nobody can ever take it away from her." He
looked pensive. "I never gave a pair of wings to Vi
vian."

Erin bowed her head. The next words were hard
"It's taken me a long time to understand how you fee
about flying, Kyle...and how you feel about the
Navy. But I think I can finally say that I am honored
to be loved by a Naval aviator...an officer...and a
gentleman."

He closed his eyes in newfound peace, then kissed
her so tenderly that Erin knew he'd just conquered the
last uncharted territory in her heart. "I'm really glad

hear that, sweetheart," he breathed against her
cheek, "because we have a little bit of Navy business
to discuss before we go to work."

Erin glanced at the clock. They were already running late. "If this is going to be serious, maybe we
should postpone it till tonight, Kyle. I want to make
sure I give you my full attention."

He kissed her again, understanding her apprehension. "The Navy doesn't always give me time to make
appointments, babe. The bottom line is that I'm going
back to Washington this afternoon with Alan, and I
don't think I'll be back before you leave for Florida to
get ready for the launch."

Erin could not have been more disappointed, but
she held her tongue. "I don't think I would have
changed a single thing about last night's goodbye if I
had known."

He smiled. "Neither would I."

"But you knew."

He nuzzled her throat with the tip of his nose. "I
wasn't in the mood to talk." He pulled back and
watched her face. "They want to go over the details of
the mission with me to see what should be scrapped
and what might be salvageable when the diplomatic
waters are calmer." Without changing his tone of
voice he added, "We're also likely to discuss new
orders for me. The Navy's really hurting for test-pilot
trainers, and I'm really itching to get back to flying
jets full-time. By the time I get reassigned to another
mission I'll be lucky to fit in even one space flight
before my seven years here are up. It might be better
for both of us to . . . just move on now and leave all this
chaos behind."

"Both of us?" Erin whispered, not certain she
understood. "You mean you and the Navy?"

"No, babe. I mean you and me. The Navy would probably be just as happy to leave me here for a while longer, but frankly I think *we* would be happier somewhere else. I'm in a position to...negotiate to some extent the location of my next tour of duty, so I could try to get orders to a base near a hospital that's good for you."

It was the first time Kyle had ever made the slightest attempt to alter his career to accommodate Erin's. His offer moved her deeply, but she still didn't know what to say.

"So what do you think, Rinny? I wish I could let you wait till after the mission to decide, but if I'm going to ask for a change in orders, this is the time."

"I...don't think this is a good time for hasty decisions, Kyle," she managed to tell him. "You may feel differently after you've had a chance to get used to... what happened."

"Maybe. But what I really need to know right now is...do you think you want to stay here and kill yourself for another few years after you wind up everything on 61-J? Or should I ask for my transfer now so we can leave as soon as we get married? We haven't really talked about when to fit in a pregnancy or two, but I was thinking—"

It seemed to come to him very suddenly that she had not yet said she would marry him. In spite of that perfect, irrevocable night of bonding they had just shared, she had still not promised to follow him around the world.

Without meeting her eyes, Kyle switched gears in midstream and announced nonchalantly, "We're going to be late if we don't get a move on. You want to take your shower first while I rustle up some breakfast?"

The silence in the room was eerie. There was a look Kyle's eyes that Erin had never seen before, and she uldn't begin to read it. She didn't even know hether to be frightened or thrilled! It was so intense, t so very guarded....

"Kyle, I love you," she started hesitantly, knowing at she could not ignore his tender words. "I—"

"I love you, too, babe," he told her almost casually he climbed out of bed. "Are you in the mood for an melet?"

It was the last thing she could have imagined he ould say. His sudden nonchalance had thrown her mpletely off guard. She tossed off the covers and opped him before he reached the door. "Kyle, I have tell you how I feel. I—"

He turned around and stopped her with a kiss that immed with tenderness and left her without words. You already told me, sweetheart," he whispered with new light in his eyes that left her baffled but not quite alarmed. "You told me everything...last night."

OR THE REST OF THE DAY concentration was impossi- e for Erin—and absolutely essential with the launch ss than a week away. The morning's orbital reentry actice was a disaster, with the whole crew sym- lically burned to a crisp. After lunch one of Erin's rgical instruments floated away in the water during actice surgery in the neutral buoyancy simulator, d the mock patient nearly bled to death. Her re- heduled conference with the New York City zoo vet ad given her considerable insight into simian surgery, t precious little enlightenment on operating in a eightless environment.

By the time Erin left the center she desperately need- a moment in Kyle's arms. But she would not see

Kyle again until she was done with 61-J. It seemed indicative of her future.

He had left her this morning with sweet hungry kisses and encouraging words. He had promised to be waiting for her when she returned from her flight and wished her the finest space voyage ever achieved by man or ape. He was, in fact, more enthusiastic about the mission than he had ever been. Too enthusiastic, it seemed to Erin. It almost didn't ring true.

Worse yet, he had never mentioned their marriage again. He had never discussed a change in his orders. He had refused to listen to a single pessimistic word on any subject; he had teased her, tickled her, praised her, and generally bent over backward to leave her feeling absolutely marvelous about the entire world.

So why does that scare you, Erin? she asked herself as she walked into her empty house that night. *Why wouldn't* Kyle *go out of his way to be loving and supportive at a time like this?*

Part of her was sure that he was just being noble, but part of her remembered that strange look on his face when she hadn't jumped right up and agreed to marry him. Had he written her off? She'd wanted to tell him yes, she'd marry him. But there were still too many questions to be answered.

No, Erin, there's really only one question. What's first in your life—Kyle Tatum or a career in space? And just when she had thought she was ready to answer, Kyle had inexplicably stopped asking.

She came home to a phone call from the base hospital that left her with no time to dwell on her quandry. Katie's baby had chosen to come a few weeks early, which was not really a problem; but the size of his shoulders was. After eight hours of hard labor, the doctor had decided that an emergency cesarean was

sential, but Katie absolutely refused to give her con-
nt for surgery until she talked to Erin.

"Rinny!" Katie sobbed when Erin marched into the
oor room fifteen minutes later, "I thought you'd
ver get here."

"Shhh." Erin put her arms around her. "I came as
on as they called. Why did you wait so long to tell
e?"

"I know...I know how busy you are. The mis-
on...is in just a few days and you've got to...give
ery spare second to Kyle." Her face was flushed and
eaty. Every word cost her an anguished breath. "I
dn't want to get in the way."

Erin rocked her as she cried, whispering words of
mfort while her heart was full of self-reproach. *Is
is what my whirlwind schedule has done?* she
astised herself. *I'm a surgeon who doesn't even have
ne to operate, a friend who doesn't have time to
and by a friend, a woman who doesn't have time to
a wife.*

"Listen to me, Katie," she whispered, offering the
unger woman tiny chips of ice. "I've conferred with
e doctor, and he knows what he's doing. I want you
give him permission to operate. Now."

"I want to see Billy!" Katie wailed, her sunshine
sposition shattered by fear and pain. "Damn the
avy! Why'd they have to take him away from me
w?"

Kyle's shipboard speech flooded Erin's memory.
is is it, Erin, she told herself, facing the full truth
e'd hidden from all these months. *This is marriage
a Navy pilot. He'll be gone half the time you need
n. It's not just a tragic scene from a movie.*

Yet now she could see the other side of the coin—the
lot coming home to the empty room on base because

his wife was halfway around the world. She could imagine how Billy was feeling right now, separated from his young wife when she needed him most. Kyle would go crazy if he couldn't be with Erin when she gave birth to his child!

The image was so real it frightened her. *Do you want his baby, Erin?* she asked herself. *Do you want a baby at all? And even if you do...*

"Katie," she tried again, pushing away her clamoring thoughts, "It's your *duty* to sign those papers so the doctor can fulfill his obligation. A Navy wife has to learn to hold her chin up. Be strong. Make Billy proud of you."

This time she reached her. Trembling, Katie whispered, "Are you sure it's okay?"

"Yes."

"I won't die?"

"I won't let you die."

"What about the baby? If I'm unconscious will you take care of the baby? Hold him until I come to?"

"Yes, I'll hold the baby."

"Do you promise? Don't let them stick him away in some crib until I wake up!"

"I promise. Will you sign the forms?"

"If you'll hold the baby," she repeated, but the fire had left her voice. In a matter of moments the papers were signed and Katie was gently lulled to sleep.

It was not easy for Erin to watch an operation without being able to help, but she was not authorized to work in the base hospital and she wasn't needed anyway. The doctor was skilled and she trusted him, but her hands felt idle. She hadn't operated in more than a month; her whole surgical focus had been methods for removing the appendix of a chimpanzee. As she watched the new human life cry its way into the world her heart thudded with new awareness of the job she'd performed so many times...with such efficiency and nonchalance. *Good Lord, Erin!* she gasped as she watched Katie's tiny son take his first breath. *What orbital triumph could possibly compete with this earthly miracle?*

Erin stood perfectly still, hands restless and empty, as the doctor did everything to the baby that she would have done had she been the surgeon. And then he handed her the baby so she could do everything that she would have done had she been his mother. And she did it only because she had promised Katie.

Or so she told herself. With the blanket-wrapped baby nestled tightly against her, Erin went to the room assigned to Katie. Though the new mother would be recovering for a while yet, Erin wanted to be beside her when she woke up. She wedged herself into a plastic chair with the tiny one on her lap, his eager little mouth seeking her breast, then her finger, for a moment's satisfaction. His eyes were bright blue, just like Kyle's. His wispy hair was midnight black just like...Kyle's. His little face was red, just like the picture of...

Erin thrust away her mental meandering. She'd held dozens of red newborn babies, several just since she'd been with Kyle. There was no particular reason for this one to affect her any more poignantly. Just because she'd been denied her busy role as a doctor...just because she'd done her woman's job as mother, sister, aunt, friend...just because she ached for a man who ached for a baby....

The minutes passed quietly as she rocked the tiny infant in her arms. His presence soothed her, his warmth a comfort in lieu of Kyle's touch. After a while they got used to sitting there together; he seemed to fit a little bit better on her lap.

"Hey, little guy," she told the bright-eyed newborn who watched her so intently whenever he was awake. "I'm a friend of your mommy's. She's asleep right now so she asked me to keep you company for a while. She wants you to know right from the start that you're going to be treasured. . . not discarded willy-nilly or raised in her spare time like some garden flower."

The baby gurgled, never taking his eyes from Erin's face. In the midnight silence of the hospital room, he watched while pools of moisture filled her soft gray eyes; he watched while one tear, then another, trailed down her maternal face. Maybe they were left over from the last few painful weeks; maybe they were harbingers of hurtful things to come. But a great emptiness seemed to fill Erin's heart and then her womb, and she pressed the baby closer as if to fill it.

He squeaked his pleasure at her female warmth, then closed his eyes as he buried his head in Erin's shoulder. In a gesture as sure as love and as old as woman's time, she kissed the top of his feathery-haired head, then nuzzled his petal-soft neck until it was wet with tears.

CHAPTER FIFTEEN

SIX DAYS LATER—after a lifetime of dreams and effort—Erin Elizabeth Ness found herself on the middeck of the space shuttle *Odyssey* waiting for takeoff. The jumble of feelings of the last few days was all a vague haze in the outer reaches of her mind. Every ounce of her concentration was on the scene before her.

She was lying on her back, studying the wall of cupboards that had now become her ceiling. She wore only her jump suit and a helmet—the oxygen masks of earlier flights were no longer necessary, though they were easily accessible in case of an emergency. All around her the cabin instruments were attached to walls with Velcro and straps. Erin was buckled in, both for safety during the launch and to hold her in place when the spacecraft reached zero gravity. Quinto was strapped, wrapped and wired beside her. He was heavily tranquilized but she still felt a tremendous concern for his safety.

His operation was not scheduled until morning. In the meantime, Erin had other work to do. Every task to be performed, every button to be pushed, every instrument to be used was as familiar to her as her own kitchen. They had rehearsed each move hundreds and hundreds of times; there should be no questions, no mistakes. There should even be time to stargaze—literally—out the myriad windows that flanked the cabin.

It was a beautiful day in Florida. The sky had greeted her that morning with a cerulean smile accented by fluffy cotton-candy clouds. A good-luck telegram from Kyle's parents had arrived the night before, and Erin wished her own parents could have shared her excitement. They would have been so proud of her....

Erin had talked to Kyle on the phone half a dozen times since he'd left for Washington, and every time his tone was the same—peppy and loving. He was very excited about being CAPCOM for her mission. He'd refused to be serious about anything but 61-J, and he'd sidestepped all of her attempts to discuss any aspect of their future in anything but general, optimistic terms. Even his response to her maternal awakening with Katie's baby had been pleasant but lukewarm. Erin hadn't fought as hard as she might have to convince him that she was finally moving toward motherhood; an even bigger roadblock still barred their path. She loved Kyle; but Kyle had surrendered his life to the United States Navy, and he expected her to surrender herself to it, too. Could she ever do it? Could she give up a lifetime of magical moments just like this one, waiting for *Odyssey* to pierce the sky?

At the first sound of the engines, adrenaline surged through Erin's veins, and her stomach clenched as tightly as her fists. *This is it!* her heart cried. *This is it!* her brain clamored. "This is it!" Jeb shouted to his crew.

The spacecraft began to vibrate...to pulse with a power unlike anything Erin had ever felt before. It was the one thing the simulator could not quite reproduce—this awesome sense of raw power, like riding a great blue whale bareback at a tidal wave rodeo.

Odyssey shuddered and heaved; white steam shot past the windows, reminding Erin of the world outside. The universe outside! Hers to play in for five whole days, like a child turned loose in a galactic carnival midway. Medicine was the furthest thing from her mind.

"Ten, nine, eight, seven, six, five, four, three, two, one...." She couldn't hear the voice anymore. Her whole body rippled with the thunder of the takeoff, the pressure of triple gravity jamming her back into the seat so hard she could hardly breathe. Her bones and muscles shook so fiercely she could not control them. And then she knew, victoriously, in a special place inside her, that *Odyssey* was in the air, banking to the left, yes, leaning toward the sky, lifting her toward heaven.

She glanced at Quinto, acutely aware of the difference between man and ape as she soared on the crest of mankind's glorious creations. Her exhilaration was too intense for words. Gradually the jarring began to subside as the blue sky turned to black in the tiny porthole near her face. Time was measured by magic. And then the spacecraft turned one more time, and a huge blue marble came into view.

"Earth!" Erin breathed, a magical sense of wonder replacing the thunder of the ride. "Oh, Kyle! How I wish you could see this. How I wish..."

It was a rapturous, ecstatic moment. Her pulse galloped not unlike the way it did when Kyle touched her. The simile surprised her. Was there any comparison between these two brands of pleasure? If she had to make a choice—and sooner or later she was going to have to make a choice—which one would she choose?

The answer hovered in the air as she undid her seat belt and floated off into space.

"ODYSSEY, this is Houston," Kyle repeated for the fifth time in the last hour. "How's the chimp?"

He really wanted to ask how the surgeon was, but he held his tongue; he didn't want to disturb her. For sixty-eight minutes Erin had been operating on Quinto while Paul assisted and Mark took copious notes to back up her tape-recorded comments. Roger, sitting beside Kyle in Mission Control, had acted as head cheerleader and consultant. He was nearly dizzy with exuberance.

Kyle's own excitement was considerable. He knew that Erin still didn't understand his change of heart about her mission, probably even suspected that he had some ulterior motive for showing so much enthusiasm for 61-J at this late date. But the simple truth was that from the moment he'd found the snaps on her blue lace teddy, he'd stopped needing proof that he came first in Erin's life. He didn't need to hear her promise to marry him; he didn't need to see her give up the mission. Quite suddenly he had realized, in a place too deep within him to probe or challenge or analyze, that he really did come first with Erin Ness.

He was surprised, but no longer hurt, that Erin didn't yet know this. But she would in time. In the interim he would give four more years of his best to NASA and support her while she did the same. Once the flags stopped waving and her name became a footnote instead of a daily headline, she would be ready to go with him. They were already bound for life.

He didn't know how they would work out the technical details. He didn't know which sacrifices would be made by Erin or by him or by the Navy; but it seemed to Kyle that if Erin was able to perform the medical miracle he was now witnessing, she'd somehow manage to be her own free woman *and* a Navy pilot's wife.

He felt as though he were watching "Star Trek" on
e screen in front of him. There was Erin, dressed in a
ght suit with a surgical mask, holding miscellaneous
struments for cutting and sewing. She was strapped
ainst the side of the spacecraft—or floor or ceiling,
pending on one's point of view. Her elbows were
nned to her body for greater control. Quinto, look-
g for all the world like somebody's hairy grand-
ther, lay motionless on an operating table that was
lted to the wall. Every part of his body was strapped
the table. It was a surrealistic scene, and yet Kyle
ew it was the heart and soul of the reality Erin had
en working toward all her life.

He had seen surgical operations on television be-
re; he had watched countless space flights on the
reens at NASA. But never before had he felt as
ough he himself were on the spacecraft; never had
s own hands tingled as though they were performing
rgery. Never had the thrill of victory belonged to
m when the actual achievement belonged to another
rson! And yet, with Erin a hundred ninety-nine
iles away, her body weightless in the majesty of
ace, he felt no separation between her soul and his.
e had orbited the globe because *she* had.

I love you, Rinny Ness. His heart applauded as she
mpleted the appendectomy, throwing up her hands
a gesture of pure triumph. He hoped she could hear
e hidden message in his voice as he announced,
Congratulations, Doctor. The press hounds have just
bbed you 'Super Surgeon of the Skies.' "

Her voice came back to him across the twentieth
ntury's most sophisticated network of ultraelec-
onics, lilting and exuberant. "Tell the press they can
st call me half of the Shaw-Ness Surgical Team. I'll
ve them a chapter and verse report at the press con-

ference after we land. But the bottom line is, Quinto'
going to make it and we've learned almost enough to
pull a human through emergency surgery up here!'' He
euphoria was contagious as she asked him, ''May I tal
to Roger?''

A month ago Kyle would have felt jealous an
pushed aside by the question. Roger had dominated he
attention during the surgery; with hundreds of peopl
listening she had spoken to CAPCOM Commande
Tatum with the utmost reserve and discretion. But now
it all made sense to him. Now, at last, he understoo
Erin's passion for space and surgery. Her triumph wa
worth every moment he'd had to wait for her love.

*And it's a love worth waiting for, Erin Elizabeth
Tatum,* he whispered in his heart. *I haven't had time t
move back to our house, but by the time you land I'll b
set for a homecoming celebration you just won't be
lieve.*

''Sir—'' a young male voice reached him from wha
seemed like a great distance ''—I'm sorry to distur
you, but this is urgent.''

''Urgent?'' Roger chuckled from his place besid
Kyle, snatching the memo from the aide. ''The greates
event in medical history has just taken place. What o
earth—no pun intended—could possibly be more im
portant than that?''

''*Odyssey*, this is Houston,'' Kyle started again, con
fident that Roger would take care of the message. ''Yo
folks breaking out the champagne up there?''

Before anyone could answer, Roger slipped the pape
across the desk to Kyle. He was surprised; he ha
assumed that whatever the problem was, Roger woul
take care of it for him.

''I'm sorry, buddy,'' Roger murmured in a low
soothing tone that Kyle had heard him use with be

aved families of patients who were about to die.
t's a message from your mom.''

ᴛʜʀᴇᴇ ᴅᴀʏs after Erin removed Quinto's appendix in
ro gravity, the crew of the space shuttle *Odyssey*
nded at Edwards Air Force Base in California amidst
eering crowds of local astrobuffs. It took Erin the
st of the day to fly back to Houston, tie up things at
e space center, and drive the last three miles of her
credible journey. She was exhausted but exhilarated
 she reached her gingerbread nest, and still a little
aky from the flight. But she had done it! Orbited the
obe, performed surgery in space, triumphed over
tigue and stress and conflicting emotions. There was
 denying the exultation that still filled her.
But there was also no way to ignore the anxiety that
awed her stomach when she pulled into her empty
iveway. There was no sign of welcome; there was no
gn of Kyle.
Roger had been vague when he'd disappeared ab-
ptly after her surgery on Quinto. Now he seemed to
ve vanished from her life.
Erin opened the front door and stared blankly at
hat she'd once lovingly considered their home. She
d told the housekeeper to take the week off. Now
o of the ferns were decidedly brown, and dust
ated a pile of quilt squares in the corner. Worst of
, the bed was still unmade, proof that Kyle had not
ice come home.
"Damn you, Kyle Tatum," she whispered almost
verently as tears misted her vision, "I never cried
fore I fell in love with you."
Vibrant memories of Kyle wrapped around her as
e tried to face the possibility that he would not be
ming back . . . had never intended to come back since

that last tender morning when she'd crushed his hopes again. Then, as now, her career had been at war with her love for him. Nothing had seemed more important than going into space.

Well, she had gone. She had come back. To nothing. To a house without Kyle's smile, to a bed without his touch. And now she had to ask herself, was it really worth it?

Her galactic adventure was over. She'd triumphed over weightlessness and made a stunning medical breakthrough. The press corps was drooling for her debriefing tonight. The president had even called to congratulate her while she was still in orbit! She had reached the absolute apex of her professional career. She was proud. She was deeply gratified. She was . . . lonely.

Never had she been this empty in her life. Never had her choices seemed so nakedly, painfully clear. Never had a decision seemed easier to make.

Urgently she told herself that Kyle couldn't really have left her. He had promised to be here, and Kyle Tatum never broke a promise and never showed up late without an earthshattering excuse. He would come. Somehow, he would arrive with an explanation that would not rip her heart from her chest. And when he did, she would tell him that she loved space travel and was thrilled at the possibility of going up again. She would also tell him that she missed surgery, that Quinto's operation had been the most satisfying part of the flight, and she could see that the time would come when she would be ready to return to earthbound surgery full time . . . whenever his tour with NASA ended. In four years, four months—or next week! And she would tell him—if only he gave her this one last chance—that no matter what project she was orking on when the time came for him to go, *she ould leave Houston anyway just to be with him.* She ould never let anything come between them again.

Erin covered her face with her hands, glad that no ne could see her weep. She had taken a glorious trip, nd she desperately hoped she could repeat it a dozen mes. It was worth all the work, the fatigue, the stress, ie struggle to prove she had the "right stuff." But it as not worth coming home to this Kyleless house. It as not worth a lifetime without his dimpled smile, his nder touch, his lips against her ear when he said her ame. It was not worth the look she wanted to see on is face when she told him that she wanted to have a aby as soon as his time was up at NASA.

But she didn't know how to tell him, because he asn't there to tell. Again she checked the house for a ote, for some flowers, for some more of his things. hen a new sensation crept into her consciousness...a oman's sixth sense when her man is in trouble.

Something is wrong. He loves me. No matter how 've hurt him, he would never frighten me like this fter that last special night. He would never—

When the doorbell rang, Erin rushed toward it with isions of disaster swirling in her head. Had he been ying? Was the lure of fighter jets just too strong? lad the grief she'd caused him affected his judgment?

"Roger!" she gasped when she opened the door and ound her friend's face behind a mass of red roses. I'm so glad to see you!"

She threw her arms around him as best she could eside the wall of leaves and thorns. He hugged her nd stepped aside.

"I'm grateful for your enthusiasm, Erin, but I must onfess I'm only the delivery boy." As he handed her ie arrangement of flowers she noticed a ribboned letter "J" entwined in the middle. "There's sixty-one of them, Erin. I counted to make sure. Kyle gave me this long list of precise instructions, the first of which I already blew. He was adamant that you would not return from a trip like this to an empty house."

"Oh, Roger," she whispered as she set down the flowers, so full of love for Kyle that she could hardly mutter the other man's name. "Where is he? Why isn' he—"

"I did my best, Erin, but I had engine trouble. I had to walk the last mile and a half." He grinned. "I never thought I'd be able to do that again."

Instantly Erin was a doctor. "Are you okay? Does your back hurt?"

He waved a hand. "I feel great. I refuse to be treated like an invalid any longer. I'll be fighting with you for the top spot on our next medical mission, Erin."

"No," she stopped him warmly. "Next time let's go up together."

"It would be a pleasure, Dr. Ness."

"And an honor for me, Dr. Shaw." Then her eyes grew wary. She had to ask again, "Where is he, Roger? Why isn't he here?"

"My instructions are to avoid those two questions until I deliver three things. The roses, a kiss—" he brushed her cheek fraternally "—and this package." He produced a tiny white box. "Only then am I supposed to let you read this letter. He apologizes for the use of NASA memo forms but it was all he had time for."

Ignoring the box for the moment, Erin snatched the letter and tore it open, absolutely desperate to read Kyle's hurried words.

Sweetheart—

I'm terribly sorry I can't be here to welcome you home, but my father has had a heart attack and is still in very critical condition. I have to stay with my mother in Washington as long as she needs me. I'll be home just as soon as I can. Keep the bed warm.

For richer or poorer,
Kyle

P.S. I'll call you as soon as the press conference is over. I'll be rooting for you all the way.

A thousand different feelings ricocheted through Erin's heart as she read the letter. He still loved her! He still wanted to marry her! All her dreams were about to come true! Except...his father was dying, and he was not asking her to stay by his side. He was wishing her luck on her career instead. "He expects me to waltz through a public spectacle like a celebrity while his family is in crisis?" she said aloud, more to herself than to Roger.

"That's exactly what he expects you to do, Erin. In fact I'm supposed to insist that you do exactly that. He doesn't want you bogged down with guilt or any question marks. His father has the finest cardiologist in the whole damn Navy looking after him, so there's nothing you or I can do to help."

"Roger, Kyle couldn't do a thing to help you when you were in a coma, either, but he stayed with you just the same." Of course Kyle didn't have the whole country waiting for him at a press conference! But she didn't even give that a thought before she made her decision. "Give me the name of the hospital, Roger. I'm going to Washington."

"Jeb won't let you, Erin. He'll go berserk. Since 61-J was a surgical mission, the press is going to want the surgeon who operated on that chimp. Kyle was quite explicit about this. This time he *does not want to rain on your parade*." He paused to make sure that she really understood the change in Kyle. "His last words were something to the effect that if he could let you go into orbit and be sure you'd come back to him, he ought to be safe letting you go on earth."

Erin shook her head. *Oh, how I love you, Kyle Tatum.* "Oh, Roger, don't you understand? The most important thing I've learned in the past five days is that there's nothing on this planet or above it more vital to me than Kyle's love. Don't you think it's time for me to live the lesson?"

Roger grinned. "I told you, I'm just the messenger. Following my buddy's orders."

"And you did a fine job," she praised him, knowing that Roger was mutely applauding her decision. "Now give me the address so you can get out of here and let me pack."

It didn't take long to arrange a flight and gather her things, but thinking up a compromise to present to Jeb was another matter. He couldn't forbid her to go to Kyle, but if she didn't offer him a reasonable alternative to her attendance at the press conference, her career could be so gravely jeopardized that she'd be free to leave Houston tomorrow! Postponing her call to the base as long as possible, Erin's hands toyed with the wrappings of Kyle's gift. Her thoughts were still with Jeb. Roger had said the press would need a surgeon. . . .

She barely had the lid off when the sight that lay before her stole her full attention and hammered on her heart. Buried deep in the folds of soft white cotton was a tiny bar of gold, delicate and fine, shaped in the time-honored glory of a Navy pilot's wings.

IT WAS SIX O'CLOCK when Kyle ushered his mother into the lobby where a television was already tuned to the NASA debriefing. Admiral Tatum's doctor had just reported that his condition was now guarded but stable, and mother and son had breathed a joint sigh of intense relief.

"Honey, look," his mother nudged him as they sat down and glanced at the screen. "They're all men. Where is Erin?"

It was a valid question. Quickly Kyle's eyes scanned the cluster of three-piece suits: Jeb, Mark, Paul and...Roger! He couldn't believe it. He hadn't seen Roger in a suit in six months. Nor had he seen Roger wearing a smile of pride and self-assurance in a very long time.

"Commander Henson, where is the astronaut who performed the surgery on the chimpanzee? We understood she would be with us today." The words were barely courteous; the disappointment audible.

Jeb smiled. "A family emergency has detained Dr. Ness this evening. However, we are very fortunate to have with us the other half of our 61-J surgical team, Dr. Roger Shaw. Dr. Shaw, as many of you know, was grounded on this mission due to injuries he sustained in an auto accident some months ago, but he has worked very closely with Dr. Ness from her earliest days on the crew. At her request, he is going to speak on her behalf tonight."

Instantly all the cameras focused on Roger. He looked awed for only a second, then his charisma beamed out over the assembled microphones.

"Dr. Shaw, what was your role in the surgery that

took place on the recent shuttle flight? How do you fee
about being replaced? Do you think you could have per
formed the surgery any better? Do you . . .''

Roger answered each question with dignity and in
creasing poise. Over and over again he reiterated hi
respect for Erin, their close professional relationshi
and his complete confidence that she was as good o
better a surgeon than he was. ''I'm not saying I couldn'
have done the job as well,'' he told the press with a grin
''but quite truthfully, I don't believe anyone could hav
done it better than Dr. Ness.''

Kyle listened with pride, certain that Erin was re
sponsible for giving Roger this opportunity to share th
limelight. It occurred to him that since she wasn't at th
conference, he could call her right now. The waitin
was finally over.

Before he could move, his mother picked up he
quilting bag and assured him, ''I'll be fine alone, Kyle
You go find Erin. She's probably on her way her
now.''

Kyle shook his head. ''I didn't send for her. I'm sur
she just arranged this so Roger could—''

''Trust me, Kyle,'' Betty Tatum declared with a smil
on her face that melded love for her son and lingerin
concern for her beloved husband. ''Erin is the othe
half of your own soul. Nothing could keep her awa
from you at a time like this.''

Before Kyle could answer, he spotted a feminine im
age of blue hurrying down the hospital corridor, head
ing straight for him.

She didn't look anything like a surgeon, or an astro
naut, or a professional lady busy with her own intensiv
life. She looked tired and windblown and incredibl
vulnerable. One nervous hand fingered the tiny pilot'
wings pinned to her dress. Her eyes were full of anguis

ven before she saw him...and full of something else
nce she did. She looked like a woman who had just
ome home.

But Erin Ness had circled the earth seventy-four
mes before she'd come to realize that home was
hatever patch of ground on which Kyle Tatum stood.
he didn't need to tell him; didn't need to say a word.
he dropped the suitcase on the floor and let her eyes
onfess her mute surrender. His eyes confessed the
ame. In that aching moment of silent promise, all
heir future and all their past washed between them,
vhispering nameless answers to once-burning ques-
ions no longer needing to be asked.

It was Erin who broke first, tossing away all vestiges
f her roles as a professional and a celebrity to run
own the hallway and throw herself into his arms.
Kyle grabbed her in a crushing embrace that took all
er breath, but Erin didn't care. Nothing mattered but
he sweet relief that only his touch could give her. She
lung to his neck as he kissed her half a dozen times in
vild jubilation, whispering her name again and again
s he twirled her in mad, dizzying circles.

And then Erin was spinning into a different kind of
rbit—the kind that lasts a lifetime. She was a moon to
is planet...a planet to his sun...a satellite lost
orever in his orbit of love.

An epic novel of exotic rituals
and the lure of the Upper Amazon

THE
TAKERS
RIVER
OF GOLD

JERRY AND S.A. AHERN

THE TAKERS are the intrepid Josh Culhane and th
seductive Mary Mulrooney. These two adventure
launch an incredible journey into the Brazilian ra
forest. Far upriver, the jungle yields its deepe
secret—the lost city of the Amazon warrior women

THE TAKERS series is making publishing histor
Awarded *The Romantic Times* first prize for Hig
Adventure in 1984, the opening book in the serie
was hailed by *The Romantic Times* as "the ne
trend in romance writing and reading. High
recommended!"

Jerry and S.A. Ahern have never been better!

TAK

Share the joys and sorrows of real-life love with
Harlequin American Romance! ™·

What readers say about SUPERROMANCE

"Bravo! Your SUPERROMANCE [is]...super!"
R.V.,* Montgomery, Illinois

"I am impatiently awaiting the next SUPERROMANCE."
J.D., Sandusky, Ohio

"Delightful...great."
C.B., Fort Wayne, Indiana

"Terrific love stories. Just keep them coming!"
M.G., Toronto, Ontario

*Names available on request.